The COINCIDENCE
Anthony Lewis

I will protect my owner

with my life - Snob & Snow

© Copyright 2006 Anthony Lewis.
All rights reserved. No part of this publication may be reproduced, stored in a retrieval system, or transmitted, in any form or by any means, electronic, mechanical, photocopying, recording, or otherwise, without the written prior permission of the author.

Note for Librarians: A cataloguing record for this book is available from Library and Archives Canada at www.collectionscanada.ca/amicus/index-e.html
ISBN 1-4251-0253-0

Printed in Victoria, BC, Canada. Printed on paper with minimum 30% recycled fibre. Trafford's print shop runs on "green energy" from solar, wind and other environmentally-friendly power sources.

Offices in Canada, USA, Ireland and UK

Book sales for North America and international:
Trafford Publishing, 6E–2333 Government St.,
Victoria, BC V8T 4P4 CANADA
phone 250 383 6864 (toll-free 1 888 232 4444)
fax 250 383 6804; email to orders@trafford.com
Book sales in Europe:
Trafford Publishing (UK) Limited, 9 Park End Street, 2nd Floor
Oxford, UK OX1 1HH UNITED KINGDOM
phone +44 (0)1865 722 113 (local rate 0845 230 9601)
facsimile +44 (0)1865 722 868; info.uk@trafford.com
Order online at:
trafford.com/06-2010

10 9 8 7 6 5 4 3 2

To my Father, who taught me the value of the word honestly from when I was a young child ~

To my Mother, who always cooked healthy and tasty meals for me ~

To Tony Fricker, who has been a great help in completing my book

THE COINCIDENCE
By Anthony Lewis

CHAPTER ONE

When I joined the company, I had just celebrated my 16th birthday and it was my first ever job. After I left school I used to dream of being a journalist, a photographer or a medical doctor, but when my grandmother died I knew that my dreams would never come true. It seemed to me then that my whole world had collapsed and completely destroyed my life. I wouldn't be alive now if I hadn't talked to grandma's ghost. You see I had no one else to help me or even to understand how I felt. Grandma was the best friend of my lonely heart.

We used to live in a Council flat behind West Hampstead Underground Station, on the fourth floor. I would watch the people as they sat on the tube each evening. The trains were always packed when the commuters finished work and were trying to get home. I had so many friends to play with then, they all lived in the same block of Council flats. One said he wanted to be a train driver so he could sit at the front of the train. Another boy said he wanted to be a policeman with a smart uniform. At that time we enjoyed playing together and we didn't want to know about anything except playing and eating.

When I was about eight or nine years old, grandma was reading me a bedtime story, she was crying as she stroked my hair and whispered, "I love you very much Louise, I wish I could be with you until you are grown up. You will have no one to look after you if God takes me right now."

I often asked grandma where my Dad and Mum were. She would tell me that they were in heaven and that I must be a good girl, go to school and look after myself. This particular time I asked her, "Where are you going, grandma? I will follow you wherever you go." She kissed my cheek and laughed. I said, "If God wants to take you away I will get very angry with Him. Why would He be so terrible? He took my Dad and Mum so He can't take you."

She sighed and said, "If your mother was alive, she would be very proud of you. You are a brave little girl. One day you will understand all about life and how to survive it, but for now you are just a little princess to grandma."

A year later I was at school and we were learning about life and had sex education classes. It was very exciting and amazing for a few of us. Some of my class were planning to experiment! "Are you coming with us, Louise?" They said.

"I'm sorry I can't come with you, my grandma is waiting for me."

"Oh shit!" They shouted. "Don't tell her, she is so silly, she might spoil our weekend plans."

"Leave her alone, she is okay," I sobbed.

After I left school I didn't bother about any of them at all. I think I missed lots of lessons; you see I had a problem with shyness. I couldn't face anything to do with sex. I even thought sex was shameful, dirty and disgusting. At least that was always my feeling anyway. My grandma was an Irishwoman, who married an Englishman by the name of John Bornne. He worked in the library until he suffered from heart disease. They only had one daughter.

Grandma once said to me, "I was a virgin; I never had sex before I got married." When I was at school she told me that I should never have sex before marriage. It was bad and not having it would protect me. That was another one of my grandma's stories. When I tried to explain why we had to have sex education at school, so that we would be properly informed about pregnancy and disease, she would put her hand to her chest and say, "Oh Mary Mother of God! Dear me, it is so terrible. Please Louise, promise me you will never have sex before you are married. How can people face

God in church when they have made love to so many men, it is shameful before God." She truly believed that sex was bad before ones wedding day. She even thought men were so evil that after having had sex with one woman they wanted to go around like bees and suck the honey from other flowers and then fly away to a new one.

My grandma kept telling me about my body. "You see, if you let a young boy touch your breast and squeeze them, they will go soft and out of shape. I can tell just by looking at them which girls have had sex. Oh! It's not nice, please Louise, if you love your grandma don't do it. I will tell you a big secret - after you get married you should be a good wife. When you're in bed with your husband you must give him a lot of enjoyment and the best of entertainment. Even after you have children you must be good at both roles: a good partner in bed and a great mother for your children." I didn't understand the meaning of this until after my teenage years.

When I look back into the past, I can still remember West Hampstead, nothing much has changed. When you leave the underground station and cross the road, the railway station is still there and if you turn left there used to be a NatWest bank. It was there for so many generations, just a small branch on the corner. I remember all the staff and the branch manager were so friendly, always smiling at the customers. They would call you by your surname and my grandma was very close with the manager. Sometimes they both went inside his office and left me sitting next to the cash counter. All the staff called Grandma Mrs. Bornne. They closed down that NatWest branch a few years later and now it is a corner shop but even now, when I walk past, I always think of them. Opposite the bank there used to be an Indian take-away. It served really hot curry, which was so tasty. Now there is a new building there. On the corner, next to the bank, there was an old pub, where there was a fight nearly every Friday night. It is under new management now and looks better than the old one. Next to the pub was a corner shop; grandma always shopped there as it was convenient for her to buy milk and potatoes as it wasn't too far from our place. Mr. and Mrs. Patel were the owners at that time. One thing I forgot to mention was an English Opera School. It was there before I was born and is an amazing place. It is still something that the English can be proud of.

One day, during a beautiful summer weekend, Mrs. Patel and her daughter Anita came to grandma's flat. At that time Anita was my closest friend, we were the same age. Anita was one of the new generation of Indians, she was so self-confident and hardly ever spoke to her mother in her native language. Instead she would speak to her in English and this usually ended up in an argument. Anita always thought of herself as English and she had me as her friend at that time.

"Come in Mrs. Patel," Grandma invited, "and Anita; please sit down. Would you like some tea or coffee?"

"No thank you Mrs. Bornne," said Mrs. Patel,

"Yes please grandma," chimed in Anita "I would like some orange juice." Mrs. Patel turned to Anita and burst out in Indian. Anita answered in English. "I'm thirsty Mum; I want to drink some orange juice."

"Okay Anita, you go into the kitchen with Louise, off you go." They had come to invite me to Anita's birthday party and when we returned from the kitchen Mrs. Patel told Anita that they had to go soon. Grandma said it was okay for me to go to the party and Anita jumped up and gave grandma a big kiss.

Anita and I were planning for the party already. Anita was always lovely; if she wanted something she knew how to get it. I miss my teenage years; I never got any kisses from boys, even though I was sixteen, the same age as Anita. Her family was very strict. She wasn't allowed to have sex and her mother kept an eye on her all the time. She once said to me that if she ever got the chance she wanted to try it once.

After Mrs. Patel and Anita had left I noticed that grandma was busy taking clothes out of my suitcase. "What are you doing grandma?" I asked.

"I am looking for your dress. You know I almost forgot that you are going to be sixteen soon. If Mrs. Patel hadn't come to invite you to Anita's party I wouldn't have remembered. You are still my baby Louise."

"Yes, I know grandma; I am still your little girl."

It was the first time in my life that I had been invited to stay in someone's house. I was so excited; grandma looked at me with her kindly eyes and said, "You look like your father." Then she sighed. She looked so tired to me. I promised grandma that I would be a good girl. "I know you will always be a good girl. Are you ready to go Louise?"

"Yes grandma; I think Mrs. Patel will be here soon." I picked up my bag that grandma had packed for me. I just felt sad, I don't know why; maybe it was because it was the fist time for me to be away from home for a night without grandma.

"I think they are coming."

"Yes there they are," Grandma exclaimed. Anita was running in front of her mother and when she met grandma she gave her a big kiss.

"Thank you so much grandma, for letting Louise stay with me tonight. I'm sixteen today grandma." "I wish you health and happiness Anita. I haven't got anything special for you, but Louise has a present for you and she will give it to you later."

"Thank you so much grandma, I love you," Anita said.

"Hello Mrs. Bornne," said Mrs. Patel.

"Hello Mrs. Patel, would you like to sit down?"

"Yes, thank you Mrs. Bornne, but I don't need anything to drink at the moment; I just want to have a talk with you. I am so tired with Anita and I almost wish we could exchange children. You can have Anita and I will have Louise."

"Oh! They are both the same Mrs. Patel, except that Louise is very quiet. She is very stubborn in her own way."

"Anita's sister is so good; she is so different from Anita," sighed Mrs. Patel.

"Yes, that's why she can have everything she wants and I can't," moaned Anita.

"I don't want to say too much Mrs. Bornne; I will come and talk to you later in private."

"All right Mrs. Patel, you're welcome to come and see me anytime."

When we were in the car Anita was so angry with her mother that she was very quite until we got to her house.

"Is anybody home? Can you open the door please?" Said Mrs. Patel. She spoke some words in her own language to Anita but instead of answering in that language she said "I have told you so many times Mum; if I am with my friends we speak English only."

Mrs. Patel apologised to me and said, "I only asked her to open the door by herself."

"It's okay Mrs. Patel." I said. Anita grabbed my bag and my hand, took me straight up to her bedroom and locked the door.

"Sit down Louise, we haven't much time to talk. My Mum will come soon and help me to get dressed in a sari; She has to help me as I don't know how to do it. My Dad and Mum are arranging for a very rich Indian family to meet me and if they are satisfied their son will be engaged to me."

"But you are so young," I said.

"My Mum said I can marry when I'm eighteen," replied Anita. "She doesn't want me to go to university, just like my sister. She was married to a rich man, an accountant, and now she just looks after her son and does the cooking. Then there is my big brother, who is a doctor. He never goes out with anyone as he wants to keep Mum and Dad happy. He is waiting for the right girl, so you can imagine how difficult it must be to be Mrs. Patel's daughter-in-law. She wants a rich Indian family with a beautiful, perfect daughter. That is why he is still waiting to get married." There was a knock at the bedroom door.

"Hello girls, may I come in?" It was a girl's voice that I did not recognise.

"Just a moment; Okay you can come in now," said Anita, "Louise, this is my sister Aruna, Aruna this is my best friend Louise."

"Hello, Louise," said Aruna, "I have heard a lot about you and that you are good in school and very polite."

"Thank you," I replied.

Aruna continued, "Mum ask me to bring both of you an orange juice, she will be here soon. I will see you downstairs later."

When Mrs. Patel came up to Anita's bedroom she opened a jewellery box which contained lots of gold items. In her hands she held a beautiful, pink, silk sari with a silver and gold trim. I looked at Anita and she smiled and said, "I am going to get dressed now but if you need anything please just help yourself." I went to open my bag. I hadn't asked grandma what she had packed for me, so when I opened it I got a bit of a surprise when I saw a plain, cream dress. It was so pretty and I wondered where she had got it from. I decided that when I got home I would ask her and thank her for putting it in. The dress was hand made and very fashionable; I loved it and knew it would give me much confidence when I joined the party. At first I didn't care much, I was just happy to come because it was Anita's birthday. When I came out of the bathroom Anita looked rather shocked, she said to her Mum, "Look Mum, Louise looks like a princess." When her mother turned to look at me her mouth fell open,

"You look so different, you are so pretty Louise."

"Thank you Mrs. Patel," I turned to Anita and said, "I think you remind me of someone so much, but I can't think who it is. You look so beautiful in your silk sari."

"Oh yes; this is my birthday, but my mother has dressed me as if it was my wedding day," Mrs. Patel looked at her and shook her head.

"Okay girls, I am going to the kitchen and will call you later."

As soon as Mrs. Patel had gone Anita turned to me and whispered "Do you know Louise? You look like a little princess."

"So do you," I said "a princess of India." We were laughing when we heard a car stop in front of the house. Anita jumped to the window.

"They are coming," said Anita "Put your head out the window Louise. That is my brother, he is a doctor; I will introduce you later. The other person is his friend Dr. Andrew. I really fancy him so much. Another family is coming to visit me to see if I am suitable for their son. You see Louise, I haven't got any friends, because my family life is so complicated. I am not very happy with the old culture, I was born here and I want to do western things. I don't want the old fashioned way."

"But your Mum and Dad love you," I said.

"I know, but we don't live in the same world," Anita sighed. There was a knock at the door,

"It's time for dinner girls," said Mrs. Patel.

"Okay, we are coming."

When we got downstairs there were so many people in the sitting room so Anita took me over to her brother. "Louise, this is Dr. Padachee, and this is Dr. Andrew. This is my friend Louise." Mr. and Mrs. Patel called Anita over to meet the special guests. I had noticed both of them looking interestedly at Anita, who was wearing bracelets from her wrists to the top of her arms; Her mother had forced her to wear them. Aruna was busy talking to Dr. Andrew. Dinner started with a very traditional Indian dish. I looked at Dr. Padachee, who was sitting next to me, and noticed that he had quite a long face and didn't look like very Indian at all. He was a charming man with a kindly face.

"Can you eat spicy food Louise?" He asked.

"Oh yes Dr. Pada; but not too hot," I said. He placed a few choice pieces of food on my plate. "Thank you, I will be fine."

Mr. and Mrs. Patel were busy talking to the guests and Anita smiled at me in her secret way. After dinner all of the guests went into the sitting room. We went out to the conservatory next to the kitchen. Anita had managed to get close to Dr. Andrew and Dr. Pada asked me about my studies.

"What are you going to do after school?" He asked.

"I don't know yet," I replied, "but if I get good grades when I finish my A Levels I want do medicine like you." That night he gave me a lot of information and boosted my confidence. I looked over at Anita, who was trying so hard to behave like an eighteen year old. She was with Dr. Andrew until her sister Aruna came to interfere. She came over to join us and said what a boring birthday party it was and that everyone was too old.

She said, "Do you know my parents tried to sell me to a man? They really don't understand what a young teenager wants."

Dr. Padachee looked at his younger sister and said, "You have to learn the lesson by yourself."

Mr. and Mrs. Patel called us to say goodbye to the guests and Anita and I went up to her bedroom. She told me that her Mum kept her eyes on her all the time and never let any boys near her. As long as I live I will remember her last words to me. She said, "If I ever get the chance I will experiment with sex."

When we got up the next morning we saw Mrs. Patel in the kitchen, preparing our breakfast. She was packing up some Indian sweets. "These are for grandma," she said "don't forget Louise." I never ever thought that day would be the last time I saw my dear friend until so many years later.

CHAPTER TWO

I think it was my bad dream, when I got up every morning I wanted things to be like the old days but it wasn't the same. Grandma used to go to church every Sunday and I would go with her until I was sixteen. Then I was too shy and sent her and picked her up in the afternoon. One Sunday morning I made a cup of tea as usual and went to her bedroom. I spoke to her, opened the curtains and then saw that she was not just sleeping but had passed away. Once I realised she had left me alone in the world I cried so much. I called our G. P. He and Father John were so wonderful and organized everything for grandma's funeral. I was very grateful to both of them. I had to confront so many problems. The Council wanted to take the two-bedroom flat away and the social worker wanted to help me go back to college. I made my own decision and was going to get a job so that I could do without the social worker.

Grandma had left me a little money, which amounted to nearly two thousand pounds so I moved out of the Council flat in West Hampstead and got a small bed-sit in the Finchley Road area. I didn't want to see Anita or her parents and wanted to be alone as I was not well in my mind. I went to the church and sat there for a long time every day. I didn't go to see Father John as I felt better when I was alone. I started to talk to grandma at night so she could be with me and look after me.

It was in May, after my birthday and, as it was a sunny day I walked from where I lived to Hampstead Heath. I walked past the Royal Free Hospital and saw the Medical School. Once I had intended to be a student there but now I didn't want to think about it or even see it.

"Louise, Louise," I heard someone calling my name.

"Hello, Dr. Pada" I said in surprise, "what are you doing here?"

"I was going for a walk in the park, wait for me here and I will be back."

When he got back Dr. Padachee said, "Okay Louise, I have finished my duty. Please get in to my car and I will take you to my friend's place; are you hungry?"

"No I'm not thank you doctor."

When we got to the flat he said, "Please sit down Louise I'll get you a drink; make yourself comfortable." When he returned he brought me an orange juice and explained that we were in his friend's flat.

"Thanks Dr. Pada," I said.

"You know you are very naughty. Why didn't you tell Anita when you left West Hampstead?"

"I didn't want to disturb your family anymore. I am very grateful to all of you for your help."

"We were all worried about you, especially Anita."

"I know and I'm sorry but I have my reasons," I explained.

"Yes, I think I understand. You are so young and I don't want you to make a mistake. Will you promise me something Louise?"

"If I can doctor," I said.

"If you have any problems please let me know and I will try to help you Louise."

"I promise I will do that but could I ask you to do me a big favour?"

"Of course Louise, of course I will."

"Please don't tell Anita that you have seen me."

"Why Louise?"

"I will tell you one day; I promise."

"Okay, but let me know where you are living,"

"Yes I will."

"That's a good girl," he said and I left.

After that he visited me once or twice a week. Dr. Padachee was a busy doctor and never stayed for more then half an hour. He came to make sure that I had enough food; to check what I was doing and whether I was looking for a job. One Friday evening in September he came to see me; he looked so tired and I gave him a fresh orange juice that I squeezed for him myself. I gave him a letter to read. "Is it a love letter? If it is from your boyfriend I don't want to read it; I am too old to read such things."

"No please open it and read it," I pleaded.

When he finished reading he came to me and kissed me on the cheek. I grasped his hand and cuddled him. I didn't let go and put my head on his chest. It was the first time I had cuddled anyone since grandma died. He held me in his arms. "I am sorry Louise I should not have done that but I am very please for you, congratulations. It is a very big firm and they will look after you well. I am sure you will have a good future working with them."

Before I started work Dr. Padachee popped in with a big shopping bag. I was so tired and I wondered if I would get a big kiss or not? Dr. Padachee gave me the bag and said, "Dear me! Miss Louise is now such a beautiful young lady. May I have a kiss first?"

"Yes, maybe just one, let me see." I opened the bag and exclaimed, "Oh boy!" All I could see was a sexy bra and panty set. "It is so beautiful."

"These are for you to go to work in." He said.

"Thank you so much Dr. Pada." "Once again we kissed. This time he kissed me all over my face. It was the fist time in my life that anyone had kissed me on the lips and it was a kiss I shall never forget. This was the first time since grandma passed away that I had felt warm and happy and I had so much confidence. Dr. Padachee gave me so much support. He was a tall, handsome man with black hair and sexy eyes. I felt secure but I had to keep my mouth shut and pretend it was not real happiness, but I did need it. He was very kind to me at that time and I didn't want for anything. I was going to start a good job and I had a small bed-sit and so many books; I loved books, they were my real friends. Dr. Padachee gave me a few books which was very helpful to me. He came to see me again and gave me a lot of vitamins, fruit, bread and cheese. He said I must eat properly as I was a growing girl and not working. He looked at me and I looked at him with a naughty look; he smiled and said, "I can see you are growing up, but this is not the right time for you. I need to tell you so many things but I promise it will not be long." I cuddled him and didn't let him go. I put his hand to my cheek and sighed, "You could teach me how to do it."

He whispered into my ear, "I will very soon. I am going to teach you the proper way to do it."

CHAPTER THREE

On my first day at work, as I walked through the main door, the security guard told me to wait in the waiting room. There were already three other people sitting there but when I looked at my watch I saw that it was not quite nine thirty. They must have arrived very early. We just smiled at each other and soon a woman walked into the room with some documents in her hands. She called out, "Is Many here?"

"Yes," said the man sitting on my left.

"I am David," said a man sitting across from me.

"And my name is Patricia," Said an attractive girl on my right.

"So you must be Louise," said the woman.

"Yes," I said.

"Good morning everyone, it's nice to see you are all early. My name is Teresa and I am going to take you to the Training Room upstairs." Once we reached the Training Room she said, "We will spend a little time to plan for today; please sit down. I would like to welcome you all to our company and will shortly explain our Company Policy. First of all I need to know a little bit about your experiences. Perhaps I could start with you Many?"

"I have been working in a retail shop for about nine years."

"That is a long time isn't it?" Said Teresa

"Yes it is," Said Many.

"And what about you David?"

"I was a sales assistant for ten years."

"And what have you done Patricia?" Asked Teresa.

"I have worked as a cashier in a supermarket for fifteen years."

"And finally we come to you Louise?" She said.

"I have just finished school." I replied.

"So that's why she looks so young," said Patricia.

Teresa continued, "I am pleased to meet you all. If you have any to questions I am here to answer them for you. I have been working with this company for twenty years, ever since I left school so I have never worked for another company. Let me tell you what we do here. If you are prepared to work hard we will give you good pay rises. We will also give you a twenty-five percent discount on store merchandise. If you want to be a leader we will train you to be a Shop-floor Manager. If you would like to work in the countryside we can transfer you to another branch. We also run a pension scheme, so you don't need to worry when you retire. Everybody has equal opportunity. Okay, we will have a tea break for forty-five minutes and then we will continue. We will have lunch at two o' clock than a break for afternoon tea and then we can all go home. Follow me and I will take all of you to the dining room."

When we reached the dining room she explained that prices were very cheap for breakfast, lunch and afternoon tea. She showed us where the trays for self-service were stacked and then took us to the Rest Room. "If you want to relax you can do so here and if you would like to see the shop floor you can walk around. I will see you all later in the Training Room." She said.

"Thank you Teresa," we all chimed together.

"You are welcome," Said Teresa

When we all got back to the Training Room, Teresa said, "I would like to explain our Company Policy. We allow all our employees four weeks holiday but after three years they get five weeks holiday. As I mentioned earlier, you are entitled to a twenty-five percent discount on all merchandise. After the company year-end, in April, your Department Manager will write a report on you and your pay rise will depend on your report."

"Excuse me?" Queried Many.

"Yes Many," Said Teresa.

"What happens if you work very hard but your Manager doesn't like you?"

"That is a good question Many. In that case you will need to see the Human Resources Department and they will have a discussion with your manager. I will put on a video, which explains the company's system, and then I will come back and see you." After the video she asked Many, "What do you think about our Company Policy, Many?"

"I think it gives its employees a very good opportunity to work hard and a good chance to achieve a high position."

"What about you David?"

"I agree with Many. I think the company appears to be very fair with its employees."

"Do you agree with them Patricia, Louise?"

"Yes we do," we said together.

Teresa said, "I will let you go and have some lunch now and when you have finished I will see you back in this room. I will then take you to the departments you will be working in."

When we got back to the Training Room Teresa took us round to our departments. "This is the Menswear section and you, David, will start here from tomorrow. Hello Mr. White."

"Hello," said a tall, middle-aged man in a dark suit.

"Mr. White here is the floor manager. May I introduce David Holle? He will be working in Menswear. David, I will leave you with Mr White until I come and collect you for the tea break."

"Thank you very much Teresa, I'll see you later."

"Patricia, you will be in Ladies Fashion from tomorrow. Many and Louise will be together in the Stationary Department."

I remember that once I started work, from the very first day, I wanted to tell Dr. Pada that I would do well in my career. On the Friday, when he came to see me, I was so happy and I told him everything about the company. "So, do you want to stay?"

"No Dr. Pada, I think I will go back to study for my A Levels. I can do them in Evening Class and there is a college just near where I work. I have got an application form and I think I will start in January."

"That is great news Louise," said Dr. Pada, "That is my girl. I am so happy to see that you are working for a good future. You know, I have been so worried about you Louise; you don't know how often I think of you."

"I do know, Dr. Pada. But firstly, if your family knew, you would get into so much trouble and second, I thought you were going to get married soon."

"How did you know about that Louise?" He asked.

"Anita told me," I replied.

"You see Louise I am not very happy about it but I have to please my parents. I am the only son they have to make them happy. I used to love someone when I was a teenager but my father and mother didn't like her."

"I do understand," I said.

"You can't understand Louise, you don't know how it is," he sighed.

"Oh but I do know Dr. Pada," I cried, "Anita understands and she wants to be different from you. She has a very strong personality."

"I know that she will never let our parents force her to marry but I can't. I am their only son."

"Don't worry Dr. Pada; I won't give you any trouble I promise."

"I know you won't Louise but do you know men? Louise, some times men are very demanding; even if a man doesn't love the woman he just wants to grab any woman who is next to him. You are growing up quickly and you are very beautiful; I don't know how long I can protect you. I think I will be fine without you, Louise, I mean in the future, if you have to leave me but I don't want to hurt you Louise."

"When the time comes I will be fine." I whispered.

CHAPTER FOUR

When I was at work I really enjoyed my section. I was in charge of all the candles and brought stock up to the shop floor and then put a price tag on the items. I was busy all day long and my section was not very far from Many. He was at the Pen Counter and we were both happy with our jobs.

"Hey! Louise do you want to go for a drink," Many said one evening.

"I am sorry," I replied "I can't today. Let me take a rain check."

"Okay Louise, don't worry. By the way, are you living with someone?"

"No," I said, "I live by myself; my grandma died a few months ago."

"I am sorry to hear that. You know Louise, life is so difficult but we have to cope, we have to let it go. I now live with my mother, who is eighty-two years old. A few days ago she had a heart problem so I moved back to stay with her. I am broken hearted and have just finished with my boyfriend."

"Oh Many! I'm so sad for you."

"I know but we have to accept these things Louise. I had been with him for six years. After we split up he got a new boyfriend and I had to begin a single life again. I was sad for a few week but then I thought; 'he is happy with his life, why should I be sad?' I go out every weekend and there are a few clubs I can go to and find someone for a one night stand. We must enjoy ourselves. Would you like to come with me Louise?"

"Yes Many I would like to go with you. I will let you know when I can make it." Many and I were very close friends and always had lunch together. Sometimes he told me dirty jokes.

We were so busy during the Christmas Season, especially on my section. Candles were the best seller and it was my first successful year. Even Many was great in his position. The company took in a lot of money. I remember so well that our Department Manager bought gifts for all of us in the department. Many give me a Christmas present; an expensive perfume and I give him a silk tie. At the end of January I went to college.

At about the same time we were sad because our department manager got promoted to a higher position in another branch. We all liked him because he was a good boss. Also at that time I had a lot of willpower and managed to do my studying. I felt that I could work hard and climb to the top of the ladder. I went to college twice a week. Dr. Padachee would visit me on Friday nights but sometimes he just dropped in on a Sunday for tea and went off to work. He was so kind to me and in late spring, before my birthday in May, he asked me about my savings and wanted to see my bank balance. I showed him what I had in my bank and he nodded his head and looked at my face. "How long are you going to carry on studying?" He asked

"I don't know," I replied, "but I want to go to university if I get the chance."

"I am sure you will go far Louise," he said.

During my second year at the company I had an appointment to see the Staff Department to discuss my progress and they offered me a job in the Buying Office. This was in the sub-basement and I had to work Monday to Friday. Although the pay was good I had to deal with the Head Office. That year I was going to complete my second year at college with five A Levels. "Congratulations Louise. Well done, I am very proud of you," said Dr. Padachee when I told him. To be honest with myself I had forgotten I was eighteen, because I was so busy with my studies and at work. I hardly had time to look at my face. I missed all of my teenage years.

"What are you thinking about Louise?" said Dr. Padachee.

"Oh nothing," I replied, "I was just thinking that the year has passed so quickly and that I want you to know you have done so much for me and without you I wouldn't be in the position I am now."

"Its not true Louise, you are the one who has pushed yourself so far."

CHAPTER FIVE

Late one Friday night in October I had a premonition that something was going to happen to me. It was just an instinct but I felt I had lost something somehow. I loved my job and I had gained so much confidence; I wanted more promotion but I also wanted to become a full-time student at university. I couldn't do it all; inside me I seemed to have lost something. I still needed Dr. Pada but in what way I didn't know. When he parked his car I got into it and he took me far away. I just closed my eyes and was half asleep; I didn't know where I was until Dr. Pada woke me up. It was dark, winter time, but I could see a beautiful canal.

"We will stay here for two nights," said Dr. Padachee. "I have prepared everything for you already in this bag. Have a nice hot bath and then we can go for dinner. I will explain everything tonight." When I thought about it I realised that such things were always in my dreams; always such happiness in my real dreams. I didn't eat a lot because I was still in shock; I was so nervous and did not know what was going to happen to me. I had always wanted to experiment when I was young. Dr. Padachee gave me a beautiful dress made of lace with pink flowers. I couldn't breath. Dr. Padachee told me to relax and everything would be fine. When we returned from dinner he lit a candle in the bedroom. I knew it was stormy outside the cottage; I was so cold and so thirsty. It was so painful until he licked me clean with his tongue; his touch was so gentle and I was dreaming that I wanted it again and again day and night. After we got back to London he continued to visit me every Friday night. He never stayed long in my place; we were so much in love. At the same time he would tell me he hated himself; that he wanted to be someone else so he could marry me.

Before Christmas I got some great news. I had applied to the Housing Association for a one bedroom flat and they had offered me one in Westbourne Grove. I wanted to let Dr. Padachee know that I was so delighted. I would have my own toilet and bathroom! Since I had left grandma's place I had never been happy sharing a toilet with the other people in the house. That week, on the Friday, he didn't come to see me. I was so desolate and wanted to go and see him at the hospital but I couldn't do it. He had been to see me every Friday since I had met him. I forced myself not to cry, but it didn't help. I went to work as usual and when I was at work no one knew that inside my heart was breaking. The next Friday, when I got home from work, I noticed an envelope with his handwriting. When I saw it my eyes were cloudy with tears. Before I opened the letter I asked myself if I really loved him; maybe I did at that moment as I had no one else except for him. When I opened the letter I read:

Dearest Louise

I don't know how to tell you this but I have known for some time that I would hurt you very much. I must be the first person in your life to make you cry. When you lost your way I hated myself as you must hate me now, but I have to leave you because my parents have engaged me to a woman I don't love. I am going to marry her in India. I might be over there for a while so that I can try to forget you. I have to commit myself to my new wife even though I don't know her.

Please forgive me. You are a wonderful lady intelligent, clever and so self-confident. I am sure you will go far in the future so please don't give up on yourself when you don't have me. Be strong and consciousness, protect yourself and plan for the future. Trust your own soul, your confidence is inside you; don't give up hope. I will remember you as long as my heart beats. Look after yourself and don't destroy yourself. I don't want to leave you but I must because of my duty. Look at things objectively then think and speak.

When I was young I saw a baby bird as it hatched from its egg. It didn't know that the snake wanted to eat it; it didn't know that the world was so cruel and dangerous and the snake wanted it as his prey. The nestling was covered in fluffy down and its wings were not strong enough to fly so his mother had to take him down to the garden and show him how to dig for worms. Soon he made his own way, as you will, in this world. The world belongs to you, good and bad, happy and sad, it is only you who decides and no one else can help you. Spread your wings and show the world your own ability, you can do it. I am sure you will do your best without me and I trust you will use your talents, confidence and ability to make your life full of success. Take care of yourself.

Best wishes

Dr. Pada

P.S. Please accept the enclosed cheque and put it into your savings account, you might need it.

I didn't know how I would survive. I read the letter again and again. I was lost at first. I had lost someone who was never coming back; I had lost someone whom I respected. What was I going to do? I was in so much pain at that moment. On the Saturday morning I picked up the phone and dialled.

"Hello?"

"Oh! Hi Many, I hope I'm not disturbing you?"

"I have only just woken up actually but its okay Louise. What time is it now?"

"It is ten o'clock Many."

"Oh dear, I'm sorry I am so tired, I came home rather late last night. You must be in serious trouble."

"Yes," I said, "can you come over to see me Many?"

"Of course Louise, I will see you at two o'clock at Finchley Road Station."

"Thank you so much Many," I said.

"No problem. Bye Louise."

"Bye Many, see you at two."

When we met outside the station Many said, "Oh dear me Louise I think we had better go back to your place; you look awful. You should take it easy Louise." When Many entered my bed-sit my tears never stopped. I gave Many Dr. Pada's letter and when he had finished reading he look at me and said consolingly, "Even though I don't know him I can sense that he is a lovely person. I am sure he has got good reasons. Even though he is a young doctor he has experienced life."

"I am so sorry Many, I have no one else to talk so I had to tell you," I sobbed.

"I understand very well," soothed Many, "I have had the same experience before and it was so painful. It takes time and you have to be strong. I will be your friend and I will teach you how to just put it behind you. Sooner or later you will get your old feeling back. You see Louise, this world is so cruel and people want to get more than they give. The clever ones are stronger and can live. We have to struggle from the day we are little sperm in our mother's womb. You are luckier than me; you can plan to do lots of things. You are so young; I am older than you and what have I got? I have nothing. I still live in my mother's house as I can't afford to buy my own place because I am only a sales assistant. I had no ambitions when I was young. I am quite sure that if I stay out of trouble in this company, this is the place I will work in until I retire. That is why I don't care if anyone calls me Gay. I am happy with the way I am and I accept that I am gay; as long as I don't make trouble for anyone else. Whatever you feel happy with you can do Louise, but I know you will want to be alone sometime. Are you feeling any better? I'll make you a cup of tea so you just lie down on your bed. You know, I think you should take a few days off."

I took Many's advice and stayed in bed for three days. I didn't want to eat anything and all I could do was drink lots of water and have some soup. When I returned to work my dairy showed that I had an appointment to see the General Manager on the Friday afternoon. The interview was held in a private meeting room. I noticed that he was quite young. The gist of his report said that I was performing very well and that I should achieve good success in my career. The report went on to say that I had been in the Buyer's Office for only a short time but that I was able to control all of the merchandise. I thanked him politely and he asked me if I would like to move to the Head Office after Christmas.

When I left the office I heard Many's voice asking me if I wanted to go to the West End with him for a drink.

"No thanks Many," I said, "I don't feel quit right so I had better go home and rest."

"Okay then, if you need me you can give me a call tomorrow."

"Thank you Many, you are so kind to me," I said.

"You are my pal, take care Louise."

"I will, see you next week."

CHAPTER SIX

I was alone in the church and lit a candle. I prayed to God and just sat in the church for a long time. When I got home I saw a letter on the floor. As I opened it my hands were shaking. *Oh! Thank God* I sighed to myself. It was only a letter of confirmation about the flat. I wanted to move to a new place and I also wanted to study and wondered what I was going to do. I didn't think I could cope with my plan. I said to myself, *lets move to a new flat and maybe it might help me to forget all about Dr. Pada.* I was so terribly tired and I had to help on the shop floor. Everybody had to come and support the department. They needed people to wrap the candles in wrapping paper. That Christmas was the best for the past ten years and my candles had sold so well compared to previous years. I was very pleased as it meant my pay rise would be very good.

It seemed so strange to me that I got my mortgage so easily. I had intended to get my own place first; I didn't want to stay in a bed-sit. Maybe I could start my new life and forget about Dr. Pada. It took me nearly two months to move into my own flat. I looked at my clothes, which were in my suitcase. I didn't have a bed to sleep in and had no furniture because, when I left grandma's flat, I couldn't take them with me and gave everything to a charity for the homeless. I walked around the flat; I went into the sitting room which had a beautiful balcony. I could open the door and go out in summer; I had the same thing in my bedroom. The solicitor said that this was the only flat that belonged to the Housing Association, all the rest had gone to private owners. I liked the back of the kitchen as I liked looking out of the window. Sometimes I could see planes flying past every three minutes or so.

I told Many that I had moved out and wanted to invite him for dinner. Unfortunately we never made it at that time as we had to work late every evening for the Christmas rush. We had to do overtime and in the mornings we had to put stock onto the shelves. We had a full days work and then we did the cleaning. To be honest I had to sleep on the floor before I got a bed. I slowly got better and didn't think about Dr. Pada. The place had changed me completely, the environment of a new area. One Sunday morning I went to church. I was so happy to start a new chapter in my life.

The next day, when I got to work Many said, "Good morning Louise."

"Good morning Many," I said.

"Congratulations Louise." He said.

"What for Many?" I queried.

"Oh come on Louise! You didn't tell me, but I will understand if you want to keep it a secret."

"What secret Many?"

"You don't know Louise?"

"No. I am so bloody busy at work I haven't got time to talk to you now. Oh look the others are watching. I will see you outside after work."

When we met later I said, "Hi Many. Would you let me treat you to dinner, you were so good to me and looked after me when I was in trouble."

"It's okay Louise, just a coffee would be fine."

"No Many I insist on a very nice dinner. We are off tomorrow and then we have to work for six Sundays in a row until Christmas. It means we will be very tired

"Yes, we will have to be at work seven days a week."

That evening we walked into a Chinese Restaurant.

"A table for two please," I said to the waiter, "do you like Chinese food?"

"I can eat anything spicy Louise," said Many.

"I would like to try this one Many, a chicken satay."

"That would be lovely."

"Do you want soup?"

"No thank you Louise, I will just go for a main course I think. I fancy the roast duck and rice."

"I will have the mixed meat and rice and some steamed green vegetables."

"That should be enough Louise."

"Okay now, come on Many, why did you say congratulations this morning?"

"Are you joking Louise?" Many said in a surprised voice.

"Why should I Many? I wasn't when you asked me earlier."

"Okay Louise, I trust you. At first I was very upset as I thought you were my friend and I couldn't understand why you didn't let me know about your promotion. I think people in the department know; some of them appreciate your ability but others do not. They say you are too young for it and you got the position because you jumped into bed with the General Manager.

"For God's sake, what position is it?" I gasped.

"From what I hear it is as General Assistant Manager in the Head Office in Victoria."

"Oh God, Mary and Joseph! I swear on my grandma's grave that I know nothing about it," I said.

"I believe you Louise, so where is the gossip coming from?"

"I think it came from our D. M. to the Section Manager and she passed it around to the rest of us. It's just that I think a few of the staff don't like you and they are very jealous of you because you are climbing too fast."

"I do understand Many. I noticed a few days ago that their attitude towards me had changed. So, do you know when I will get the position?"

"They said the Staff Manager will announce it after January."

"I will wait until then Many."

"You really didn't know Louise?"
"As far as I'm concerned I haven't heard anything."

CHAPTER SEVEN

After Christmas I had to clear my desk and then I had to a new problem to think about: I had to decide if I wanted to stay with the company until I retired. What did I want out of life? Did I want to be a journalist or a photographer? Yes my dream was coming back. I wanted to travel around the world. *Are you mad, Louise?* A voice inside me was asking. *You have to pay your mortgage, your bills and your very expensive university for four years. No way can you do it.*

One cold Sunday morning in January, I was walking in the park and looked at a dog with its owner. She must have had money to afford such a dog. I loved dogs and would have liked one if I could but at that time I could hardly afford to feed myself. I walked past Little Venice and up to Maida Vale. I turned to look at the pub; it was a very elegant building, very old style. A sign said 'We need part-time bar staff, apply within.'

When I told Many that I was changing jobs he was astonished. "Oh my God! My dear Louise, why didn't you ask me first - why?"

"Because I knew what your answer would be if I asked for your advice, that's why I made my own decision. If something goes wrong I will be the one to blame myself."

"What will happen if you don't have enough money to pay for your bills?" asked Many. I had listed out all the money I had to spend, about six hundred and eighty pounds a month.

"What about your fees for the first year at college?"

"It will be fine. I have enough with the savings I have got."

"But Louise, your future should be okay with this company."

"I know, but this is my chance. I have got a good place at university."

"Are you quite sure you will complete the four years, Louise?"

"I don't know Many, but if I don't try I will never know."

"You are very stubborn, Louise."

"I know Many."

"Please keep in touch, Louise. Let me know if I can help you"

"I will," I said, "Thank you so much Many, ever since I have known you, you have been wonderful to me."

"Oh Louise, don't make me cry," sobbed Many, "I am sure you are going to get your degree; I was just testing you. You are going to graduate Louise."

"Thank you Many."

I was interviewed for the pub job by John, who was very surprised when I told him about my position in the company and asked me if I was sure about leaving full time employment to be a full time student. At the end of the interview he said that if I wanted any extra overtime I should just ask. I started work from six o'clock to eleven at night, Monday to Friday. The money I earned from this job was still not enough to pay the bills but I didn't want to be in one place more than five nights a week. I had a few friends in the pub, such nice people; most of them had finished university and were just working for the experience. They would soon go travelling around Europe or elsewhere. There was one person who was a special friend. Martin had been working there longer than anybody else and John had given him the position of Assistant Manager in the pub. He was a very honest person and was studying part-time for a Master's degree in Law. "Hey Louise, this is Patricia my girlfriend, Patricia this is Louise, she has just started work here."

"Hi. Louise."

"Hello, Patricia."

"Just call me Pat, Okay? Is Martin looking after you, Louise?"

"Yes, he is, he is a very good person."

"You don't know him Louise. Before you met him he used to fight a lot over girls. He used to go out with so many women but he just settled down a few months ago."

"What made him stop?"

"Well, he took out an American student one night after working in the pub, she was the daughter of a colonel and he fought hard to be with her; she was crazy about him. I think the colonel gave him one last chance to say goodbye to his daughter, but I am happy now. Women like to talk about the past and never forget things, easy isn't it? Okay, I'm off to work, I might see you tomorrow Louise."

"Goodbye Pat"

"Nice to be meet you, Louise."

John was so kind to me. He had a flat upstairs and there was a place for staff to live in. He had divorced two years earlier, after twenty-five years of marriage. His elder son lived in Australia and his second son, who lived with him, was twenty-six years old and was self-employed. John was like a free man and went out with a lot of women. I respected him because he was a good boss. When you needed help or when you had any problem at work he sorted it out immediately. The customers who came into the pub had a lot of respect for him and he had no trouble getting them to leave at closing time. When I finished my studies I sometimes went to the pub and did my homework or chatted with Martin. Sometimes I would have a sandwich before I started work. I worked five nights a week but I was still very worried about my monthly payments. My income was barely enough to cover all my bills and I had to take money out of my savings in the bank to make ends meet. I had to earn more than this job paid but I didn't know how to get the money. I had to pay tax, even though I was a student. I couldn't afford to continue taking money from my savings as after one year I would have emptied my account.

CHAPTER EIGHT

One fine Sunday morning at the beginning of March, I went out to clean my balcony and looked over to the park. I was thinking something strange; I thought someone was staring at me. When I turned round they had gone. I felt so cold; I took my book and I turned the pages over again and again. I didn't understand my feelings until I looked deep inside my heart. I told myself, *I need help; I want another job, where can I go?* All was quiet; then suddenly the answer came into my head; just two words: 'Camden Town'. I didn't know what it meant as I had never been there before. I used to have a friend inside me when grandma died, but I had forgotten all about him when I got to know Dr. Padachee. Some years later I realised he was what they call my subconscious.

One day that Spring I took the bus to Camden Town and walked around the market and it was then that I started my own small business. I was so miserable at first; I had to get up very early on Saturdays and Sundays to collect the ticket number for where I was going to set up my stall. As I was a new face in the market the Market Manager could put me anywhere he wanted. Someone told me he could be very rude if he didn't like you and we had to keep our mouths shut if we wanted to run a business in Camden Town Market.

"Number five, where are you? Do you want to do business or not?" shouted the Market Manager.
"Yes I do and I am here," I said.
"Do you know where your stall is?"
"No I don't."

"Follow that guy there, he will show you. Wait a minute, what are you selling?"

"This is my first time and I am selling a few handbags and some jewellery."

"What kind of jewellery?" He huffed. "If it is silver you have to pay now. Saturdays it is twenty-eight pounds and Sundays thirty-five pounds. You have to pay for today only and this is your receipt. Okay you can go and set up your stall now."

It was a sunny day in spring but I felt cold. I had got myself a small table to lay my stuff out on. It wasn't very nice at all. I displayed the jewellery on the table and said to myself, *Next week I will prepare my own display.* At the end of the day I got back to my place with sore feet and decided I needed to buy a stool. I looked at myself in the mirror and said to myself, *I can do it; I need more money.* I had left all of the handbags in storage at the market, which I had to pay for, and just took the silver jewellery home with me. I went to the kitchen and made a cup of tea. I looked at my sales list and calculated that I had taken a hundred and ten pounds. I deducted the cost of the merchandise and the stall rent and I still had fifty-eight pounds left. I went and had a bath and read my book until I fell asleep.

Sunday was so different from Saturday, there were so many sellers. I thought I had come early but I was wrong. I had to stand in line and got ticket number thirty-two. "Where is my stand going to be?" I asked. "I wanted the same place as yesterday so my customers will know where I am."

"Get in the queue please. It is first come first served. We haven't got time to talk, we just want to set up our stalls and sell."

I moved to a central spot next to a pub; it wasn't too bad.

"Good morning dear," said a woman at the stall next to mine.

"Good morning," I said.

"Are you new here?"

"Yes I am."

"That's what I thought; I haven't seen you here before."

"I just started yesterday."

"Ah! I wasn't here yesterday. Did you have a good day?

"It wasn't too bad," I said.

"My name is Sandra and I have been here for so many years."

"You can call me Louise."

"That is lovely," she replied.

"Do you make good business here Sandra?" I enquired.

"Oh Louise, to be honest with you some days you can earn a few hundred pound like on a Sunday, when there are a lot of tourists in summer, but in the winter it is hell; it is so cold. Nobody wants to walk about in the cold weather but you still have to pay the rent and sometimes I haven't got enough to pay the rent Louise. I see you have your first customer, have a good day."

"You too Sandra," I said. We were so busy that Sunday in spring and at the end of the day we were all happy.

"I hope to see you again next week Louise."

"Yes Sandra I hope so too."

"One thing I should warn you about, you must be careful; there are some bad people in this area and if they find out that you have made a lot of money during the day they might try and steal it."

"Thanks Sandra, I will be careful." In fact I had seen with my own eyes that you could buy drugs in that place also I had seen people fighting with the police. But for various reasons we all had to be there to earn some extra cash-in-hand and this was the way of Camden Town Market. I desperately needed to earn cash on Saturdays and Sundays and I was very grateful to be in the market. As it was a part of my degree I worked there for three years.

I asked John if I could work three nights a week as I got very tired working five nights. I had no time to do my homework. I noticed that none of the other students on my course did any work at all for the first term. I was worried and I sometimes I wanted to join them. I had a few friends in my class but some of the others were such snobs. Everybody had their own group and it was just me who went out to work. One day, after classes were over, I had just put my notes into my bag and was making for the door when someone said, "Are you in a hurry Miss Elizabeth Louise?" It was the first time in my life that anyone had called me by my full name.

"Yes I am," I said in surprise.

"Can you stay tomorrow after my lesson?"

"Yes professor," I said.

"I would like to see you in my office?"

"Okay professor."

"You can go now."

"Thank you professor; goodnight sir."

I had to tell the professor everything. He nodded his head at the end he told me to make sure I had better results after September. I told him I would try my best. I noticed that out of all of us in the three groups I was the only one who had no time to join in with them. We would just say hello, or good morning. I must have seemed to be very strange person to them.

"Good morning Louise."

"Good morning Jason," I said, "How was your first year Louise?"

"Not too bad," I replied "but not too great either. What about you?"

"It was great," he enthused. "I was just going to ask why you never join in with us?"

"I will soon Jason," I promised, "It's just that at the moment I have lots of things to do."

"Are you free this weekend?" He asked, "We are all going to the club."

"I would like to Jason but let me make it next time."

"Hi Jason, there you are, I have been looking for you everywhere. We are all ready to go and have been waiting for you in my car. We are all hungry for our lunch."

"Do you want to go with us, Louise?"

"I'm sorry Jason I don't have room for anyone else in my car."

"It's okay Jason," I said, "I will see you in the afternoon class. Enjoy your lunch Jason."

"Sorry Louise I'll see you later."

I told myself, *don't worry Louise, you can drive, but you don't need a car right now.* I smiled to myself and thought, *Louise you haven't got enough money to buy a car.* Was I jealous of Alison? Maybe yes, she was a snobbish blonde; her father was a businessman and her mother had had plastic surgery and looked younger than her real age. Alison had a Mercedes sports car to drive herself to university and when she got out of her car she looked like a model, who had just walked out of a magazine. A lot of boys wanted to be her friend and she made Jason so special. Jason was the most handsome of all the boys and was in the top grade in class.

"Hey, hey," he called out, "I'll catch you later. Wait for me Louise I want to apologize about this afternoon. I don't think Alison meant what she said."

"No don't worry about it Jason."

"Can I walk with you?" He asked.

"Yes of course Jason," I replied.

"So you are not in hurry today?"

"No, I am not working tonight"

"What did you say?"

"I said I am not working tonight."

"So the day you were running out of class you mean to say you were going to work?"

"Yes that's right Jason."

"Oh boy! I don't believe it."

"Please, I beg you don't tell anyone what I have told you. Only you and the professor know."

"I really must apologise to you. We all thought you were a bit of a strange person. That is why they were talking behind your back. They were all wrong about you."

"What did they say about me?

"Oh nothing really," he bluffed. "It must be Alison who spread these things."

"You make me want to know more Jason, what did she say?"

"Don't worry Louise I will explain to them that it isn't true."

"So you won't tell me Jason?"

"No, Louise, you don't need to know. But I do want to know if you can come out with us this weekend."

"I am very sorry Jason I want to go out with you but I have to work in the morning. Let's make it another time Jason."

"Okay Louise. You do know that I want to be your friend Louise?"

"Thank you Jason. If you want to be my friend you should understand and let me go to work now, otherwise you will not see me at university for the second year. Goodbye Jason and let me know about your weekend."

"I will Louise, I promise."

Once I started working in Camden Town at the weekends I was so relieved that I didn't need to worry about money any more. I knew I could survive for the time being. I learned a few things from Sandra, who was always urging me to save money for the winter. I could see from my own experience that there were some dangerous people around selling drugs on the street and that there was a mixture of worlds; the new generation and the old. I couldn't imagine that anywhere else in London would be like Camden Town. Of course there was The Portobello Road Market but the two of them had very different atmospheres. When I was earning my own pennies I had to believe in luck. I am very sure it must be as if I had good luck on a Sunday I could sometimes make a few hundred pounds but if it was a rainy day I had to count the pennies to pay the rent. I couldn't expect to earn anything like I used to get from the company when I knew that at the end of the month my wages would be paid into the bank. Now I realised that money did not grow on trees. There were so many stalls, all selling the same merchandise and I had several competitors.

One day Sandra said to me, "Are you closing now Louise?"

"Yes Sandra," I said, "I have to go to work in the pub as I have asked John if I can work extra hours on Saturday nights."

"Don't worry Louise, today has not been a great day for everyone. We will do better tomorrow."

"Thank you Sandra."

Saturday night at the pub was so busy; it was just crazy from the start. I just managed to say hello to Martin and we had no time for anything except pulling draught beer. It was a night for making a lot of money by entertaining hundreds of customers who just drank, and drank. I had a few regular customers who always bought me a drink but, instead of taking drinks, I had asked John if I could exchange them for cash. He allowed all the staff to keep the cash. It always surprised me how some people drank beer like water; some of them must earn a lot of money to spend it so easily. Martin was bloody fast, so quick and accurate; he was a great person to work with at weekends. He could make a lot of cash and lots of customers were impressed with his service. Last orders was at eleven o'clock sharp, at which time we would ring the bell and this meant that the customers had to drink up and by eleven-thirty the pub had to be clear.

"Hey! Louise can I give you a lift home?"

"No thank you Martin, in fact I can walk home."

"Not tonight Louise, it is too late and besides you look pale. Come on, jump into the car, that's a good girl. You see, it took less than ten minutes. You have a good Sunday rest."

"I will do Martin."

"Goodnight Louise."

"Bye Martin."

I had a hot bath, turned on the radio to listen to soft music and sighed to myself. *Thank God tomorrow is Sunday, maybe I will have a good day at Camden Town. I could make a lot of money.* I had to think positively to give me the willpower to get up early.

"Hi, this way Louise," said Sandra.

"Hi, Sandra have you got your ticket yet?"

"Not yet Louise, Daniel is in a funny mood today; maybe he knows we had a really bad day yesterday, he is being so kind to us. We have a new trader."

"Oh yes, the queue is so long; I hope I will get a position next to you. There he is. After he has given you a number you can set up Louise. What number is it Lewis?"

"Number14."

"That is a good location Louise; it is near the canal next to the pub.

"Good morning dear."

"Good morning, you must be a new trader."

"Yes I just start a few weekends ago and I was over there with Sandra, she is very nice person, I'm Steven."

"I'm Louise."

"Have a good day Louise."

"And you too Steven."

I was so happy with my sales; it was the best day ever for me. I packed-up my stall quite early as I was worried I might be getting sick; I felt so tired.

"Are you packing-up now Louise?" asked Steven.

"Yes Steven," I replied.

"Are you working tomorrow?"

"No I am at Uni," I said.

"Wow, that's great to hear. I will see you again next week?"

"Yes Steve."

"One thing Louise, please be careful as there are a few bad people around Camden, so watch out for yourself."

"I will," I said, "thank you."

I thanked God for a great day but I was getting worried as winter was coming; then I thought winter is too far away to think about. I heard the phone ring. "Hello," I said.

"Hi it's Martin, where have you been?

"I was working."

"Are you kidding?"

"No I am not I will tell you on Wednesday."

"Do you need any money? I can lend you some."

"No, thank you Martin, I have to work to get some extra. What I earn at the pub it not enough." "Poor you Louise, but you can ask me if you want."

"Maybe when I'm doing my second year," I said.

"Anyway, I called to ask if you wanted to pop in for a drink, I will pay."

"I am so tired, let's make it next time Martin."

"Okay, I will see you on Wednesday. Take care Louise."

"Thank Martin bye then."

CHAPTER NINE

I started my second year at Uni and had to work so hard. I was very busy with so many things to worry about. In Camden Market I had done good business before Christmas but after Christmas the market was empty; it was so cold nobody came to Camden except other traders. Sandra and I had to make our own drinks to save a penny. I still had to find my fees and didn't want to think about the bills. I was going to be broke; every pound I had went to pay for the university and books. I was dependent on my wages from the pub. During January, February and March, we were so poor every weekend we sometimes couldn't pay for the rent. I shall never forget that money does not grow on trees. I was rather depressed at that time.

"Good morning Louise," Said Jason.
"Hi Jason."
"How are we?"
"I am not too bad thanks, what about you?"
"I am so pleased with my first year. My father and mother are also pleased but I think I need to do better than my first year."
"Congratulations Jason, well done."
"You didn't tell me about your results."
"I'm not too happy; I need to improve in a few subjects."
"I can't believe it; you never go out with us."
"I am working Jason."
"Oh yes I know Louise; we have accepted your excuse. By the way are you working this evening?"
"No, not on a Monday," I said.
"Can we meet for coffee?"
"Okay Jason." I agreed.

"Excuse me for interrupting Jason."

"It's okay Alison."

"I've been looking for you everywhere; we were supposed to go for a coffee. I have been waiting for you in the car."

"We don't need to go by car; Marylebone High Street is just round the corner."

"I want to go by car okay Jason?"

"I will see you later, bye Louise."

I tried to think positively about beautiful blondes; there were three of them in the class; they didn't have to work hard like me and they could get what they wanted. They had every opportunity to get top grades in the class but they didn't make the effort. I thought of a lot of reasons why I wanted to do well in the second year.

"And what would you like Louise?"

"A cup of tea please, thank you."

"Two pots of tea please"

"Come on Louise tell me, your life seems to be all work; do you live alone?

"I suppose I do."

"So, I have something to ask you Louise; can you help me?"

"I can't tell you if I can or if I can't; you have to tell me your problem."

"I don't want to go out with my friends any more. I want to be my own person."

"What makes you feel you want to be apart from them?"

"I don't know; I feel I am wasting my time every weekend. We go to the club, discotheque, smoke drugs and then what next? You know Louise; I don't need to tell you."

"I know, sex, yes that's what we humans are doing; there is nothing wrong with it. Why do you want to leave your friends? There must be another reason Jason."

"I know I have got my parent's money and I didn't work hard last year. I should do better than I am doing and now we are into our second year I want to do my best."

"I am so glad to hear that Jason. Your idea is so great and I am very pleased to be your friend."

"You see Louise, when I look at you I see you are the only one in the class who is working hard but your grades are the same or better than most of the others in the class who don't go out to work at night."

"Thanks Jason what you say is very true. Can you tell me about your life?"

"Of course I can."

"Have you had sex with anyone in your group?"

"Yes I have; with Alison but at the same time she was going out with another person."

"So you are very jealous of him?"

"No Louise, not at all. What I have done in the past was just for fun; I have learned that it is not the right time and that I should concentrate on my studies. I don't know how to tell my friends that I don't want to be with them any longer."

"Well, I do understand your situation."

"Please give me some advice Louise."

"I will try to think of something because we are friends and we are in the same class. You need to give them a good excuse but I don't think it is a good idea to stick with me and ignore them. Why don't you look for a part-time job? You could do very well in a bookshop or any kind of part-time job. Tell your friends that you are in trouble with your parents and you have to earn some of extra money."

"Yes, that's a good idea. I will start from tomorrow."

"Could you let me know how you get on Jason?"

"Of course I will; thank you for your advice."

"Thank you for the tea Jason."

CHAPTER TEN

Business at Camden Town was bad and it was getting worse and worse.

"Good morning Miss Louise."

"Morning Mr. Daniel" I said.

"I heard all of you have had a bad time, do you still want to be in this market?"

"I suppose so Mr. Daniel. I need the money."

"Why don't you work in an office?"

"I can't, I am at Uni."

"Oh I see, how many years to go?"

"This is my second year."

"Jolly good. Let me see if I can find somewhere better and I will tell you Miss."

"Thank you Mr. Daniel." Mr. Daniel was the Market Manager and was a very strange person. He can be a nasty man if something doesn't go his way. He has been known to throw a trader out of the market when he complained that he was having a hard time during winter and wanted to have the rent lowered. Mr. Daniel would shout and say, "Oh yes, when you do good business in the summer I never put the rent up. If you don't want to do business in Camden just go, I don't need you; if you don't like it you can go somewhere else, I hate you." But later he would be nice again. He liked the traders to be happy and make money in the market, but he didn't know we were suffering.

"Hi Louise, over here."

"Hi there," it was Jason.

"Can I sit with you?"

"Of course, how is life treating you?"

"I have great news for you."

"What is it?"

"I have got a job."

"Oh well done, do you mean a real job?"

"Yes, Louise. At first I was not quite sure if I would get it or not; I went for an interview and there were a few people there before me. I got it two weeks ago."

"And you didn't let me know!"

"I told you, I wasn't sure I would get it. This is the first time in my life that I am doing a job I love. When I think about it I blame myself; I should have looked for work long ago."

"Where is it?"

"It is at the bookshop that you recommend; I am very grateful to you and I am so happy. There are a few other students from university but they are from a different college. I want to work more hours."

"Where is your friend?"

"Which one?"

"Oh come on Jason didn't you notice?"

"No."

"Everyone in the class knows she hasn't been to lectures for a week."

"I don't go out with them any more, I haven't got the time, but I might give her a call."

"Good, just in case she is not well."

"I will see you Louise, I am very happy."

One Saturday morning, in order to improve my sales for the next year, Mr. Daniel came to speak to me in private and said, "Miss Louise, don't tell anybody but I want to help you to do good business in the market. I have one stall inside the hall that I think might be better for you in winter as it is not too cold. Go and have a look at it and let me know if you are interested."

"Thank you Mr. Daniel," I said.

I do like Mr. Daniel; sometimes he looks at me and I can see he feels sorry for me. I told him I liked the stall but thought it might be too expensive. He said, "You pay nearly sixty pounds outside for two days, I will charge you seventy pounds but you won't have to pay for storage. You can lock up and I will give you a key. You don't need to get up early and wait for a ticket as you have your own site. If I wanted to give it to someone else I would ask them for more money but you are at university and I want you to get your degree. Let's try it for a week and you can let me know if you can make more money outside than you can inside."

"Okay Mr. Daniel, I will try from next week."

I thought that in the long term, if I could open in summer, when I had my holidays, it would be better because inside the hall the market was open seven days a week so I should make some extra money.

I hadn't seen Jason at Uni for two days but I didn't want to ask one of his friends. I thought it must be something serious as he never missed out on classes. As I crossed Baker Street on my way home I saw Jason in front of the coffee shop. "Oh goodness Jason, you look so ill, would you like to drink some tea?"

"No thanks Louise, I need to speak to you in private. Are you going to work today?"

"No, it is my day off."

"Thanks Louise, shall we walk in the park."

"Yes sure, let's get some fresh air; have you been sick?"

"More than sick, I don't know how to tell you, it is so difficult to put into the right words."

"Just open your mouth and talk," I joked.

"It's not funny Louise."

"I know it's not, I assume that is why you missed class for two days."

"Alison is pregnant," he blurted out.

"How many weeks?" I said calmly.

"You are not shocked?" he asked surprised.

"Not really," I said, "I knew something had gone wrong; she didn't attend class and you had disappeared."

"Oh please Louise, I can't cope; she is blaming me for destroying her life and her future. She wants me to see her family or she wants to have an abortion."

"That is cruel Jason. Are you absolutely sure you want to be a father?"

"No I am not. I have been thinking about it for two days. If you remember, I told you I had stopped going out with her because she went out with a senior boy from Uni. Then I got a job and I swear to God I haven't had time to see her. What can I do Louise?"

"You have to make sure whether you are the father or not."

"I am positive."

"So you don't need to go and see her family, but you must give her support."

"She won't listen to me; she says she will commit suicide if I refuse to be a father."

"I hope not, she would never do it. Alison loves herself more than anything. Tell her to keep the baby; her family is very rich and she can take a year off Uni and then come back."

"You don't understand Louise. It will be so hard for her family to accept it."

"So you are a father and I am not, can you agree to see her family?"

"No. That would mean I would have to tell my father and mother. No I can't do that. I must complete my degree."

"I don't need to tell you that you are really so silly. When you went out with her and enjoyed having sex with her, did you think about your degree?"

"I suppose not," he sighed.

"You guys never think about contraception. And don't tell me you had too much to drink and got drunk."

"I forgot."

"What happens if she has HIV, what will you do then? You said she was sleeping with someone else as well."

"It was all my fault Louise; I swear I will never do it again."

"She said she wants an abortion but I think that is not fair. If she sleeps with a man without protection she must know she might have a problem and now she wants to kill an innocent foetus; that isn't right. The best thing she can do is to tell her parents she has made a big mistake and I think her parents will understand."

"What can I do?" He bleated.

"You said you wanted to study, so came back to Uni and I think the problem will sort itself out on its own. You must explain things to her in a subtle way and be gentle with her; she is very upset at the moment and needs good advice from you."

"Thank you so much Louise," he said.

CHAPTER ELEVEN

I was so glad I made the right decision about the corner shop in Camden. I moved into the hall and made a lot of money. I thought to myself that I should tell John, the manager of the pub, I wanted to do only three nights a week so I could concentrate on my studies. I decorated my stall and put some new stock out. I was expecting to have a lot of fun during spring and summer. Sandra and Steve were very surprised that Mr. Daniel was so kind to me; they both agreed that he must have felt sorry for me as I had to support myself; he was much less terrible than before.

One Saturday, when I got off at the station, I was window shopping before crossing the road to my flat. A sign said 'Home Made Soup, Sandwiches, Tea, Coffee', oh how I missed my grandma's soup; it was so delicious. Feeling hungry I went into the café.

"May I have a bowl of vegetable soup please," I asked.
"If you want to drink it here it's okay."
"It is nice and hot but I see you are getting ready to close."
"No, no we have to clear up before closing time; we just live above the shop. I have seen you walk past every weekend but you always seem to be in hurry. Here you are, and I have brought you some toast as well as you look pale."
"Thanks."
"Take your time."
"Are you open every day?" I asked.
"No we close on Sundays, do you live nearby?"
"Just across the road."

"Yes, as I said we have seen you before but this is the fist time you have come in here."

"Yes I was missing my grandma's soup. This is very delicious soup; I haven't had any for such a long time."

"How old is your grandma?"

"She was nearly eighty when she passed away."

"Oh I am so sorry to here that. You can drop in here any time and we will give you a special price. This is my partner, David and my name is Jim."

"Call me Louise. I promise I will pop in again."

After that I popped in nearly every Saturday and became David and Jim's regular customer. Not only for soup. Sometimes they made a very nice dinner and kept it for me to take away. They were both so kind and I paid them very little money.

Jim and David were a couple; they lived above the shop but they also had three flats to rent in our area. They only sold to local people but they enjoyed doing it as it was something to keep their lives interesting. They both went to church every Sunday and on Saturday evenings they would both say, "Don't worry about tomorrow; we will pray for you and you will have good business in Camden Market." In the spring, it was in April, I was so busy in Camden that they would make me a take-away if I wasn't working at the pub.

In the second week of April it was Jim's birthday and I gave him a special present and they both invited me to have dinner in their flat. It was so nice and they both asked me if I didn't mind if they could be my uncles. I agreed on the basis that they had to let me pay for my take-away meals, which were not very expensive anyway, but at least I had a proper dinner.

CHAPTER TWELVE

During that spring, I started my year at Uni so well. Jason and I were very close and we never mentioned his past. We all laughed and had discussions in class; everybody was working so hard trying to get to the top of the class and we called ourselves 'The Great Team' and we promised to help each other. Things had changed so much and we got along so well together, much better than the first year. Alison didn't come back and I think the two girls who used to be her close friends gave up the disco club. They also gave up smoking drugs and both became friendly towards me. Some of the subjects I missed and they gave me a lecture. We were all in the same boat; all the students in my class were looking forward to going up to the third year and we sometimes talked about getting ourselves good jobs somewhere around the world before we settled down. We often laughed at our ideas and someone said we would have to wait for another two years. Jason said we were right to dream and I said our dreams would come true.

"Hello, Louise, I would like you to meet a new customer; she has just moved to Maida Vale, near the Venice Canal. Lucy, this is Louise my close friend."

"Hi Lucy, nice to meet you; I hope you will come and visit us again."

"Oh yes this is a beautiful pub. I love the location and the character of the building and the people here are so friendly. I promise I will come here often. I came here on Monday and Tuesday but I didn't see you."

"I know; I only work three nights a week."

"Why, are you too tired?"

"Yes, that is one reason; also I don't have much time. I am studying at Uni."

"Wow! That is great, you look so young; I thought at first that you were eighteen."

"I am going to be twenty this year."

"So we will have a great time together when you are twenty-one."

"Sure, Lucy," I said.

"Excuse me for disturbing you; there is a cheese sandwich for you upstairs Louise. I made it myself and you can pour your own tea."

"Thank you John, you are so kind and I do like your sandwiches. I am going now Lucy; I will see you later."

"Enjoy your sandwich."

"I will."

She seemed to be a nice girl, she had told me she was working really hard and was studying as well. One day, I thought, she would get a good job.

"I don't want her to work in the pub when I am not here."

"Why not, where are you going?"

"I am going to retire in a few years."

"Oh my God! You look too young to retire."

"Thanks love; you must be a new neighbour."

"Yes I am, I just moved into this area."

"Well, it's nice to have you here. I have been working in this pub for forty-four years love. You said you were new to this area; if you need a hand or have any trouble let me know. Just ask for John, I live above the pub."

"Thank you so much John, thanks a lot."

"You're welcome love."

When I came down, I saw Lucy sitting outside with her friend. It was quite a cold spring but John had put a few gas heaters outside as a lot of people liked to sit in the garden. I couldn't have guessed what part of the country she came from if I hadn't heard her voice. I could tell by her accent she was an Englishwoman or she could have been born here. She could have been Chinese, but no, maybe not, as her eyes were large, not narrow like a fish's eyes. Why was I interested in her? I knew I liked women with a lot of confidence, and she certainly had confidence. I liked her character; yes she was friendly, but not with everyone in the pub. She was a woman who had very expensive tastes; her clothes, her Mercedes car, even though she had a foreigner's appearance she oozed self-esteem. I liked her and noticed that she was interested in me as well. She came to the pub on the four nights that I worked but she changed men like she would change her shoes; she didn't care.

"Martin, do you like Lucy?
"Yes, I do"
"I didn't think men wanted a woman with too much confidence"
"What do you mean?"
"Do you prefer stupid women? Sometimes men like that kind of woman because men want to be the leader. Lucy is a business woman with a lot of experience."
"In what way?" he asked.
"In business, I mean she must have got her own career, her own business. The way she talks like she is the boss; she doesn't care whether people like her or not, but she is a charming person."
"Do you like her Louise?"
"Yes I do like her. She must be a rich woman. Here she comes with a handsome gentleman."
"Hi both of you; how are we?"
"We are fine thanks."
Martin asked for his usual. "Double or single?"
"Double please." Lucy liked Campari with ice and lemonade; she never drank anything else. She could cope with three or four doubles.
"What about you Abdul?" Lucy asked her friend.
"I will have a pint of lager please." Abdul seemed very smart; when they sat next to each other, he was cool and had a sharp

pair of eyes. I thought Lucy was very much in love with him; more than any other man she used to bring to the pub.

"It's good to see you Louise; I would like to know when you have a day off so we can have dinner"

"Thanks Lucy, but I'm afraid I haven't got much time at all."

"What are you doing on Saturday and Sunday?"

"I am working at the market."

"Oh my goodness! How many jobs do you have?"

"Well, I don't earn enough here to pay for my living. I have to pay my mortgage and other bills; I also have to pay for Uni, so my money is very tight Lucy."

"Poor you; are you free on Monday and Tuesday evening? Yes but I have to prepare my stock for the market at the weekend. Soon I will be free on Saturday and Sunday nights."

"That's great please could you let me know."

"I will Lucy."

The year went so quickly, I had a lot of fun in Camden Market and to be honest my business was booming at the weekends. I would get home with a big smile on my face on Saturdays and Sundays. My two new uncles said it must be God who was looking after me as my business had been so good since they started praying for me. They said that their business had also improved that year.

"I think there have been a lot of tourists this year Jim."

"Yes I know,"

David said, "It is from God, he has sent thousands of them to this country."

"Yes, yes I agree. How much is my dinner today?"

"Today we made a quick roast, quick stuff with lemon roast tomato. Not tomato! I mean potato, and a banana fritter. Altogether that is one pound and fifty pence please."

"I'll give you two pounds and you can keep the change. By the way I have some wine for both of you. It is so popular in Camden; I hope you like it, if you do please let me know."

"How much did you make today Louise?

"Nearly three hundred pounds love."

"Jolly good, well done you sound like someone from Camden," David said and we all laughed when I tried to speak like a cockney.

"Don't forget to pray for me and tell God I say thank you. The two pounds is one pound for God and one pound for the poor."

"Thank you love, we will tell God for you."

CHAPTER THIRTEEN

All in all I didn't have much time to myself. I had to prepare for my exams and I worried a lot as I wanted to get to the top. This was very important to me. I thought I should tell John that I definitely wanted to cut another night off my duty at the pub. After the summer term we went to celebrate at the pub near the Uni. Some of my friends were going home to stay with their families. Jason was desperate to make some extra money but we were all very happy. One of my friends said they couldn't wait until the next term as we were going to be seniors in year three. Someone yelled from the back, *'Come on give us a speech; we won't be together for at least two months.'* Another said *'Oh no mate I'll keep it for when we are in year four.'* We were all so drunk and it was the first time in my life that I was really sick for two whole days. I hated it, I hated being sick and promised myself I wouldn't do it again. In the summertime I opened my stall on busy days, I cut down my work in the evenings and I dreamt that I would be very good in year three. I prayed to God every night as I wanted to be someone who would know my own abilities. I would never forget that I was the person he threw away, because I had nothing. I was still very hurt inside; I never showed it but I had a big scar in my heart.

"What are you thinking Louise?" Said Jason

"Oh I was thinking about the past. Do you have a past?"

"Yes of course but I thought that in this world you didn't have a past, only the present; working in the pub, working in the market and attending Uni; that's all you have done since I have known you Louise."

"Oh that is unfair; you look down on me, do I look so angry?"

"Oh no, no Louise, that is the truth; I am so sorry. You are so special; let me tell you the truth. You have so much confidence, much more than me; your mind is thinking forward and you want to prove something in your life; you want to get to the top."

"That sounds better. I forgive you Jason."

"Thanks, you're a princess."

"Don't be silly Jason; come on tell me, did you win the lottery? Why are you taking me out to dinner?"

"I told you I missed you."

"Thank you, Jason."

"It's nothing special no, no. I needed to see my close friend that's all, how is life?"

"Just like you; working very hard, have you heard any news?"

"No, she just won't let me know where she is living. I want to know if she kept the baby; I think she did keep it; I can feel it. I want to go around the world Louise; I want to forget the bad times I have had."

"You will forget and begin a new life very soon Jason, very soon."

"I wonder; I wanted to ask you something but please don't get angry."

"I won't," I said.

"Do you have any boyfriends?"

"At the moment I don't have one and I don't want anyone. I think we have so much time to think about love. If I had a boyfriend it would just be for fun, like you said. I have no time, what about you, do you have a girlfriend?"

"I am alone at the moment and you are my only friend in class. All the others think we are a couple, we look like twins."

"Very well Jason, best friends are forever."

"I agree with you one thousand percent, Louise."

CHAPTER FOURTEEN

One day in May, when I passed the door to the pub, I saw a big birthday cake set out on a table. It had a statue of a bull and a small candle. I stopped to look and wondered where everybody was. If Martin was working, where was he?

Suddenly I heard, "Happy birthday to you, happy birthday to you, happy birthday dear Louise, happy birthday to you."

"Oh John, Martin, Lucy thank you all so much."

"Hey don't cry; you are a big girl now twenty years old, Wow! Here's a card for you, keep it and you can read it when you get home. Go on; cut the big cake for us, hey! This is a very special day for you Louise, from me and Martin."

"I don't know how to say thank you to you all."

"The bull is from me to remind you that you are stubborn."

"Thanks a lot Martin."

"And this is for you Louise. Are you working in Camden this week?"

"Yes, I am open nearly every day now that I am on holiday."

"I might pop in and see you; I haven't been to Camden for a long time."

"Good. If you do come I am in the hall. Camden has changed a lot, it's not like it was before."

"That's what I heard."

"Where is Abdul today?"

"He went away on business and will be back next week."

"I see, do you miss him? I was just wondering as he's always with you."

"I must go home, Louise, I'm a bit tired."

"Yes you look pale. Thank you Lucy."

"You're welcome Louise."

When I got home I read the birthday cards; they were so nice. The first was from John and he had put a fifty pound cheque in it. I then opened Lucy's card, which contained a gift voucher for a hundred pounds. I looked at Martin's bull; I liked the bull more than the money. I didn't mind the cheque from John but I was not comfortable with Lucy's present. I didn't know her that well and I didn't want anyone feeling sorry for me. I had to keep it though as she might have got upset if I refused it. She was such a mysterious person; she still came to the pub with a different man all the time. I liked Abdul, he was cool. I looked at them all but just keep quiet. It was not my business, maybe all these men were just friends of hers; that's what the friend inside was telling me.

It was late in May when I came back from the market and I saw a man sitting outside on the balcony of the next door flat with a blondish girl. He had his back turned to the street so I couldn't see his face. Even though I could only see his back I could tell that the man was ashamed of something. He put his face close to the girl and seemed to be very gentlemanly. My friend inside me was saying, *'Maybe his face looks terrible Louise.'*

'Look,' I said to myself, *'I want to look at the man, I feel so good about it so please leave me alone. He is the kind of man that I want to know.'*

'No, no keep your eyes away from him, you will get hurt again.'

'I know, I know, I just want to see his face, is that okay?'

'No it's not okay, why don't you open the door?'

'Oops sorry, I don't know.' Maybe there had been something wrong with me since that day. I was so happy to get home and open my sitting room door. Then I hid behind the curtain looking to see if he was outside on the balcony. Well he was not, then I smiled to myself, I must be mad, never mind I would soon see his face.

"Hi Lucy I am here."

"Oh, Louise, you are so great; your stall is so attractive."

"Thanks Lucy. Please help yourself to anything you like, just pick an item as a gift from me."

"No I couldn't, I will pay for it if I like it; besides you need the money."

"I know, but you gave me a valuable present. Friendship means more to me than money Lucy."

"I am very impressed with your stall. I really like that scarf."

"That colour suits you, it is so nice; let me put it in a box for you."

"Are you sure?"

"Yes I'm positive; sure."

"I have been walking around Camden and it has changed so much. It seems great for young people."

"Yes and lots of other people too. You have to be careful here as well."

"I know."

"Would you like a drink?"

"No thanks Louise. I would like to ask you Louise, are you free this evening? I would like to cook you dinner."

"That is very kind of you. I'm sorry but I can't make it this evening, can we make it next week? Is that okay?"

"Yes, that is fine; you seem to be so busy. You have a few customers now."

"Thanks Lucy."

"And thanks for the beautiful scarf."

I looked forward to going home each weekend just in case my next door neighbour had invited the girl I had seen during the week to stay. When I got home I was very disappointed I didn't see them. I went for a hot bath and put on my radio to listen to music. As I had done good business my uncles Jim and David said I was in a funny mood and asked me if I had met a man.

"Oh no, not at all; I don't think I miss my grandma any more and I am going to behave as a mature woman." That was my answer.

"Good girl, if you have anyone we would be happy for you."

"Oh no, no, I haven't meet him yet."

CHAPTER FIFTEEN

That year, in June and July, it was very hot. I lay down in the sitting room with a load of books; I love to read. I don't remember how long I slept but when woke up I could hear a woman's voice sighing, "Oh God you are so wonderful! I miss you, I miss you so much." Then she said, "You are the best, you are superb, please, I need you; please don't stop; please do it again, oh God! How wonderful you are."

I realised that I was not in my bedroom and had been asleep in the front room. I went to my bedroom and dreamed about what I thought I had heard until morning.

"What are you cooking for me, Lucy?"

"The first course is chicken satay and then king prawns grilled with green chicken curry and rice. Do you like spicy food?"

"Yes I do, but not too much. I can eat Indian food; I will be okay if you serve Indian food. I didn't know it was so simple to cook."

"It's not too difficult." She told me to sit outside. I looked at the canal and saw a few boats were passing by.

"You know I think that boat has come from Camden. I like to look at the water, it cools me down. I am very sure I am connected with water; it is charming and smooth on top but it has got power underneath."

"Here we are."

"Let me give you a hand."

"Red or white wine?" she asked.

"Would you mind if I said no? Tomorrow I have to work in Camden. I would prefer a cold drink."

"Oh Lewis it is no fun if you don't drink."

"I'm sorry Lucy but it makes me sick if I drink."

"Okay, you take care of yourself."

"Thanks. I like your apartment; it is so beautiful; it must be very expensive."

"It is. But when people are very rich they move out to Chelsea or Knightsbridge but Maida Vale is not too bad for some of them and to think, Maida Vale was not too expensive a few years ago."

"I'm sorry Lucy, I wanted to ask you ages ago, but I didn't, are you self-employed?"

"Yes I am; I have my own business and I have a few properties."

"You know I think you are such an intelligent woman, not from the past."

"I nearly committed suicide when I was young. Now I have got everything that money can buy and the only thing I cannot buy is love. My dear Louise, I am searching for love; I haven't received real love from a man's heart and I am sure if I try to catch it, it will run away from me. I need it and I can't live without it."

"What do you mean?"

"I am a very passionate person as you have seen. I have so many men friends at the same time; I spend my money to get what I want; they all love my money."

"What about Abdul?"

"No, I don't include him. He is a mysterious person, we get along very well and we are in tune with each other. In bed he is the best, we can be together for two or three hours a night. But I don't know anything about his private life. If he wants to come and see me he makes an appointment; he is very polite and sometimes can go all night. He can just kiss me and he makes me feel as if I am going to die. When I am in his arms I forget the whole world. I am crazy to have sex with him and if I could pay him a million pounds to be with me for ever I would."

"What do you mean by that?"

"He has never asked for even one penny from me, that is why I am suffering. I don't know where he is; I don't know where he lives or what he does for a living. He is very strange."

"Does he call you?"

"Yes, sometimes. I am sorry to involve you, it is very unfair and it's not nice of me."

"I am very pleased to be here, I really don't mind. I know you and I have no friends, so whatever you tell me about your private life will die with me. What did you do before, Lucy?"

"It's a long story. I have been cursed since I was born. My parents didn't want me."

"Why?"

"In the Chinese way they didn't want a girl. My father and mother wanted to have a boy. Let me start with my grandfather. He arrived in Siam without a penny and sold iced coffee on the street. At that time, I think it was during the Second World War, he helped to save the Commander's life. When the Second World War came to an end he became a builder. My grandfather had two wives, but neither of them could give him a son, although he had several daughters. When he grew older his wife employed a servant to help clean the house and at meal times. He was very rich and had about a hundred buildings for rent or sale. One night, when his wife went away to visit one of her daughters for a few days, my grandfather slept with her. She was younger than his daughters, somewhere in her late twenties and he was in his late fifties. My grandfather fell madly in love with her and his sex life was rejuvenated. That is what my grandma told me and apparently I look like him. My grandma loved me very much and said he was with the servant all day and he could make love with her until night time."

"How could your grandma stay with him?"

"Oh well, in that generation a Chinese man was the big boss and his wife had to keep her mouth shut. Instead she had to prepare his food. He was so happy when he was with the girl until she got pregnant. I think God knew what was going on; she gave birth to a baby boy. My grandfather loved him more then anything. God was so unfair to his first wife; my grandma had to look after the baby boy and he brought joy and love; everyone loved him. Still my grandfather never stopped loving her. She relaxed for less than six months and he never stopped loving her. He went out to work, came back for lunch and after lunch he took her to bed and was with her for at least two hours he then went back to work and at dinner time he played with the boy. Then he went to bed with her again. She soon gave him a second boy and he was even happier. He asked his doctor to help him until in the end he died in her room. He had a heart attack and his last words to my grandma were that he wanted to make love to her until he died."

"And he did." I said, "So you are the daughter of her first son?"

"Yes I am, my father is the older son of my grandma, but I don't like him, he married my mother and I have an elder brother and a younger brother. My father hated me so much."

"What made him to hate you?"

"I don't know."

"If he hated you, why did he spend so much money to enable you to study in this country?"

"Oh no, you must be joking Louise. My uncle sent me to live here."

"I see."

"I respect him very much and I love him; he is so kind and generous. Before my grandfather died he still kept in touch with the Commander and one day he came to visit him. My grandma told me they spoke in private and the Commander was the one who gave the money to help my granddad in his business. A few months later he went back again but this time my grandma had a breakdown and cried for a long time. He took my uncle with him to England and since then my uncle has never seen my granddad. He died before he returned to his country. My uncle always wrote to his family to keep up his mother tongue and my grandma has kept all his letters. He was so different from my father; maybe he had grown up in another country; we all respected him. In his days in Bangkok a few people graduated from English Universities, especially Oxford University. When he returned my grandma didn't remember her own son; he was so handsome, taller then his brother. He had several jobs on offer but he decided to work for The Foreign Ministry. Through his own ability he became a Minister at The Foreign Ministry within a few years. You know Louise; if I tell you the whole story I will keep you up the whole night."

"But I am very interested to hear all about him," I pleaded.

"I promise I will tell you next time."

"You must keep your promise," I said.

"I will Louise, I will."

I told myself I wanted to know more about Lucy; I wasn't sure, maybe she was very rich in her own right, maybe she just had so much confidence or she had lived a very interesting life.

CHAPTER SIXTEEN

I had so much entertainment from watching my next-door-neighbour; he often had a new fake blonde sitting with him enjoying a pot of tea on his balcony; I was so pleased to learn such intimate lessons without having to pay for them. I knew I had to learn a lot more about romance; I had missed so much in my teenage years. I had once been excited being with Dr. Pada but when I wanted to learn he left me.

I developed a bad habit on Friday nights, I would tiptoe into my sitting room with my heart pounding; I wanted to see his face, how sexy he could be. There he was and I hid behind the curtains, wanting to know what he was doing.

One Friday night I heard the Beep...beep...beep, of a car horn.
"Hi Chris what floor are you on?" a girl was shouting from her convertible in the road below.
"Here I am," he replied and went out onto his balcony. "I'm on the first floor," he shouted.
"Where can I park my car?" She yelled back.
"Don't ask silly questions, go and find a meter and pay."
Then she got up to the flat I heard her complain, "Why didn't you tell me you had moved to a new flat? I had to lie to your secretary that I had an emergency."
"I was about to tell you; my office just called and they said you were on the way to see me. Please, take a seat I want to have a word with you."
"I miss you. You haven't come to see me for two weeks."
"But I gave you a call. I am very busy at the moment."

"Yes I do understand that you are busy but you have a big house in Knightsbridge and I haven't been there for ages and now you have bought a new flat."

"Excuse me Natalie maybe you have forgotten your situation; what did you promise me? If you don't remember I will remind you that I gave you a two bedroom flat at Chelsea; it's where you wanted to live and you don't need to work as I support you every month. You must let me have my own time."

"But I love you."

"But you shouldn't come and bother me."

"But I am not."

"If you are not bothering me why have you come to this place?"

"I just told you, I miss you. Now I see why you are ignoring me."

"What is it?"

"You have got a very beautiful neighbour who looks younger than me."

"What are you talking about Natalie? I haven't seen her."

"Don't lie to me; she is next to your bedroom. I want to see her."

"You can't just walk through someone else's property, you have to show respect to my neighbour. You are so rude; please don't behave like a child. I will make you a cup of tea."

"Okay Chris, but I'm telling you she is too young for you, she is probably a student."

"You are so silly Natalie; I haven't seen her since I moved in."

The next day, when I got back from work, I saw a white lily and a note just outside my French windows. I opened them, picked up the note and read it:

Dear neighbour,

I am very sorry about yesterday evening and I want to apologise as it was my friend who went into your property. I have just moved in and I hope you will forgive me for disturbing your private area.

Thank you

Chris.

I took the flower and his note and thought to myself that he was a gentleman and that I would have to be careful. On Saturday night of the same week, I was reading my book in the front room, my heart was beating, it was so gentle and heavy, he was the one who played the orchestra and she was the one who was singing a beautiful song. It was beautiful from the beginning and it was so wonderful at the end, it lasted about two hours.

CHAPTER SEVENTEEN

We were back for our third year of university.

"Hey, hey," Jason said, "You look very mature Louise."

"Do I?"

"Yes, you make everybody happy." We shouted and kissed each other; the third year was very important to all of us. We were all together and were looking forward to our final year. We had to stand tall and get to the top. Jason was the leader; someone blew a whistle;

"Yes we will, yes we will Jason."

I had to pay for my fees, books, bills and my mortgage that month. I was so broke and wondered how long I could carry on if my business was not too good. All the money I had saved up, which had amounted to quite a lot, several thousand pounds in fact, had just disappeared. I had been saving up for such a long time. The tears poured down my cheeks, I had no one. I had to work so hard but was still very poor, my heart was empty. I stopped at Jim and David's to pick up my dinner.

"Oh dear me you don't look well Louise! Sit down and I will make you a cup of tea. How is your third year going? Is it too much for you?"

"No, David."

"I think Louise is in need of a holiday, look at her life; she never seems to enjoy herself, work, work, work since she was sixteen! She never goes abroad and needs some love."

"We give her love."

"The love I'm talking about lover is she needs willpower. For example; when she finishes at university she will need someone to be proud of her, someone who can comfort her, do you understand?"

"Oh I see. How do you feel Louise?"

"I will be fine, don't worry Jim," I said.

"Here is your dinner. If you don't feel better please give me a call."

"Thanks Jim."

"No, no you keep your money; this is a special dinner for you."

"But you promised you would take my money."

"Next time I will. Go and have a bath and have a rest and please take care."

"I will."

"Good girl."

When I crossed the road I didn't see the car. When it stopped very close to me I just dropped the package with my take-away in it. To my surprise the car didn't drive away, the driver got out and came over to me, "Are you okay?" He asked.

"Yes, it was my fault," I said. I couldn't look him in the face but I recognised his voice. I just looked down and tried to clean myself with a cloth.

"Oh look I have spoiled your take-away."

"It's okay."

"No it's not I am going to buy you dinner."

"No sir, I will be fine."

"Let me take you home at least."

"Thank you sir I just live near-by."

"Don't call me sir; do I look like an old man? Look at me, that's better; let me take your bag. Come on get in the car, which way do we go?"

"Go straight on and then turn left. If you stop near the park I can walk from there."

"No I insist on taking you home girl; you do not look well."

"Yes okay if you must."

"Right, so you live near my place. Let me park my car and I will take you to your flat. That is a good girl."

"I am okay."

"No you are not. Now what flat are you in?"

"I am fine."

"I will go and buy you some dinner to replace the one you dropped."

"I'm not hungry."

"Just tell me what your flat number is?"

"I'm on the first floor."

"So you are my neighbour? Very good; now you go and have a rest and I will come back later. How do you feel?"

"I am okay."

"That is good. I'm going to get you dinner."

"No please I can do it."

"You just sit down and relax. Your flat is just like mine. By the way I am very sorry about my friend the other week; did you get my note?"

"Yes I did, you didn't need to send it."

"I'm glad I did. This is a vegetarian soup and some salad. I don't think you need a heavy dinner. Just drink your soup and I will come back later."

"No please."

"I am going to sit here until you drink your soup; then I will go to my flat. That is a good girl."

"I am not a girl."

"I know, but you look like a little girl to me. This is my card, you can call me Chris."

"Nice to meet you," I said.

"And it's nice to know my next-door-neighbour. I haven't seen you at home in the evenings."

"I go to work."

"Oh I see, do you work every evening?"

"No just a few nights."

"I never see you rest in the day time."

"I have to attend Uni."

"Well, well, so that's why you look so tired. You should have a good rest at the weekends."

"I have to open my stall in the market."

"Oh dear God! I don't believe this is a true story. How can a small person like you be so strong and have so much energy?"

"I don't, that's why you nearly hit me on the road."

"I am very worried about you. Don't you want to introduce yourself to your neighbour?"

"I'm sorry, you can call me Louise."

"I'm glad to know you Louise."

"Thank you for the soup."

"You are welcome Louise. What year are you in?"

"This is my third year."

"Well done, one more to go. Your parents must be very proud of you. I will leave you to rest now; may I call you tomorrow?"

"Yes, I will be here at about the same time."

"I don't mind I can just walk through from the balcony. Take care and have a good rest Miss Louise, good night."

"Good night."

I wondered if this was the man that I wanted to know so much, the one that was in my imagination. He wasn't cruel; in fact he was very handsome and attractive. It was no surprise to me that the woman called Natalie was so crazy about him. I didn't want to think about it. If all those blondes were so impressed by him, what hope did I have?

"Jason you made me jump; I was not well last night and felt so tired."

"Yes you do not look well Louise; you shouldn't work so hard. Don't forget that next year is our last and you need to get your brain ready and your energy levels up."

"Thank you Jason, you are a real friend.

When I was at the front door of my house I turned the key and felt that someone was looking at me from the balcony. "I've been waiting for you Louise. When you are ready I'll make you a cup of tea." I gave him a smile; I was not comfortable at all. I put the book I was carrying on the table and went to wash my face. My heart was racing, I couldn't breath. The friend inside me said, *'Don't be shy; you are a woman not a young girl. Go and see him.'* I opened my French windows and walked through to his balcony.

"Here is your tea and I am going to put some toast on. I saw strawberry jam in your cupboard yesterday; you must like it so I got some for you today."

"Thanks."

"How was your day? Do you feel better?"

"Yes, thanks."

"Did you tell your parents?"

"No,"

"Why? You really should."

"I live here by myself; I used to stay with my grandma until she passed away. Then I moved to this place."

"I am sorry to hear that Louise. I did the right thing; I was supposed to go to New York today but I postponed my flight."

"You shouldn't have done that."

"I do worry about you; don't ask me why as I don't have an answer; I just wanted to make sure you were okay."

"Thank you for being so kind."

"I won't be in this country for at least three weeks but if you need me you have got my card and you can leave a message with my secretary. I have cooked a meal for you look; it is a nice roast chicken with a fresh salad and fresh orange juice; go on taste it and tell me if I am a good cook or not."

"Thank you so much but I don't want anything."

"I want to hear 'Thank you Chris'."

"Thank you very much Chris."

"That sounds nice. Now, when I am not here I want you to take care of yourself. I really want to see you graduate with a first class degree and I will be there to take a photo of you in your graduate cap and gown."

I remember that night and every word he said, his eyes, the way he treated me. He was a gentleman and I have never forgotten him, not even in the past thirty years. After Chris went to New York I didn't hear anything from him until the end of the month when he sent me a postcard:

Hi Princess,

I'm sorry but I am still in New York, I am very busy and I will see you when I get back to London. Miss you.

Chris.

I didn't think that the way he was treating me was special; maybe he was the kind of man who had to be nice to everybody. I was thinking too much; I should have known how many women he had slept with. When I went to work at the pub I saw Lucy with Abdul and she looked happy.

"Nice to see you Lucy," I said.

"Good to see you too, I missed you and was waiting to ask you if you are free next Saturday evening?"

"Let me look in my diary, next Saturday? Yes Lucy I am, it should be fine because after that week I have to go back to Uni."

"I will pick you up in Camden."

"That will be nice Lucy. You have a customer, excuse me."

I thought it would be good to talk to someone so that I could forget my stupid ideas. I couldn't stop thinking about him and I was going crazy.

CHAPTER EIGHTEEN

"Hi Lucy I am nearly ready; give me a few more minutes."

"Yes sure; have I come too early?"

"No, not at all. Today was not a great day as on Saturdays most people go to Portobello Market."

"I didn't know that."

"Yes they always do; we are busier on Sundays here. Right, shall we go?"

"I will take you to Knightsbridge; there is a tasty Chinese restaurant, do you like Chinese food?"

"Yes I do."

"After dinner I would like to have a nice pot of tea at my place."

"Sure, sure."

"Thank you Lucy that was very nice food I am very impressed."

"You are welcome."

"Tell me is this a special day for you, is it your birthday?"

"No not at all. I have something to tell you but I don't have time, so I thought I would let you know first. I wanted to tell you in the restaurant but it was too noisy."

"Is this the drink you like?"

"Thanks Louise, you know what I like."

"Please make yourself comfortable."

"I do like your flat."

"It is very cosy and it's big, like yours."

"My place is big but it's sad, the owner has to wait for a man to live with."

"Don't say that; you have got nearly everything in your life."

"That is true, but money can't buy happiness, isn't that true Louise?"

"Yes I agree, but if you have got money it can help."

"Yes I know Louise, but mark my words, money is not everything. I used to think like you but that was a long time ago. When my uncle sent me to this country, he sent me to live with an English family until I had finished my O Levels. Whilst I was staying with them, Mr. and Mrs. Smith went on holiday to Spain for four weeks. I had to stay with their son, James, who had recently returned from Germany, where he had managed to get a good job. We were very happy to cook and watch television together. One Friday night he came home late; I was in the sitting room and he came to me and started kissing me from my head to my toes; he was a very sexy man. In fact he was really great in that way and he was very handsome. At first I allowed him just to kiss me. He was such a romantic person; he kept saying the nicest things. He said I smelt nice and was so clean that he couldn't stop kissing me. I was nearly dead and asked him to let me go. I was enjoying his kisses and when he kissed me down there I couldn't resist it; it was the first time anyone had done that to me. I am sure you know how it feels when it is your first time to make love. We were in the sitting room, on the floor all night. When I got up early the next morning he began a new game. He wanted to make breakfast and give me a bath. In the evening he took me out for a beautiful dinner and when we got back we did the same thing again and again. We couldn't get enough. When his parents came back from holiday he told them he was going to buy a flat in London. At that time he was working on computers and earned a lot of money."

"He came to visit us at weekends and one night I made so much noise, I couldn't help it and he missed me so much. When we met we were in our own world even though we were in front of his parents, it was so embarrassing. He told them very clearly that he loved me and wanted to marry me. 'Oh for God's sake,' they said, 'she is a baby, she is only sixteen and she has to go back to study for her A Levels.' He said that it would be no problem and that I could study in London. His mother started to say 'What about her parents don't you forget she is a for...,' but she stopped and the word didn't come out of his mother's month. I said it was okay and that I agreed to live with him in London but I asked them not to tell my uncle."

"You know Louise I was so crazy about him I moved to London to be with him. I didn't go back to do my A Levels; it was one of the biggest mistakes of my life. I disturbed him too much; all I wanted from him was sex. I soon realised that it was not all sex when you live with a man; you have to cook and you have to work hard and be a mother to him and of course give the best sex to keep your man with you. It lasted for one and a half years and then, one day, he said he had to go and work in Sweden. He told me not to cry, but he couldn't take me with him. He was going to get big money for the contract and I could visit him if I had the chance. He told me he would call me every day and said he had put the flat into my name. He also said I had money in the bank and we would soon buy a big house and have children."

"For the first three months nothing changed and then he signed a new contract. One day my door bell rang. I said I was coming and asked the woman at the door if I knew her. She asked if I was Lucy Smith and I said I was. She told me her name was Helen and she wanted to talk to me. When I asked her what it was about she said it was about my husband. He had sent her to tell me that he would not be coming back to England and that he was staying in Sweden. She said, 'You can see I am going to give his child, he loves you but he can't tell you himself, he doesn't want to hurt you.' I was so upset I just asked her to leave my property, like immediately. I talked to him and he said he still loved me and that it was all his mistake. After that we just talked through our solicitors. Do you know Louise? Since then I have been involved with many kinds of friend. I went to discos and got involved with so many boys; in the end I became a drug addict, smoked hash, cannabis; I made myself worse than a prostitute; I didn't sell my body it was free to anyone for a one night stand."

"I had a close friend who was my drug dealer; she got it from the black market. One weekend we went to a disco club; it was nice and was packed with young people. We were drunk and smoked drugs; I didn't know who I was with. I woke up and was with this guy; he was asleep and I have no idea who he was; I just grabbed my clothes and ran away. When I got home I thought about Sue, I don't remember where I went. I told myself I would call her later. After a bath I watched the News on T.V. They had found the body of a young girl aged between eighteen and twenty. She had been found dead close to the park in Brixton; she had been raped and had suffered head injuries and her body had been badly beaten. There was no identity and the police were asking if anyone could help and to please phone a certain number. I called Sue to ask if she wanted to go out in the evening but her parents said she hadn't come home that night; they thought she was with me. When her parents and I went to the police station, I swore to God that I would change my life. I was very scared. Why, oh why did it have to be Sue; her parents were crying; it was a terrible sight to see. I was sick and I blamed myself; if I had stayed with her she would still be alive. I didn't know what to do with my future; I couldn't go back to my uncle. I lied to get his money but I didn't do any studying; I used all the money on drugs as I needed to smoke to forget about Sue."

"I went to the door and the lady asked if she could help me; she didn't even invite me to sit down as she was speaking in another language to a beautiful lady. Once I had sat down I explained that I wanted to sell my flat and that I wanted an estimate of how much it was worth. She asked where I lived and when I said, St. John's Wood, she said that was good and she would visit me the next day if that was convenient. I said I would be at home so she gave me her card and said I should just call her Nadia. The next day she turned up with a guy; she told me the price of the property, which would leave me with a lot of money and asked if I was sure I wanted to sell. I said yes and she promised that the flat would sell within a few months as it was in a good location. She was right; I sold it in less then two months. She was a kind lady and I wanted to earn her gratitude."

"I went to a clinic to cure my drug addiction. It was a very hard time; it was so difficult but I thought I could manage because I remembered Sue's face; it was terrifying when I thought of how she looked when the police showed us her body. I wrote a note to my uncle:

Dear Uncle,

I am going to tell you the truth now. I have spent all of the money that you sent to me on drugs and I haven't been to the university. However, at the moment I am in a clinic getting treatment from doctors to cure my drug addiction. I am very sorry; I shall never do it again. I will not return home to see you until I have made a lot of money. Please forgive me. I hope you will be able to understand me,

Lucy."

"So how did you make your millions Lucy?" I asked.
"When I got out of the clinic I wanted to be a new person, but you need someone to help you Louise, if you haven't got confidence to make it on your own. I called Nadia and reminded her that she had sold my flat for me a few months earlier. I told her my name was Lucy and she remembered me and agreed to see me that evening outside her office. Well, we met and I spoke to her and asked her if she would let me train in her office. I said I didn't need any money. She was a genius and so self-confident; she gave me the idea of buying an old house on the cheap and doing it up. She recommended a builder who decorated the

house; I stayed there for a year and then sold it. Nadia found me a good buyer; she is very rich herself, I mean her father is from Saudi Arabia and her mother is English; she is the big boss at the agency. Very soon my money built up."

"Where is Nadia now?" I asked

"It is a long story; she married an American Diplomat and is now in the United States. I miss her a lot; we used to go to the Park Lane Club; she always had rich men with her; she was a very lucky person. At the time she was making arrangements for her wedding we went out to a club and that night she met the owner of the club. We never actually saw him as they said he was a man who didn't like to show himself. He owned ten buildings in Park Lane, a restaurant, the club and had his office at the top of the building. I forgot to tell you; you had to be a member to get inside the club."

"So you are a member?"

"At first Nadia was able to get me into the club; it's strange, before you could become a member you had to prove that you had four million pounds in your account."

"What?" I said astonished.

"That was the rule for membership. When we got in that weekend I didn't believe there were so many rich people in London. There was a beautiful restaurant on the ground floor, a bar and a dance floor at the top. We enjoyed dancing until late. All kinds of people from around the world were there. You might see the king of a small country, the president of another, businessmen from many different nations, white, black, yellow they could all join as long as they had four million pounds. They all spoke the same language, I mean 'Rich'. The rich don't care who you are as long as you are rich. Nadia said she was very lucky to be in the club before she met her future husband. The club were very strict and there was a secret; nobody knew who the real owner was, whoever it was had been in charge before the Second World War. Do you want to know more Louise?"

"Yes please, Lucy. I think your story is very interesting."

"It gets more exciting."

"Could you tell me more Lucy?"

"Yes I will tell you more. To carry on with the story; someone said the club was connected with money linked to a secret agent and the CIA wanted to investigate it, but they never got the secret out of them as they all stuck together."

"A gentleman who liked blonds came over to say hello to Nadia; he was talking to her a lot. Nadia was wearing a long, black dress and looked absolutely great. You know Louise? I think he was falling in love with Nadia; they were dancing on the dance floor and he was kissing her. They went back to his house in the end. Nadia told me there was one blond woman who used to be crazy about him and she gave Nadia a lot of trouble. I think she was a French woman and they hated each other. One Friday night he went to the club without her and all night long he danced with Nadia; it was so romantic; I could see that Nadia was melting like butter in the pan on the dance floor. That night I left the club before her and she phoned me a few days later. She told me that she had stayed with him day and night and they had made love several times. Suddenly the blond came in and slapped Nadia in the face and he went mad with the blond. Nadia told me she made a decision there and then to escape with the American Diplomat, marry him and go and live in the USA. She wanted to settle down and leave all her problems behind; she hasn't been back to the United Kingdom since she left."

CHAPTER NINETEEN

Lucy and Abdul popped into the pub more often when I was working; we had become closer than before. I noticed Abdul cared about Lucy; there was something in his eyes. He was a gentleman, so calm and deep in his thinking. Lucy was a kind, open person, whilst he was a man who could keep a secret until he died; he had to of course as he had another woman, more then one I suppose.

"How is your third year going?"

"Fine thanks Abdul."

"I am very proud that you are so clever Louise."

"I am like everyone else; I have to earn a living."

"But you are special Louise I hope I will be here to see you succeed."

"Of course you will Abdul."

"I don't know about my future Louise. I don't know where I will go. At the moment I am with Lucy, but things might change soon."

"Hi both of you what are you chatting about?" said Lucy.

"We were talking about several things," Abdul answered.

"Can I join in?" she asked.

"Of course you can."

"May I have the same drink again please Louise? Thanks Louise. Oh I forgot to tell you, I am going away next week and this time it might be a long time before I see you again."

"I will still be working here. I hope you will be back soon. Lucy will miss you."

"No she won't miss me."

"I can see it in Lucy's face that she will miss you."

"You might be wrong Louise, if he is away too long I might get someone else; I can't wait for him to come back." I never thought that it would be the last time I said goodbye to Abdul.

Time was rushing by, my life was spent in a flurry going round various places home, Uni and the market; everybody had their own duties to perform.

"Hello Louise, how are you?"

"I am okay thanks, when did you get back from New York?"

"May I come into your sitting room?"

"Yes, please take a seat, I'll go and make a pot of tea."

"Thanks Louise. I'll come with you to the kitchen, how was your day?"

"I'm just tired."

"I think you are Louise, you work too hard."

"I have no choice."

"I can get you a job if you want."

"I have no time to clean my house, except in the evening."

"It doesn't matter what kind of job. You could be my secretary."

"In that case neither of us would ever get the job done."

"I am serious Louise."

"Can you afford my wages?"

"How much do you want?"

"I am very expensive."

"But I would be happy to pay."

"Let me think about it."

"Just let me know when you're ready Louise. I will be very happy the day you want to be my private secretary." We both laughed and I had realised by now that he was flirting with me.

"What day are you free next week?"

"I am working at the pub for three nights but I will be free on Monday and Tuesday and at the weekend."

"But at the weekends you are so tired Louise."

"I know."

"I will take you out for dinner on Tuesday, is that ok Louise?"

"If you want Chris and thank you."

"I want to do more to look after you Louise."

"I appreciate it Chris." Chris was gone for a long time. He didn't stay in his flat and his car was not out front. Since he had known me he had stopped bringing blonds to his place; I don't know why, maybe he was embarrassed that I might hear when he was going to make love. I couldn't sleep; I had so many questions; did I want to be in a deep relationship with him? Yes; he was romantic and very rich but he had so many girlfriends; did I really want to get hurt again? On the Sunday I had a nice day. This was the time to save money for the next year. Whenever I thought about my fourth year I was so proud of myself. I promised myself I would get a better job. This positive thinking kept me going to work and moving forward; it was the only thing that kept me alive. I was so tired and I was very jealous of Lucy. She was so independent and could get whatever she wanted. Although she had a rough life before her success she was a good person and gave me so many reasons to respect her.

When I got home one evening I didn't see anyone on the balcony and didn't hear him for the whole week. Where was he? Did I miss him? Yes I did. I went to the sitting room; he was in his flat and had turned on some soft music. I heard a woman's voice; she was laughing; so was he. Oh well I thought perhaps I might have some entertainment very soon. I went and had a bath, ate my dinner; David and Jim had made me a nice roast chicken; it looked so delicious but I couldn't taste it. I decided I must be sick so I went to my bed with a lot of books; I didn't know which one I wanted to read and I wasn't really in the mood to read. *'Listen you,'* the guy inside me said, *'do you want to study? Do you want a man? What do you want?'* I used to play this game when I had too many problems; I called it, 'The focus in mind'. I heard my front door bell ring.

"Hello, sorry to bother you Louise, are you still awake?"

"Yes."

"Could you let me in and I will go to my flat then I will walk through the balcony?"

"Okay Chris."

"I sent my friend home and when I came back I saw your light was still on; are you reading?"

"No, I mean I wanted to read but my brain isn't working."

"Did I disturb you?"

"No, no can I get you a pot of tea?"

"No thank you Louise, I won't stay long, I know you are very strict with your time."

"You can sit on my writing table."

"No, I prefer to sit next to you."

"But it is not comfortable."

"It is okay Louise. Did you have a good day at the market?"

"Well it wasn't a great day but I felt happy."

"I need an answer from you."

"What about?"

"Oh you have forgotten already!"

"Yes I have, I am sorry Chris."

"Do you want to be my private secretary?"

"I haven't made up my mind yet. Could I let you to know next Tuesday, when you take me out for dinner?"

"That is a good idea Louise but listen to me, it is not worth you working in the pub at night it is too late and the atmosphere is too smoky. I don't want you working at all really. You need to study hard for your final year but if you enjoy selling your jewellery in the market you should keep on doing that. I am serious Louise, I wasn't joking that day when I offered you the position; think about it. Let me say good night." He came to me and kissed me on the cheek, "sweet dreams."

He was gone for a long time and left me with a feeling of lust. I was sure that if he had stayed longer he would have made me nervous; I just didn't know why I wanted to be with him.

Did I like him? Did I love him? Or was it his money I liked? I expected that I would find out that Tuesday night.

CHAPTER TWENTY

When I had finished my work at Uni I wanted to see Lucy so much, so I took the underground from Baker Street and got off at High Street Kensington. When I got out of the station I turned right, crossed over to the church and could see her shop. She had some beautiful clothes in the window.

"Sorry madam the shop is close."

"I know am too late but is Lucy in the Office?"

"Let me check." The girl went upstairs for a while and when she came back she invited me to sit down.

As Lucy came down the stairs she said, "Hello Louise, please come into my office." She turned to the girl and said, "You can go home now, just lock the front door behind you."

"Thank you."

"What a surprise it is to see you, what would you like to drink?"

"Just orange juice, please Lucy. Thank you. Do you have time for me now Lucy?"

"Yes today I'm free; I was just thinking of you; I thought I might call you tonight."

"I couldn't wait to see you at the pub on Wednesday; I need to see you in private."

"So what made you come here?"

"I think our minds must work together, I wanted to ask you something."

"Are you hungry?"

"Not really."

"Let's go to my place. Shall we walk to the off-licence and get some drinks? Then we can go in my car, it's parked at the back of my shop."

"What are you looking at Lucy?"

"Did you see that Mercedes sports car over there?"

"Which one is it?"

"The one stopped at the traffic lights, the silver grey one with the blond in the front."

"Oh yes that is Chris, do you know him?"

"Yes I do."

"But you never told me."

"I didn't mention it because he is just my neighbour."

"How come? I thought he had a big house. I have so many stories to tell, let's get home."

It was a small world; I couldn't believe I had seen him again.

"Would you like a glass of red wine Louise?"

"I don't drink Lucy."

"I'll get you an orange juice. Do you remember I told you about Nadia?"

"Yes I do."

"He is the same person; thank God Nadia didn't marry him, he will never change; he is crazy about blonds. He is a billionaire. Nadia said he loves to pay women just for sex and then never see them again. There was one blond for whom he bought a flat in Chelsea; I think she was a model with a cosmetic company. She was very beautiful but Nadia said they both hated each other. Don't tell me that Chris fancies you Louise."

"I don't think he likes me Lucy."

"When did he move into that flat?"

"Only a few months ago; he has got lots of girls but the one you mentioned, her name is Natalie."

"How do you know her?"

"She came to see him and gave him trouble; I heard him call her names."

"How did you meet him?"

"I was crossing the road and he nearly knocked me over. It was my fault; I wasn't feeling well that day."

"What happened next?"

"Like you said, he disappeared and then he came to say hello a few times."

"Oh wow Louise!"

"But nothing was going on between us until one day he was making a joke and asked me if I wanted to be his cook and his private secretary."

"What answer did you give?"

"I didn't think he was serous so I said to him that my wages would be too expensive so he asked me how much I wanted."

"Oh boy, oh boy!"

"Then last night he called again and said he wanted an answer to his offer."

"What did you say?"

"I didn't say anything. He is going to take me out for dinner tomorrow evening and I was going to give him my answer then, that's why I need your advice."

"I have told you so much about him I think you know him better then I do. This case is one in a thousand, I think he fancies you but I'm not sure how deep you and he have gone. I hope he hasn't slept with you."

"No, not yet."

"I think he wants to help you, do you want to know the reason why? I think I am right Louise but in some ways you look like Nadia, not exactly, as you are so many years younger then her; I can't explain. When I met you for the first time I felt you were a warm and special person and because I am very close to Nadia. I think he loves Nadia and he must think that you are special too. Do you want to accept his offer?"

"I don't think so Lucy; but I want to ask you something, please don't get angry with me."

"Do you need money Louise?"

"I will be okay for this year."

"Listen to me Louise, I know you so well; I know you are proud but sometimes you have to think of yourself. I have a lot of money, I am not a multi-multi-millionaire but I do have a few million and I want to give some to you. If you want to return it to me when you have a good job you can. I know you are working very hard to earn the money to pay for your university. Think about it Louise."

"Thank you so much Lucy. When I am in trouble I will always let you know."

"You promise Louise?"

"I promise."

"I have decided to go home to live. I think it is a good time to see my family again. When I am not here you must take care."

"Why Lucy?"

"Because of Chris; he is a playboy and his life is too complicated. You don't know him well enough; he hides himself behind a mask."

"I will look after myself Lucy don't worry. Why do you want to go home?"

"I feel I'm alone in this world."

"But you have Abdul."

"That is the main point; I really enjoy being with him. I haven't slept with another man since I met him. I have a deep relationship with him and we both get along so well together; we can stay in bed all day and night."

"What makes you unhappy Lucy?"

"I think that when we women get to our late thirties we worry; we want to marry and have babies. I want to be like that; I want to have a permanent man. Before I met Abdul I used to pay men to make me happy; I didn't care how much I had to pay for one night of sex as long as I was satisfied. If the man was good it made me feel so great and the next morning he would just pick up the money when he had done his duty. If I was really impressed I would call him again. Since I met Abdul I feel I need someone to make me tea and breakfast in bed or someone who will sleep next to me. When I see a baby I want to be a mother; I want to settle down."

"You could ask Abdul to stay with you."

"No, I think he is a person who prefers to remain private. I don't really know him at all, l don't know his family, I don't know what he does for a living; I just call him when I need sex but when he is with me I forget the whole world. He is the best; he is such a wonderful man but I don't think he loves me enough to be my husband. I think this is the right time to look for a man, before it is too late. I have spoken to my uncle and he said he has got two International Schools so I can help him to look after them if I get bored, but I will keep in touch with you Louise"

CHAPTER TWENTY-ONE

I dreamed that I was walking alone, didn't want to think about anyone and felt so tired; I stopped by a pond and looked at the white lotuses, there were hundreds of them and there were so many big trees; there was a pleasant smell all round and the park was very clean. I thought that I remembered that I had been there before. As it was neither too hot nor too cold I decided to walk up the hill until I reached the top where there was a big castle. I wondered if I should go into the hall but decided it was better not to; maybe it would be very rude and I would have to hide behind the door. There appeared to be a party going on and people were wearing such beautiful clothes. I was very surprised, there must have been several hundred guests, all dancing happily. At the end of the hall was an empty throne and someone was approaching it; he was dressed like a king and everyone stopped dancing. He smiled at them and thanked them all for coming to join him on this special day. He said his son would soon be arriving with his new wife, and that they were very happy as it was their wedding day. As the couple entered they both bowed to the King and then turned to face the guests. I was so shocked to see that she look like me but I didn't know the man who stood beside her. Why did she look so much like me?

When I woke up that morning I was still thinking about my dream. It had seemed so real; I remembered the beautiful smell, it was still in my nostrils; I had never had such a realistic dream in my life.

"Why are you so quite my dear?"

"I was thinking about something Jason."

"I know you were, your mind was miles away Louise."

"I am worried Jason, our forth year is coming and I don't know how I will manage."

"Don't ever say that again Louise or I will get angry. If you can survive for the past three years you can manage the last."

"I will try Jason."

"Hey, what's with the red eyes? If you want to cry here is my shoulder for you to cry on. Are you in love Louise?"

"No not really; I am a bit confused."

"Have you slept with him?"

"No, not yet."

"So you like him?"

"Yes I do."

"Does he like you?"

"I think so."

"So why are you confused then?"

"He has invited me out for dinner but I know he goes out with lots of other girls."

"How do you know that?"

"He lives next door to me."

"Well, in that case Louise I think you just have to be nice to him and wait until it is the right time. Just be good friends with him. Do you remember what happened to me when I was a first-year student?"

"Yes I do Jason."

"Good girl. Sometimes when we are rushing forward we need to look back and reflect."

"I will try and remember that Jason. I will never forget what we planned together; that after we have completed our degrees we will spread our wings."

"You must make your own destiny from now on Louise."

I still get excited when I think about the first time a gentleman invited me out for dinner; I mean I was delighted but I tried to keep my feelings to myself. When I got home I saw a big parcel outside on my balcony. I opened the French windows and saw a little note with the box:

I will pick you up at eight o'clock.

Chris.

I picked up the parcel, tore off the paper wrapping and opened the box to reveal a beautiful dress. It was a perfect fit; of course he must have had a lot of experience at guessing a woman's size. It was eight o'clock when my doorbell rang but when I opened the door it wasn't Chris. "Good evening madam, I have come to pick you up for dinner," said the stranger. I didn't know what I felt, whether I was happy or sad. Why was he making me so confused? The gentleman took me to a car and we drove until he parked in front of a big restaurant. When I get out I looked up at the building, 'The Unity Union', that was the name of the building.

"I am so sorry Louise; I was at a meeting and had to send someone to pick you up. I didn't want you to wait, so please forgive me. You look like a little princess; never in my dreams did I think you would look so much like a different person. Are you hungry?"

I smiled at him. "Not really." His hands were as quick as his mind, he kissed me and cuddled me then he whispered in my ear that we should go inside. It was the first time in my life that I had ever been inside a proper restaurant, it looked like a palace. My life had revolved in such a small world; going to work at the pub going to study at Uni and then off to the market. In my spare time I read a lot of books and watched the news on my T.V. He led me to a corner table with a pink rose in a vase.

When I looked at him he said, "Make yourself comfortable Louise, I am still Chris; why are you looking at me like that?" Before I could answer him the waiter came and Chris said. "Ask the lady what she would like to drink and I will have the usual, thank you." I was surprised that by nine-thirty all the tables were full and if I remember correctly there must have been about two hundred people having dinner.

"Why are you so quite Louise?" asked Chris.

"I am just thinking Chris."

"Would you like to tell me what you are thinking?"

"I wanted to know why you asked me out for dinner."

"I wanted to know your answer, you promised to tell me your decision about the position I offered." I looked at him; he was so handsome, so charming and so rich. Then he said, "You can tell me later tonight, let's have dinner first."

Of course the dinner was wonderful but I couldn't even tell what it tasted like. We finished our dinner at about ten o'clock and he took me up to the first floor, it was quite dark; some people were dancing whilst others were standing at the bar. The music was so romantic. Later he took me up to the second floor; he said it was his office and above was an apartment which he rented out. We returned to the first floor and he asked me to dance. I told him I didn't know how to dance but Chris said he would teach me. I can't remember how long we were on the dance floor I only recall his voice whispering in my ear, "I want you, I never thought I would hold you in my arms again. I am so happy, I can't stop thinking about you; you are so sexy I want you day and night." The music slowed and the light got darker. I felt his body against mine and it tempted me to think that I wanted him too. I didn't say anything but instead I moved my body into his arms. "I can feel I want you so much Louise, you make me feel great, you make me feel fresh. May I kiss you?" I nodded my head and he kissed my forehead, my eyes and my neck again and again. I don't know how long we are on the dance floor, I was in his arms when the music stopped and he asked me if I wanted to go home or stay with him? Suddenly I remembered who I was, a big lump stuck in my throat; he was still cuddling me and I put my face against his chest and asked him to take me home.

He was kissing me on the cheek, "Listen to me; don't get upset, you won't see me for a few weeks as I am going to New York. If you need me just leave a massage with my secretary and she will let me know." I wanted to cry and I knew my heart wanted him, but he was playing games with me. I didn't love his money; I just wanted someone who really loved me.

My doorbell was ringing. "Hello Louise, I'm sorry to call on you so early. I couldn't wait to see you."

"Please come in Lucy. I didn't go to work; I feel so sick."

"I know, Martin told me, that's why I came to visit you, what is going on? Hey you sound so bad, did you stay with him?"

"No I didn't."

"So you turned out to be a Cinderella and you have to become a servant again."

"I will go to work tomorrow night."

"Don't worry; you must take care of yourself."

"He sent his driver to pick me up."

"Oh well."

"We danced all night long; I won't see him again for a few weeks as he is going away."

"My dear Louise I think you need to be a strong person if you want to play with fire. He is very hard to catch; he is a playboy and has got a lot of money. He can buy anything he wants; I think you must use all your talents. I have brought some fruit and things for you."

"Thanks Lucy."

"You are welcome my dear. I think you and I have both had a difficult time especially now that Abdul has gone away for a few weeks. He said he would call but I haven't heard anything yet; he can do whatever he wants to do; I won't shed a tear; my heart is set in cement. Men are so hard to trust but I do believe there must be someone good enough for us; there must be someone out there in this world. Louise, you are young, beautiful and well educated; you have a good future and should never cry over a man."

"I feel he loves me Lucy."

"He is like you Louise; for some reason he can't commit himself to you. I think he wants to make sure he has found the right woman Louise. You have to make up your mind; if you don't try you will never know."

"I am worried Lucy, I am not sure if I love him or even if I like him."

"Don't be silly Louise I am sure he will look after you."

"I don't need that Lucy. Whoever is going to be my man, I have to love him and he should love me in return."

"Oh Louise, you can say that because you are so young. I have to tell you my news; someone has offered to buy my shop and my flat. I might leave this country before Christmas but I will keep in touch with you Louise. You are a good friend Louise and I will miss you so much."

"And I will miss you too Lucy. I feel you are my sister, not just a friend."

"I appreciate that Louise."

CHAPTER TWENTY-TWO

That year my business in the market was very slow and the weather was so bad. It started at the beginning of October; people just walked around but didn't buy anything. Sandra complained to me and said that it was unusual but hoped that we could make things up by Christmas. I said I hoped she was right and then she moaned, "Dear God, life in the market is so up and down, please help us to make good business."

"God will help the best He can Sandra," I said.

"Yesterday it was raining, today it is cold; I haven't even made fifty pounds."

"I have made even less than you Sandra," I wailed.

On my way home I picked up my dinner at David and Jim's.

"Did you have a nice holiday uncles?"

"Oh yes, we didn't want to come back; it was so lovely in Spain. It was so cheap. Maybe we will retire soon and just rent the shop to someone."

"That would be good. You will have a lot of money from your flat as well."

"What about you Louise? Have you lost weight?"

"I think so; I miss your food that is the point."

"We will stay here until you finish Uni; how is the market?"

"It's got worse since I started."

"Oh God! That is bad; why don't you sell your flat and rent it out Louise? You would then have money left do study properly in your final year. I think it is a very important time in your life Louise."

"I will think about it David; if my business continues like this I will have to do something."

"Good girl, don't suffer more than you need to."

"Thank you both."

"No, no, not today Louise, keep your money, we haven't seen you for a long time; this is our treat."

"But next time you must take my money."

"We will; go home now and rest."

"Thank you so much."

When I got home I made a cup of tea; I felt sick and tired but I knew I must be strong. I thought maybe a hot bath would help me feel fresh. I didn't eat my dinner but decided to work out how much money I was really making. When I finished I found that I could just about cover my rent; I wasn't making any profit at all and if my business continued the way it was over the next three weeks I wouldn't be able to afford my monthly outgoings. I tried to think positively and told myself that maybe next week the weather would be fine and anyway business in the market was always up and down. I told myself that I had better do some studying the next day so I resolved to attend class.

"Hi, good morning my dear friend."

"Hi Jason, hi Sam."

"Did you hear the rumour?"

"No, what about?"

"One of the girls in our class has found out that for this third year there is going to be a big bonus for all of us. They are going to set a very difficult final exam and only the best will go on to year four."

"That is good; it means that the best students will go on to achieve a high quality degree. That will be you Jason, you are so great; you too Sam."

"Did you know Louise that I am going to leave my job next week? I have decided it is not worth it as I must do my best to earn a really good degree; then I can get a good job."

"Are you?"

"Yes Louise. You see, time is passing so quickly and we need to overcome it. If we fail, I mean if we don't get very good grades, what is the point of studying for four years? I would have wasted my time and I only have one chance for success. I think this is very important for us Louise."

"I agree with you Jason. Yes, I agree with both of you, do you think we will we make it?"

"Yes we will." The telephone rang and I picked it up.

"Hello Louise could I pop in to see you?"

"Oh Chris, where are you?"

"I'm just next door, very close to your sitting room."

"Okay, I will go and open the French windows."

"Hello darling, let me kiss you, I have missed you so much."

"I thought you were in New York. You said you would be over there for a few weeks."

"At first I intend to stay but I have to attend a meeting in Paris, so I dropped in to London on the way. I will go back to New York again once I have finished in Paris."

"I see."

"Are you okay Louise?"

"I'm a bit tired Chris."

"You must be. How is Uni?"

"I am doing quite well but not enough to stay in my group; I am at a lower grade, I am very worried and I must concentrate more."

"Okay sweetheart, I won't disturb you again."

"No I mean myself not you."

"Are you upset Louise?"

"No Chris I am not upset."

"I promise next time I will let you know where I am going to be. Let me hug you. You are a good girl, I mean a woman." I hated myself but I let him hug me and kiss me. I was in his arms and he laid me down on the floor; his body on top of mine. He whispered in my ear, "You are growing up girl, don't be scared, I will look after you I promise to God I will only be with you. No more new girls. Please let me, I have missed you so much since that night; I can't stop thinking about you and I want you so much. Let me do it Louise." He started kissing me from head to toe; he was so great at kissing and I let him do it. I had no strength; he was the master, an expert.

As he licked all over my body with his tongue I said to him, "Chris please, I have let you into my life, please do it, I am dying." He moved up and looked into my eyes. He was just about to open his lips and continue to kiss me when we both heard someone shouting outside his flat."

"Chris, Chris, open the door. I know you are in your flat, your car is here. Open the door Chris." Poor Chris, his face went pale and he looked sick. I suggested to him that he had better let her in.

"But she might give you a lot of trouble."

"Don't worry,"

"You don't know her Louise, she might hurt you."

"No she won't, let her in."

"Please promise me that whatever happens you will stay with me. I will support you until the end of my life, even if I do not belong to you, even if you are not mine, thank you Louise."

"Where are you Chris? Why didn't you open the door? When did you get back to London? You didn't call me. Look at you! Oh my God! Look at your hair have you been making love with someone? Oh God!" Instead of crying she ran across the balcony, "Where is she?"

"Natalie, please listen to me, for the past three years I have given you everything you wanted, I don't want to have to repeat myself over and over again. I am not in love with you any more; you used to be a lovely lady, beautiful and very sweet, but look at you now, you have changed your face with plastic surgery and you are no longer my Natalie."

"I am still beautiful. I did it all just for you; I wanted you to love me Chris."

"Don't you understand? I have given my heart to someone else. How much money do you want?"

"No I don't want money, I want you Chris. You tell me you have someone else I think I now know who she is; I bet she is your next-door-neighbour. I think you have just made love to her and I am going over to see her."

"No Natalie, you mustn't give her any trouble, like you did to Nadia."

"I just want to see her face; I want to know how beautiful she is."

"Come back Natalie. It is not your property"

"No I want to talk to her. There she is! Oh yes, you look so young and beautiful. I want to know why you can't find another man my dear. Did you know Chris was my long term boyfriend?"

"I don't want to know about someone else's business that does not involve me."

"Are you involved with Chris?"

"Yes I am but he didn't tell me about any long term girlfriend."

"I am telling you now."

"You had better tell Chris not me."

"I think you just want his money."

"Is he very rich?"

"Of course he is, all the women want his money."

"I didn't know about his money. He didn't show me his bank account. I love him and he loves me."

"You make me laugh, this man has never loved a woman; he just pays money for all his girls. If you really want to stay with him you will be sorry."

"I won't mind being sorry."

"So you are attracted by his sexual ability?"

"That is the main point; I think he is the best."

"Well then, so you want to continue to be with him."

"If he wants me."

"Did you know that before he moved into this flat he loved me so much? You are the one who has taken him away from me, why aren't you ashamed of yourself?"

"Why should I be? If he loves me." Without any warning she turned to Chris and slapped his face and started hitting him with her two hands.

"I am going to destroy his flat." As soon as she said this she ran out of my sitting room and threw everything in Chris's flat on the floor. I felt sorry for Chris so I hugged him.

"You go and stay away for a while until she is okay; take care Chris." He kissed me and went away.

That night I prayed to God before I went to bed. *'Thank you God and Jesus Christ for looking after me; I have no one else in my life to love me and to care for me and I am suffering; I am not happy so please look after me. Amen.'*

CHAPTER TWENTY-THREE

A week later I got a phone call telling me that I had a delivery item. When my front door bell rang I went to open it and found a big bunch of pink roses with a little card attached.

To my dear Louise

Love

Chris

I didn't know how I felt, happy or sad. A few days later I got a hand written letter and a beautiful bunch of roses. They were also from Chris but I didn't want to open the letter; I kept it until the Sunday night:

Darling Louise,

I am very sorry to have given you so much trouble, it was all my fault. I never wanted to make you unhappy. I am not going to return to that flat anymore and I promise nothing like that will happen again; I want to protect you from Natalie and if I live next to you she will disturb you again. You need to concentrate on your studies. I will sell the flat very soon but I will keep in touch. I will wait until you finish university and then I will ask you to marry me?

You are always in my heart,

Chris.

December was a time to say good bye. One evening when I was working at the pub Lucy came in to see me.

"Tomorrow night I am leaving, I have to be at Heathrow for check-in at eight o'clock in the evening. Will you be free Louise?"

"Are you kidding Lucy? You can't leave me without notice."

"I am sorry Louise, that's why I had to see you tonight."

"Yes okay I will see you off because I don't know when I will see you again. I will meet you at Terminal Three."

"I have to go back to my hotel; I will talk to you tomorrow evening Louise."

"Okay Lucy."

"Take care Louise."

"I will, and you too."

After my last lesson I went to Baker Street station and jumped off the tube at Paddington. I thought I had better get the Heathrow Express. I felt it was me who was going away, I was so excited. I had never been to another country. The train took me to Terminal Three and when I got off I went to the check-in area. She was there at the British Airways counter.

"Hey Louise, you are early, I only have a few bags and I have checked them all in. I am sure I will have a good sleep in Business Class. Shall we go for dinner Louise?"

"I am not hungry Lucy; I don't think I could swallow any food."

"So let's have a cup of coffee. I wish you could come with me now Louise, so we could be on holiday together."

"I wish I could too Lucy."

"Have you had any news from Chris?"

"He just sent me a bunch of flowers that's all? And he sent me a letter. He is going to sell his flat as he doesn't want Natalie to give me any more trouble."

"Then he will come back to you?"

"I don't know Lucy. I have no one and today you are leaving me."

"You known me Louise, I will keep in touch with you; I won't forget you."

"This is life, we have to survive."

"You know how I feel Louise? London is my home, I grew up in this country; I will miss it all but it's time to go. When I went to Europe I never missed anything, this is the first time I have felt that I might never come back again. I am going to miss everything. Before I forget, here is my address on this envelope, don't lose it. I had better go." I felt I was going to be sick. We just hugged at the gate, we couldn't say any words; she walked through and turned back to wave her hand.

CHAPTER TWENTY-FOUR

Once again we had a bad time in the market, all through October. I was constantly wondering how I could keep my business going, none of us were making any profits and it rained and was so cold every weekend.

"Are you alright love? You look so pale."

"I think I have got a bad cold, Mr. Daniel."

"You must look after yourself love; this has been a bad year." I had no time to go and get my dinner from David and Jim. I went home by taxi that Sunday evening; I felt so sick I just crawled up to my flat. I couldn't move my head; I couldn't even move my tongue as my throat was so dry; I felt utterly miserable. It was a warning sign that my health was at a low point. I called John and told him that I had a bad case of flu and that I didn't think I would manage to work for the next week.

"I will take the whole week off from the pub," I told him.

"That's okay love, you might be better off at home as it is so smoky here you might get even worse. Look after yourself love."

"Thank you Johnny."

"You are welcome love." I had visitors who brought me some soup, they were both so kind to me and I was very grateful to them. I didn't go to Uni for a whole week; I phoned in and reported that I had a serious illness. I got cards from everyone in the class trying to cheer me up. *'Get well soon, our final year is coming soon. Xxx Jason.' 'Be strong Louise, come on man. Xxx Sam.' 'Hi fight it. Xxx Simone.' 'We are all waiting for you. Xxx Simon.' 'How dare you get sick! Xxx Paul'* All of them with so much love. I put my cards above my bed and I loved them all. I heard my front door bell ringing, I assumed it must be a taxicab driver; they always go to the wrong house.

"Hello Louise, it's me, please let me in. Oh God you are sick Louise! Darling I am so sorry, I was so far away from you; I love you; how do you feel? I will call my doctor."

As he said this he made a call outside my bedroom and not too much later he went to open the front door. I couldn't speak as I had lost my voice; I just closed my eyes. They were talking and he asked when had my cold started, I just raised my fingers and the doctor said to him that I had very bad flu and asked why I had left it so long. The doctor gave me an injection and said that I had a bad case of flu but that few people had died from it. He gave Chris a prescription for me and said I would sleep for a long time.

"I think she should be better next week but until then don't let her out and make sure she takes her medicine."

"Thank you Dr. Patel."

"Just make sure she is okay and don't leave her by herself."

"Yes Dr. Patel."

I slept for a long, long time and when I opened my eyes I saw Jim and David were talking with Chris I don't know how many days I was sick and I don't remember when it started.

"I am happy to be your nurse as you are a very good patient; please drink this soup; David made it for you. I'm afraid I must stay with you until you get better otherwise Dr. Patel will kill me. Don't worry I will sleep on the floor." I nodded my head and waved my hand. I wanted to say no, no but I had no voice.

"Oh no, no," he said, "I will be here next to you." He pointed his finger to the floor and he said, "Don't try to say a word; I am going to have a bath and I will use your T-shirt and my shorts. Tomorrow I will go to my house." I slept for many hours because of the injection and the medicine.

When I woke up in the morning he was in the kitchen. "Here is some tea, toast and jam for your breakfast my darling. Dr. Patel said you are not strong enough to move. No, no you must have a little bit. I will wait to make sure that you eat something and if you don't eat I won't go out. I need to go to my house and my office and then I have to do some shopping. David and Jim will come to visit you before they open their shop. I am so glad you have no voice because you can't say no. I am the one to tell you what to do so don't look at me like that. I am only joking; do you need anything? No, okay I will see you later darling." Chris left and I felt so relieved. I was not used to someone staying with me. I was still not strong enough so I just closed my eyes. I had taken the tablets the doctor had left for me and was so tired that even when I sensed that someone else was in my room I couldn't open my eyes. I thought it must be David and Jim as they had a key. I listened to them talking for a while.

"Are you hungry darling?" It was Chris and I nodded my head. When I opened my eyes Chris was looking at me. "You have some wonderful soup here sent in by David and I have lots of shopping to do. You look much better. Listen Louise, I need to tell you so many things and I will tell you about my problems but first you must drink your soup."

"Yes."

"That's a good girl, open your mouth; this is good for you. I'll make you a cup of tea; you will love my tea. Don't you want any more soup? That's okay; in a few days time you will get your voice back. At fist I didn't want to tell you; I didn't want to hurt you. The first time I met you I think I fell in love with you. You were in my thoughts and I fell for you. I think you know that I have slept with many women and my biggest problem is Natalie. I bought the flat next to you as at first it was convenient for bringing girls in for one night stands; then I met you and felt so guilty when you saw me with different women and when Natalie gave you so much trouble. I am nearly forty and I am fed up with the way I carry on; I want to change my life. I will try and sort things out with Natalie; I must confess to you that I used to spoil her too much. Ours was a long term relationship but once she got fed up with me and went out with a French millionaire. She came back to me again but although I didn't love her I enjoyed having a relationship with her; she was the best."

"Hey don't cry I have more to tell you. Maybe you will hate me but I must explain myself to you so that you can understand who I am. I gave Natalie everything she wanted; the rest of the girls just wanted my money but now I am getting old I want to have the right woman to be a good mother to my children. I promise you that if you can wait for me I will clear these women from my life and then we can start to have a family. From now on you don't need to go to work at the pub or the market; I will support you until we get married. What I want from you is to be with you for some time and have dinner. Most of my time I will be in New York but I will let you know where I am. If I go on business I won't leave you. Please trust me and let me kiss your tears away. A few years ago, when I was full of life, I used to have a different blond every night of my life. Once I met a girl in my club; I called her Princess because she was so beautiful, so perfect; she had got brains and was a real businesswoman. We danced all night long and I felt that I couldn't live without her. I took her to my house and we went to paradise until morning; I didn't want to go anywhere, I just wanted to give my life to her. That morning Natalie came in and slapped my face. I was so shocked. I sent my Princess home without a word and went away to my father's place to make up my mind whether to marry her. When I got back to London I discovered that she had married another man. Ever since that time I thought I would never find the right woman to marry until I met you. I want you to know me, the real me, and I will leave it up to you whether you give me a chance or not. I will wait for you until you say yes; my life means nothing to me at the moment. I feel for you so much."

I shall never forget that time in my life when I was so sick and Chris looked after me for three nights. He nursed me and cooked for me. He told me about his past life; he even explained very clearly about himself but for me it wasn't enough to agree to sleep with him. Of course he would wait until I said I was ready to marry him but I thought it wouldn't make any difference if I married him, he would still continue to travel for his business and I would get phone calls telling me he was in such and such a place and that he would see me soon. I asked myself again and again, *'Do I love him? Or do I Love his money?'* I never got the right answer. I knew that what I really wanted was for him to be with me so I could talk to him; for him to be a good father to my children and for him to be with them most of the time rather than living in New York for long periods by himself.

Once I had recovered from my illness he left me for another long term business trip. He gave me a card to draw money out for my spending but I didn't touch his money at all. I left the pub and gave up my stall at Camden Town market; I wanted to catch up on my lessons; I had missed so many whilst I had been sick for three weeks. I had good friends and a very good professor who gave me extra lectures. I felt I needed to catch up with everyone and prepare for my final exam. I wanted to get through to my final year; I would never forgive myself if I failed. I joined David and Jim on Sunday mornings to pray in church; I went swimming when I had time and I went out with Jason to see films if we had a nice Friday during the week; he is a very special person for me.

"You know Louise I like you so much, I have not looked at anyone else since I finished with Alison."

"That is good. You have more time for your studies."

"What I meant was we are all human and we need to enjoy ourselves."

"I know that Jason, I like you too and you are very special to me. If I didn't have so many problems in my life I would ask you to be my boyfriend."

"So why don't you ask?"

"I don't love you Jason."

"Who do you love?" he pleaded.

"I don't love anyone at the moment. At first I thought I loved him but I found out that it was not love. I will only sleep with a man I love. Don't get upset my dear Jason, you are so clever, so handsome and so independent. I have known you for three years and soon you will be living far away from England."

"So what?"

"So you will forget all about me. A man loves a woman in his mind, not in his heart; when a man moves far away it will not be too long before he will want to meet another woman. I mean you might be one of the rare ones who are always honest and true but they are very rare."

"How do you know Louise?"

"I learnt it from someone."

"Okay, I guess I will have to accept that I will just be your good friend."

"No, good friend is not enough, you are my best friend Jason."

"I will see you on Monday; look after yourself for the exam."

"I will Jason and thanks for the special lesson."

"You are welcome Louise."

I was very happy to stay at home in the evenings and I had my weekends off to sort out my studies. I had to be careful with my spending but I was okay.

"Does he support you Louise?" David asked.

"No David, Chris offered to help with money but I didn't touch it."

"How do you live?"

"I have taken a student loan and I re-mortgaged my flat."

"Why didn't you accept his money?"

"I don't think he loves me enough."

"I am sure he does Louise, if he did not love you he wouldn't give his money to you."

"He always gives money to girls he wants to sleep with."

"Yes I agree with you, Louise," Jim said, "He is a very rich man, look at his car; a Mercedes Sports! I think he is a playboy but he does seem to like you very much."

"Maybe he does Uncle David; I will give him a chance to prove himself."

"Why Louise."

"I think he has got someone else in New York."

"Good girl," Jim said, "When you have finished at university you can do a lot of things; sometimes money doesn't give you happiness."

"Thanks for comforting me Jim."

For several weeks I waited for Chris to call me; he didn't phone and he didn't send me any cards. We had a few days off over Christmas; Jason went home to see his family and I was invited over to be with David and Jim. I gave them each a nice jumper and they both gave me vouchers for one of the big shops in Oxford Street. They explained that they didn't know what I would like but they thought that women loved to buy their own clothes. When we opened our Christmas presents we were so happy. David cooked a nice turkey but I couldn't eat much.

"Have you heard from him?"

"No, he must be sick."

"He should call and tell you where is he."

"I don't know uncle; he just disappears, he is very strange, I think there must be something wrong."

By January I had got bored with winter as it was so cold. I joined an evening class at the college; it was a Chinese Medicine course as I liked herbs and plants. I couldn't wait for Chris to come back though I tried not to think about him. It was in February when I heard news of him. He was in Europe; he sent me a bunch of roses and a little card:

I miss you my darling; I will see you soon.

Chris.

CHAPTER TWENTY-FIVE

Bangkok...

Dear Louise

First of all I must to tell you I am so sorry, I haven't forgotten about you even though I haven't been in touch. Since I passed through the departure gate at Heathrow Airport my life has changed completely. I miss London so much more than I thought I would. The plane took more then eleven hours, without stopping, and both my uncle and my farther were at the airport to meet me. When my feet touched the ground my instinct was telling me: you are not Lucy anymore you left that name behind at Heathrow Airport. Now my real name is Sivanee; the first moment I saw my father and uncle my tears started falling. There was my father, who I had not spoken to since my mother died; he seemed to look older than before and my uncle looked so young. When I hugged my father and my uncle at the same time I was so happy; I was crying.

My father said he had been counting the years as they went by and he had prayed for me to come home. When we were in the car my uncle talked all the time. He said our family had changed and maybe I might not know that our family name was now one of the top ten families in the country. He said father was a millionaire now so I had to think carefully before I did anything here in Bangkok. He warned me that I was not in England now. He hoped that I wouldn't be upset, but in England no one cared what I got up to; not in Bangkok. I thanked him and said he must tell me more. I had to learn about my new life here and that was good. I asked what kind of business the family was involved in now and was told that it was still to do with building equipment but the main thing was steel. My uncle said that there were a lot of new properties to build and sell and that my older brother had taken over the business whilst my two half-brothers were helping him. We were a big family now and Tiger Steel was a great company.

They drove me to a house in Silom; my uncle had bought the house when he came back from England. He told me to have a rest and he would come back to pick me up and take me to see the family in the evening. If I needed anything I was to ask Pachom and she would look after me. Pachom is the name of the old lady who is my uncle's housekeeper; she looks after the house with her husband Lung Mint; I later called him Mint as the name is too difficult for me to remember. Mint is the gardener and they live in a bungalow at the back of the house.

I love the house; I went upstairs and walked around, it was so beautiful, a mixture of European styles. I felt even happier when I saw that the British Embassy was opposite my bedroom. I felt that I was in London. I walked to the next room; I think you would love this room; there are hundreds of English books as it is my uncle's library and study. Next to that is his bedroom; I saw a black and white photo of him when he was in England; he was with an Englishman and woman who looked familiar to me but I couldn't think who they might be. There were two more rooms but I didn't bother with them and returned to my room. After I had finished my bath I went to bed and had a good dream. I don't know how long I slept but when I woke up I thought I was in London.

"Are you awake Lucy?"
"Yes uncle, just give me twenty minutes and I will be down."
"That is so quick Lucy, just like a real Londoner," uncle said.

"Yes uncle, London never changes; you still have to be on time." He was smiling.

"This is my housekeeper Pachom; she is worried that you don't speak Thai."

"Of course I can speak Thai, how could I forget my mother tongue? But give me a chance; don't laugh uncle I heard that when you came back from London it took you a few months to get used to it."

"I'm not laughing because of that, I am laughing because I think you are lovely."

"Oh, okay then."

"Shall we go? Your family are waiting for us and they all want to see the beautiful lady from London."

I have to tell you Louise, I love my uncle, he is so nice and a very lovely person. He looks so respectable all the time. I want very much for you to meet him. My uncle and I were not in the car for very long; he told me that the family had moved from the house where I was born to a new house. It was bigger and better then in China Town here, they call it Sukumvit Fourteen; it is not very far from my uncle's house. When we got there I saw three houses surrounded by a fence. Uncle said the middle house was my dad's and one of the other two was for my older brother. Apparently my younger brother was living with my dad. It was amazing, I didn't remember everyone but I did remember my own brother. I said hello to my stepmother in Thai; the rest were my stepbrothers; who were all married and they had so many children. I looked for my grandma but my father told me she had died a few years ago but he would take me to pay my respects later. I hugged my brother for a long time then my half-brother.

"I am sorry," my father said, "we are missing one of the family, he isn't here at the moment."

"Who is he?" I asked.

"Your younger half-brother," he said.

"Oh I see."

"He is a big man and he is a troublemaker," my uncle replied laughing.

"Is he?"

"Just some of the time, but he is working very hard," my brother said, "plus he is still single."

"He likes to muck around," my father said.

In the end I told them that all my presents for them were in the car. I had brought so many and suggested that they could chose what they liked. I had more arriving in a few days. Someone called out from the kitchen and announced that dinner was ready. We all sat round the table; it was a big, round kitchen table and had one of those Lazy Susans you see in Chinese restaurants; you can turn it round in the middle of the dinner table; there was so much food.

I forgot to tell you, my brother has two sons and my half-brother has two sons and a little girl, she is two years old. When he arrived he said hello to everyone and asked how we were. My stepmother got up from her chair but my father told her to sit down and let him feel guilty; oh boy what a party! Everyone stayed quiet and he walked past the kitchen door; he stopped and looked at me; I turned my eyes to look at him; he was very tall with dark hair. He was such a good looking guy, so charming from the first moment. I stood up and said 'hello younger brother,' he came towards me and shook my hand. He spoke to me in English and apologised, saying that he had forgotten that I would be there today; he spoke quickly. My father asked him if he wanted to have dinner with us. He said no as he had already eaten.

"I am so sorry," he said.

"Yes you should be sorry and it is not enough just to say sorry," my uncle said. He moved close to uncle and bent his knee.

"Yes sir, Minister." He shook his hand. I looked at my stepmother; she looked relieved. I have to tell you Louise, my brother Joe is the one who makes me feel that I want to stay in this country. After dinner we had coffee in the sitting room. My uncle said we had lots to talk about.

"I know you are missing London, it was your home," he said. "It took a long time for me to forget London; in fact I still miss it. When I returned to Bangkok I had a great job, an important job, so I didn't have much time to think about it and now you have Joe to be your friend." Joe had arrived in Bangkok just a year before me. He had been sent to Australia when he was twelve and then he went to live in New Zealand until he graduated. I am not very surprised that he can't speak our own language. My uncle is still good looking but he has now left his job, he was the Minister of Foreign Affairs and retired early for his age. He has got two private Secondary Schools and one of them was the first private school where you had to speak in English only; it was a boarding school as well. He doesn't stay with me in Bangkok; he has got his own private estate in the North of Thailand. I haven't been to the North yet.

My brother Joe and I have been doing some research in Bangkok into why there is so much HIV. Did you know? Ninety-five percent of prostitutes have got it. Joe took me out to visit some night clubs, discothèques and dirty massage parlours; in fact we saw every kind of entertainment that is on offer in Bangkok. Joe said there are at least two other places in the world like Bangkok; Rio and Amsterdam. I asked him why the girls liked to work in the clubs. He replied, "Well who wants to work in a factory earning thirty pounds a month when you can work in a night club, dress up like a princess and earn good money? You can see how beautiful they are."

"Where do they come from?"

"The most beautiful girls come from the North. The girls who are prostitutes have to work day and night for their living. They send some money to support their families who can't work."

"So this is a way of getting good money but why have they got HIV?"

"I think it is because they are part of the profession who sell cheap sex; I mean, once they get older and haven't managed to save up enough money, they don't know how to get another job, so they have to carry on with their career. Some men are careless and do not put on a rubber; the next day they go off to someone else and then return to their wives; this is the way HIV infection is rising in Bangkok."

"What about the young girls in the discothèque?"

"That is another problem. There is a large group of students here who live on their own and go out for fun. They connect with a drug seller and at first they want to try the drugs for fun; then they become addicted to them. When they have no money to buy drugs they start to sell themselves."

"I think this is so terrible Joe."

"I know."

"I am sure the government will try to improve things in the future."

"Well I just hope so, but over the past six years it has got worse."

Joe took me to Pattaya, it used to have a beautiful, clean, silver beach when I was a little girl. We used to go there with the family and grandma. Now you can't even sit down and relax as the beach is packed with 'business women' who are trying to sell their bodies. They just walk around the beach offering their services to any man who is lying down in the sun. It was amazing. I told Joe I wanted to go back to the hotel and when we got there Joe said he would take me to see Paradise in Pattaya that evening. He said it was the best place for entertainment and I wouldn't believe that it was real life. We were staying in a five star hotel right next to the beach, I really liked the hotel as I could just get into the lift and it would take me right down to the sea. Joe asked me if I was hungry but as I wasn't he said he would see me at dinner.

We had a beautiful, romantic corner in the restaurant; Pattaya can be so wonderful if you are with someone that you love. Oh Louise, I want you to see it here when the sun goes drown; it is so beautiful; I cannot put it into words. When it is dark I can see the lights around the village and think; what a shame this town is full of women selling sex and pushers selling drugs. I wish I could be by myself. Joe asked me what I was thinking about and I said I supposed I was missing London. 'Just London,' he said, so I told him maybe it was someone else but that it was over.

Joe is an expert on food; he ordered some seafood and a bottle of white wine. You know Louise, white and red wines are so expensive in my country; the prices are ridiculous; that is another reason I miss London; you know me Louise, I like drinking Campari and I like all kinds of wine. Joe is always speaking in English when we are together.

"I have never drunk this wine in London, it is so cheap."
"I know sister; don't forget you are in Pattaya now."
"I am sorry, you are right Joe."
"Uncle told me that you have worked very hard and that you are a successful businesswoman in London and that you have made millions on your own. The whole family is very proud of you."
"Thank you Joe for telling me that. Do you want a cigarette?"
"No thanks Lucy, I don't smoke."
"How come?"
"I used to smoke but I gave up."
"I will try to give up soon Joe."
"You don't need to Lucy."
"So why did you give up?"
"I used to go out with a girl and when I smoked she couldn't breath."
"I see; where is she now?"
"She died."
"I'm sorry, what happened?"
"She had cancer; she was so young when she died."

Whilst we were talking I noticed that at the opposite table there were four people, two men and two blonds, Joe couldn't see them as he was sitting behind them. One of the men kept looking at Joe.

"I am happy to be your sister Joe."

"Thanks Lucy."

"If you weren't my brother I would ask you to be my bodyguard."

"I am your bodyguard now." Joe smiled at me.

"Let me pay the bill."

"No Joe, let me. I am your sister."

"It's okay Lucy I need to spend my wages."

"Thank you Joe. Next time is my turn okay?"

"Next time is yours Lucy."

When Joe stood up and turned round he stopped and gave a big smile to the gentlemen. The two gentlemen also stood up and they all shook hands. I looked at one and saw that he was tall and very good looking. He was smart and I couldn't take my eyes away from him. Joe asked them if they were free later and he would see them in the hotel bar. When we in the car I looked at Joe curiously.

"Do you want to know who they are?"

"I'm not too curious Joe, just surprised that my brother appears to be quite popular."

"I told you that Tiger Steel, our company, is one of the top ten in the country."

"Who were they?"

"You see, you are interested in them. The one with ginger hair is Robert, he works for the British Council in Bangkok and the charming, handsome one is the Ambassador of Saudi Arabia. Don't ask me why he is so smart, I think his mother is English."

"Who were the two blonds?"

"He just imported them from Russia."

"What?"

"Yes, they are both very rich and are both playboys. The Ambassador, I mean Mohamed, is the owner of an oil company and Robert is a millionaire property tycoon in London. They are both popular in local high society; it's quite funny really, they are both very close with our uncle and have great respect for him."

"Why?"

"I think they knew him when he was the Minister of Foreign Affairs. Uncle was an Oxford senior when Mohamed and Robert were finishing at Oxford University."

"That's interesting to know."

"Don't worry, you will see them again. They are both frequently in the newspapers. Right now we are outside a club for gay ladies, shall we go in?"

You know Louise, if Joe hadn't mentioned it I wouldn't have known they were boys, they looked so beautiful, even more attractive than women. We went to the next one and I want to tell you more and more about it, it was unbelievable what I saw; my eyes were so tired and we got back to the hotel very late.

The next morning I got up very early and walked along the beach to see the sun rise by myself. I sat down and had no idea where I was; the sea was so blue and nature was so wonderful.

"Good morning, good morning, may I sit with you?"

"Please do."

"I think I saw you yesterday evening."

"Oh yes I remember."

"My name is Robert."

"And I am Lucy."

"Nice to meet you, Lucy."

"Nice to meet you too."

"So you are Joe's…?"

"I am Joe's sister."

"Oh I see. You know if I couldn't see your face I would swear you came from London."

"Why do you think that?"

"Because of your accent."

"Were you disappointed when you saw that I looked Chinese?"

"No, not at all, you are beautiful."

"Thank you Robert. I have just come back from London."

"Very well, so you see I do know my accents."

"Yes I will accept that. I was sent over there when I was young."

"So that is why Joe has to show you around your own country."

"Yes that's right."

"So you must miss London."

"Yes I do."

"I never knew that Tiger Steel had a daughter."

"Just one; my uncle sent me to England."

"So you never came back?"

"No. Not until now."

"This is a good time; would you like to walk to the end of the beach? It is so beautiful."

"Yes it is."

"When I finished university I travelled around the world before I started work."

"So do you like Bangkok?"

"Of course I do."

"Have you ever been back to London?"

"Just occasionally, I don't miss London at all; I think the traffic in London is getting bad."

"Yes it is, but it is a hundred times better than Bangkok."

"Yes Lucy, but you will get used to it soon."

"I hope so Robert."

"When are you going back to Bangkok?"

"This evening."

"I hope to see you again Lucy."

"Yes sure Robert. I live right next door to the British Embassy."

"How wonderful, so I can pop in for a cup of tea?"

"No, you mean a pot of tea don't you Robert?"

"Thank you Lucy."

"I think Joe might worry that someone has kidnapped his sister."

"I promise I will visit you."

"You are welcome Robert."

When I got to the hotel, Joe was waiting for his breakfast.

"I am sorry I'm late Joe."

"It's okay Lucy."

"I think Pattaya is a very romantic place. I had no one to walk with; I was laughing as he might have seen Robert before he came down.

And now I am back in Bangkok. If I have any more news I will let you know. How is your life in London? I hope to see you after your final exam. Good luck and take care.

Miss you and London so much

Lucy

CHAPTER TWENTY-SIX

London

Dear Lucy

I was so pleased to read your letter. I had been waiting to hear from you for such a long time. I am very, very glad to know that you are okay; I do miss you and the things we used to do together. Since you left London it has become darker and colder and it rains nearly every day as usual but the weather got even worse a few weeks ago. I was very sick and had a bad case of flu and a chest infection. Chris looked after me whilst I was in bed and if he hadn't found me I might have died. It was the first time I had been unconscious. He was so kind to me and has offered me money to support me but I didn't take it and got a loan from the bank instead. I gave up both of my jobs as I had to catch up on so many things at university. Once I had done that I had nothing to do and got bored so I started an evening course in Chinese Medicine and Herbs. It is very interesting and I am really enjoying it.

At the moment I am very confused about Chris. When I was sick he was so kind to me but now he has been away for so long, I mean a few months, and he has just sent me a bunch of roses with a note saying that he misses me. He is somewhere in Europe and tells me that somehow he will sort out his problems. When I was ill he told me he wanted to marry me and have children, even though he has never made love to me. He sold his flat and since then he has disappeared from my life. He gave me a card so that I could take cash out but I have never used it. I have no hope; why should I care about him? I want someone to be here with me and to love me. I don't want his money and him somewhere else with another woman. I don't think he loves me enough. Right now I think I will give up on him. I promise you one thing though, I will do my best in my final year at university and then I will have a life of my own; I will get a job and enjoy life.

I wish you were in London; then I could phone you and ask you to have dinner with me. I miss you and as soon as I have finished my exams I will come and see you. I will try to send you more news from London but you know London never changes. I was so happy to get your letter so please, if you have more time, tell me more about yourself. I am waiting for your next letter. I look forward to seeing you very soon and hope you are happy in your new world.

Always thinking of you

Louise

CHAPTER TWENTY-SEVEN

Bangkok

Dear Louise

I was very pleased to hear from you, it was the first letter I have received from London and I was so happy to get it, it means so much to me. I miss London so much. I am still the same old Lucy; I don't think I shall ever change. I am very sorry to hear that you were not well. I wish I could have been there to help you. It must have been very hard for you to cope with work at nights and weekends and then having to study at university. I was so upset when you refused my offer but I knew you were a very proud person. I am very pleased you have now left both jobs so you can concentrate on your studies. It will not be too long before I see you again. I have so many stories to tell you.

I am sure you will never be lonely, even if you are living on your own without Chris. I promise that when you read my words with your heart you will see I am right. First of all I think Chris is very confused about himself. Either he doesn't know what he is doing or he does but is in a difficult situation. Don't get worried or depressed; you are brave, beautiful and clever. I know you well enough to know that even though you missed all of your teenage years you are not a girl who likes to muck around with sex. I am sure that when the right time comes your life will be full of colour; just be patient.

I talked to my uncle about you. He said it would be no problem at all and he is happy to get someone from London. The school principle, who works with him, is a Londoner and has worked with him for many years. The rest of the teachers come from different countries. Some are from Australia and New Zealand; anyway he is looking forward to meeting you. I asked him how much he was going to pay you; he laughed and said not to worry as he will pay you good wages if you get good grades in your degree.

Since I came back from Pattaya I have had a visitor nearly very day. I think I told you about him in my first letter. I don't go out with him; we are just friends. I have nothing to do here; I could go to work in the family business but I went to work there for a while and I didn't like the job. I don't need to help them as my father gave me a shareholding in the company. I told him I didn't want it as I have got enough money to spend for the rest of my life. I am very fed up with my routine; I feel my life is useless and hopeless. I want to go out to work again; I can't be a lady of leisure.

My uncle has just bought me a new BMW as a present to make me happy. I don't know where to drive as I have nowhere to go here. I don't even use a mobile phone as I have no one to talk to.

Sounds very weird I know but it is true. I don't want to tell you how much I miss London and Abdul. I cry at night thinking that I have made a big mistake; I will wait until the end of the year and if things don't change I will have to think of a new way of life. At home I have uncle's housekeeper, Chome, I call her Pachom, she is so lovely and I also have a private maid called Sumon. There is a guard who sits at the front gate; he is Indian, an old man with mustard coloured hair. I like to visit him because I like his English accent.

Tonight Robert and Joe are coming to take me to a dinner party; it will be the first time since I've been in Bangkok that I can wear my evening dress. We are going to a charity function at the Oriental Hotel. I like going there; it's such a beautiful place and I feel as if I am in the Hilton in Park Lane but the Oriental is a hundred times more comfortable. I am very close with Robert, he is such a playboy, lovely and intelligent; I trust him because he is close to Joe and my uncle but I think he likes to play around with girls but I still accept him as a good and dear friend.

Joe, Robert and I went to the Charity Ball at the Oriental Hotel I was so excited. Robert said that a princess of the royal family would be there as well; I had never seen a real princess in my life and I wanted to see how beautiful she was. Joe said all the guests would be high society and very rich people.

"You know?" He said, "I really hate going to these functions."
"Why do you say that?" I asked him.
"Well, as you will see, the women take out their big diamonds, wear them round there necks and walk around to the next table to show off their jewellery."
"I bet I will see the daughter of a gold mine owner wearing her sari with gold bangles all the way up her two arms." Robert said to Joe.
"I agree with you Robert."
"It is not nice to criticize ladies."
"We are so sorry," Robert said, "We go to such parties all year long and what we always see are competitions to see who is the richest at the party, who has got more diamonds."
"Thank God you didn't wear any jewellery," Joe said.
"They might think I have none to wear."
"That is good sister, wait and see if they realise you are the daughter of the Tiger Company."

When we got there it was about 9.00 pm., the place was full of guests already, and I think there must have been about three hundred guests in the hall. There was a dance floor on the left hand side and Joe led us to our table, which was in a good position. As I walked along with them, Joe and Robert seemed to know all the guests and they had to shake hands like princes in a procession. I saw the names on the tables included diplomats, companies, a Dr of the University, Ministers and businessmen. I noticed even before I sat down at our table that the card on the next table read 'The Saudi Arabian Ambassador' and there were already a few gentleman seated there, busy talking and laughing; one was a close friend of Robert and Joe but he didn't see us. I was introduced to the professor, Tony, and Dr. John; they both worked at the university. I liked them and they told me a lot of things that I needed to learn about my own country. They said I had missed so much of the history because I had been away for too long.

It was 9.45 when the Royal Princess arrived. All the ladies and gentlemen stood up and I could see her from very far away. I was on the right hand side towards the end of the queue. She looked so elegant, very bright and she looked so different from what I imagined. She looked as if she was European; at least that's what I thought from her behaviour until she arrived at my end of the queue. She stopped in front of me and said something in Thai; I really didn't understand what she said and without Robert and Joe to help me I spoke to her in English. "I am very sorry Your Highness but I have forgotten how to speak Thai to a member of the Royal Family."

I should explain to you that the Thai language it not like English; in Thailand you have to speak in a different way to royalty, it is so different from normal public speech. When the princess replied to me she was laughing and she spoke English with an American accent, I mean a real American accent.
"I do understand; I lived in the United States when I was a young girl. How long have you been back?" She asked me.
"I arrived a few weeks ago," I replied.
"So, you came from London?" She said.
"Yes, Your Highness."
"I like London very much," she said, "I have been there a few times. I hope to see you again." She extended her hand to me and I shook hands with the princess; she then moved on to

her table. I was very proud of her and my country; she is such a great princess.

When Robert came back to me he was so lovely, he said, "You have done well Lucy, Joe was worried when the princess stopped to talk to you."

"Thank you, both of you. You left me alone and I didn't know anybody!"

"Oh come on, don't moan like an old lady. Shall we dance?" Robert took me to the dance floor. This time I caught the Ambassador's eye in the dark; he was dancing with a French lady; I could hear her accent. When the music stopped he turned to Robert and said he was very surprised that he hadn't called for a long time.

Robert said, "Mohamed, I called you a few days ago, the Embassy secretary said you had gone away to New York; did she give you my message?"

"I haven't been back to the Embassy yet."

"By the way Mohamed, this is Lucy, Joe's sister; Lucy this is Mohamed, the Ambassador of Saudi Arabia and the owner of an oil company."

"That is enough Robert; nice to meet you Lucy; I think we have met each other before," Mohamed said, "But no one introduced us." He looked at Robert.

"I am introducing you now; is that okay Ambassador?"

I smiled at him, "Nice to meet you Ambassador."

"Please call me by my name if you don't mind."

"Thank you."

"May I dance with you?"

"Yes."

"Only for the next one Mohamed, I have booked her for this one," Robert said. He took me to the dance floor; I didn't talk to him until the music ended. I felt something wrong inside me but I was not sure whether to tell you.

I enjoyed talking and dancing with Professor Tony until Joe and Robert came back; they were both tired of dancing;

they hadn't stopped dancing since the music started. I was very surprised when the last dance was announced after midnight and Mohamed asked me to dance. This time he whispered into my ear, "Would you like to have afternoon tea with me tomorrow?"

"Yes, that would be nice," I said.

"I will pick you up at 4.00 pm."

"Okay, thank you." The lights dimmed and the song was so romantic: I am sorry to say good bye, the song was prompting everyone to say good night.

I HAVE TO SAY GOODBYE

I want to tell you my darling when you are nearby, I feel so good even though I am so shy,

I try to touch you I am so relieved, that you don't mind. My darling I can tell you if you look into my eyes, I am so in love with you even though I am so shy. Please let me kiss you before I say goodbye. Darling I want to tell you I feel so good when you are nearby I want to be with you all nigh. Please let me kiss you even though I am so shy. Oh my darling I don't want to say goodbye,

I know that you are not mine, could I tell you that I love you? I want you to be mine. Oh darling I wish you are nearby. Tonight I am sorry darling I have to say goodbye, goodbye my darling, I am sorry I have to say goodbye. I hope in the future I will dance with you until I die I hope you don't mine I want to tell you I don't want to say goodbye for tonight, I wish you could remember me, please look into my eyes I need you, I want you, I want to be with you all night long, but I have to say goodbye, goodbye my darling, I am sorry to say goodbye.

When Joe and Robert came back I thanked them very much for leaving me alone with Professor Tony all night long; they laughed and Robert said he wanted to finish the dance with me but unfortunately the Ambassador was too quick. They took me home after the dance and then Joe and Robert went out to the night clubs.

The next morning I thought I was in a dream and that I was still dancing with the Ambassador of Saudi Arabia, a man who is half English and is always in my mind. Mohamed came to pick me up on Saturday at 4.00 pm exactly. I told him I was very sorry but I wasn't feeling well and could we make it another time instead. I made afternoon tea for him.
"Maybe you need a rest," he said, "I will go home."
"But I would like you stay."
"Are you sure?" he asked me.
"Yes I am positive." He stayed with me until late, telling me about when he was in England. He also asked me what I did in England and why I left London. I have to tell you Louise he is a cool man deep inside his heart. He has a very sharp mind and it is very difficult to understand what kind of person he is. In some ways he is a bit snobbish but he is very polite. I have met so many men in my life but he seems to be a person I could settle down and have a family with.

Later on that week Mohammed, Joe and Robert were my regular guests for afternoon tea. They always came together and then went out to the clubs. Once in a blue moon I felt I wanted to go out on my own; I didn't take my BMW as the Oriental Hotel is not too far from where I live. I went by boat which took me along the Chao Phraya River. It went past the Portuguese and French Embassies and then passed through China Town, where I was born, until it came to its destination at Nonthaburi, which is quite far from where I live. I jumped on a bus and soon we had left Bangkok behind; it was so beautiful and I could see green trees and plantations and fruit and vegetables. I stayed on the bus for about three and a half hours. I was lost; I had no idea where I was. I told the bus conductor I wanted to go to China Town and he said I had to take the number 53 bus and it would take me there. The number 53 bus took me to my father's company; I could see the name 'The Tiger Steel Company' on the big building where I grew up. I didn't go into the building because I was very tired. In the end I came home by taxi but it still took me ages to get home; the traffic was terrible; the worst I have seen in my life; I couldn't stand it. When the taxi stopped outside the gate the guard, who is always sleeping, jumped up, looked at me and then came over to open the gate.

"Thank you Babu," I said.

"You are welcome madam." I could see two cars parked in front of the house and was very surprised to see Mohamed and Joe.

"Hello my dear sister, please don't ever do that again in Bangkok. Do you know we nearly called the police?"

"Why?" I asked.

"We thought you had been kidnapped."

"You are kidding," I said.

"No I am not," he replied, "This is not London; it is very dangerous for someone like you.

"We didn't know where you had gone?" Mohamed said.

"I am very sorry; I promise I won't do it again. Please forgive me."

"Hello, is anybody there?"

"Yes, we are in here Robert. Come in," Joe shouted.

"Oh dear, what is going on here? Everyone looks so serious; I had better go home; I think I have changed my mind about going to the grill tonight."

"Oh please, wait Robert; give me ten minutes and I will be ready." Without waiting for an answer I ran upstairs and jumped into the bath.

I have so much to tell you Louise; I have big doubts about my future; what am I going to do? I am a stranger in this land and I have to learn a new lesson every day.

When I returned downstairs they were playing cards.

"Shall we go?"

"Go where?" Joe said.

"I think we are going to the grill."

"We are not very hungry anymore."

"But I am," I said, "Please Joe just forget it; I am sorry. I don't know how to use a phone box."

"I told you I would buy you a mobile but you refused it."

"I have no one to speak to."

"You can speak to me, your brother. You don't know how dangerous it is in Bangkok. You can't even trust the taxi drivers if you are alone at night. This is not London."

"I am hungry to," Robert interrupted just at the right time.

"Okay gentlemen I apologise; I want to take you all out for dinner. I have told Robert already and we are going to the Soi Lung Sean Grill."

"Okay I will be the driver," Mohammed said, "Ladies first please."

"Thank you," I said. In no time we all got out of the car at a wonderful looking place.

"Wow! This is an English Grill," I said.

"How do you know?" Robert asked me.

"I can tell by the name: 'THE WEST HAMPSTEAD GRILL'."

"There speaks a real Londoner," Mohamed replied. I looked around the place; it was very attractive and packed with people.

"Here is the menu, have a look Lucy," Robert said.

"Oh dear, it all looks so nice."

Hampstead Grilled Steak with fresh salad

Scottish Grilled Salmon with fresh salad

Thames Caught Fish and Chips with fresh salad

Knightsbridge Grilled Chicken with roast potatoes

"They have all got names connected with London; so many things to chose from," Joe said, "I fancy Thames Caught Fish on a Friday night."

"So do I," Robert said.

"I'll order the Scottish Grill," I said.

Mohamed had the Hampstead Grill and ordered a bottle of red wine and a bottle of white wine. The food was delicious; it was a perfect grill and I had not enjoyed a meal so much since I left London. Later I got a shock when I saw the Head Chef come out of the kitchen. He came to our table.

"Well good evening," he said. We all said good evening back to him.

"Sam," Mohammed said, "How are we?"

"We missed your food," Robert said.

"I don't believe you," he said, "You haven't been here for a week."

"Oh yes," Joe was smiling, "It is all Mohamed's fault. He has been away in New York for a while and we were waiting for him to join us."

"I see. I came out to see who ordered the Scottish Grill."

"Oh this is my sister Lucy," said Joe. "Lucy, this is the Head Chef and owner of the restaurant; his name is Sam."

"Pleased to meet you Lucy," he said, "I am going to cook a very special dinner for you all."

"Thank you Sam," we said.

"It won't be long, see you again." He walked away to the kitchen at the back of the restaurant.

"So," I said to the gentleman, "This is your private kitchen is it?" They all answered at the same time.

"Yes madam."

By ten o'clock every seat was full; I wish you had been there with me Louise. I bet you would have loved my Scottish Grill; it was so fresh and tasty I thought I was in a London restaurant. I order my white and red wine from France at the moment; I have forgotten the taste of Campari and Lemonade with ice that I used to drink. The music started at about 9.30 pm; they were such romantic songs. I didn't know the name of the group so I asked Joe who they were. He said they had no name but that they were students at the university.

"Oh well they sing a very well."

"Yes they do," Mohamed agreed. Robert said he would ask them to sing a special song for me.

"You don't know which one Robert," I said.

"I could have a good guess what it might be; I Have to Say Goodbye?"

I smiled at him, "So you have seen the CD in my living room?"

"Well, I just had a look."

"Anyway, you had a good guess Robert."

Joe looked me in the face and said, "Now you can tell us where you have been all day."

"We thought you had been kidnapped," Robert said.

"I wish I had been kidnapped, "I replied.

"It would not have been funny if you had been," Joe said with a serious expression. I looked at Mohamed and he just smiled with eager eyes.

"I just wanted to look around Bangkok and see what it looked like."

"How far did you go? Robert asked.

"I went by boat until it reached its destination."

"Well done, you are very clever," Mohamed said.

"I don't know where I went then; I took a bus and then a taxi to get back home. There was a traffic jam which was so bad; everyone was smiling."

"Now you know how bad it is on the roads," Robert said.

"I know I need to learn new things every day."

"That is good to hear, but next time please don't go by yourself. Tell me where you want to go and I will take you there," Joe said.

"I will do; thank you."

Robert looked at Mohamed and said, "Come on Ambassador," he was pretending to be very polite to him, "You said you wanted to invite Lucy somewhere; have you forgotten?"

"Oh yes, thank you Robert for reminding me. This weekend Robert, Joe and I are going to the beach with a friend of mine; would you like to come with us?"

"I would love to, is it Pattaya?"

"No Lucy, it is a hundred times better than Pattaya."

"It is very nice of you all to invite me to go with you."

Robert said, "We leave Bangkok on Friday morning. We have decided to go by fast train so you can see the countryside. We will come back by car as Mohamed's driver will drive the car and pick us up."

"How wonderful; it's so exciting. I am looking forward to seeing beautiful beaches and the sea," I said.

"You will Lucy, it is a beautiful place," Joe said.

"Thank you very much."

"No, don't thank us," Robert pointed his finger at Mohamed, "It is the Ambassador's idea; you have to thank him Lucy."

I turned to him with a big smile on my face, "Thank you Ambassador." He just nodded his head and looked at me with his sharp eyes.

Joe, Robert and I went together by taxi to the Thai International Railway Station at Hua Lamphong. When we got out of the taxi we saw Mohamed getting out of his Mercedes sports car with a beautiful blond lady. My heart felt as if it had fallen to the ground.

"Are you okay Lucy?" Robert asked and held my arm.

"Yes I am fine."

"Hi there, good morning all," Mohamed said.

"Good morning Mohamed," we all replied.

"Nat, this is Joe and his sister Lucy; you know Robert already. This is Natalie my guest."

"How do you do," Joe said.

I said, "Nice to meet you."

"Shall we get on board the train?" Robert said.

"Yes sure. I think the train should be leaving soon," Joe told us. When we boarded the train we found that we had our own special carriage with private seats. The train rumbled on for several hours and we had our breakfast, after which I looked out of the window and watched the countryside go by.

There are so many stories I want to tell you. Joe and Robert were playing cards whilst Mohamed took care of his guest and occasionally looked across at the game. I think they knew I wanted to be left alone with my writing. The train passed through green mountainside and jungle. At times I thought I was in Africa. What a shame I don't know my own country. Sometimes I saw people working in farms, growing rice; it was such a wonderful picture I saw how difficult their life was and how hard they had to work; it reminded me of when I went to Europe. The landscape was so beautiful but in my imagination it seemed I was in a different world. I want to explain it to you; to give you a very clear picture so you can see it in your own mind. I am afraid I am not a very good writer but I hope that one day soon you will be able to see it with your own eyes. I wanted to stay on the train for ever but I also wanted to reach our destination; yes you are right, at the moment I don't really know who I am.

Joe announced that we had arrived and told me we had reached paradise. When we got out of the train Mohamed's security people were waiting for us and we were checked into a five star hotel. Hua Hin has a wonderful beach; it is so beautiful and peaceful and completely different from Pattaya. The atmosphere was tremendous. I was very surprised that the others were not as excited as I was; I found out afterwards that they had been here before; in fact they had been to Hua Hin several times. I couldn't wait to run onto the silver sand and lie down in the sun

I took my clothes out of my case; it was perfect, thank goodness I brought it with me from London. The phone in my room rang; it was Robert and he said, "Hello, are you ready Lucy? We are going to have lunch first and then we will go for a walk and show you round the place."

"Yes Robert, I am looking forward to it; give me five minutes and I will be downstairs. Thanks for calling Robert."

"That's okay; I will see you soon Lucy, bye, bye."

"Oh wow! You see Joe? Those two ladies look stunning," Robert said to Joe. Mohamed just kept smiling with his sharp eyes.

"Yes they are very beautiful blonds; even I can tell they must be professional models. They dress very fashionably and look like people from high society."

"It doesn't surprise me why Londoners keep going out with new fashions," Joe replied.

"Thanks Joe," she said.

"I didn't know your sister had just come back from London," Natalie said in her French accent.

"I was over there for a few years," I replied.

"If I hadn't seen your face I would have sworn you were English," she continued.

I smiled at her and explained, "I was there when I was young."

"Yes I guessed as much." She looked at me with her haughty eyes; how can I explain it to you Louise? She is the kind of woman men love to be with; she is very feminine and a good performer with great emotion. She is a real woman and very tempting for a man to be with.

We had our lunch in the hotel. They were talking about the South of Thailand, somewhere that I haven't been to yet. They all said that in the South there were some of the most beautiful places in the world for someone who loves to be by the sea, especially Phuket and a few other places; they promised to take me there one day.

We went for a long walk around the area and I noticed that most of the people we saw were families on a weekend holiday. We sat down on the beach and I lay on the sand. I suggested to Natalie that we go for a swim. I can't swim far from the beach, in fact I am not too good at all; neither was Natalie. The boys just lazed around and smoked cigarettes. When we got back Robert said we were going to a dinner and dance that evening and that they would be playing golf in the morning. He asked if we wanted to go with them. I looked at Natalie and she nodded her head at me and said she would rather go to the beach, if that was okay. I said that that was a good idea. We walked back to the hotel, each of us in our own cocoon of happiness.

Robert and Joe seemed to be the most delighted; they were like young kids running around and playing games. I was in my beautiful bedroom and thinking about Natalie. There were so many questions I wanted to ask Robert and Joe but I hadn't had a chance to open my mouth.

When I got down to Reception Natalie, Mohamed, Joe and Robert were drinking at the bar. She was wearing a long, creamy, lace dress; I could tell she had expensive tastes or perhaps that was the way people dressed if they became members of high society. When I was in London I was involved in the fashion business and I understand these things, but I could still learn a few things from her. That night I wore a black satin dress in a plain style, it was open at the back and front with a small stripe; I looked so thin, as I hadn't eaten much since I arrived from London because of the hot weather. When Mohamed saw me he stood up and bowed his head; he is so polite and he is so handsome. Due to his position as Ambassador of Saudi Arabia and the owner of an oil company he had of course had everything prepared in advance using, his own private security people.

On the way to the restaurant, Robert and Joe were talking to Natalie; Mohamed and I just listened to the conversation. She mentioned to Robert about a few things from the past, I heard her say, "Do you remember, Robert, when you were in the Unity Club and they had to put all of you into a taxi? You were drunk and had been dancing until 3 o'clock in the morning."

"Yes of course, I shall never forget," Robert replied.

I was feeling so drunk or perhaps I just imagined that the world was so small and round like an orange. "Are you feeling okay Lucy?" Mohamed asked me.

"Oh yes, thank you. I just feel a bit dizzy; would you mind if I don't go to the dance?"

"Please come with us you will feel better," Natalie said.

"I think I feel sick."

"If you don't want to go for a dance, we won't go tonight, we will have a rest instead," Mohamed said.

"Anyway, we have to play golf early in the morning," Joe said.

"I am so sorry everyone; I have spoiled your program."

"I think we better rest," Robert agreed.

"We will make it another night," Mohamed said to Natalie.

You know Louise, I was so shocked; I didn't understand why this woman, who was involved with Chris, was also involved with Mohamed; it is unbelievable to see her in this situation. I was so surprised; why was she with Mohamed at this moment; I could see that the relationship was more than simple friendship.

Very early in the morning I went for a swim and later I lay down on the clean silver sand and closed my eyes. I was thinking of you and wishing I could be with you and telling you how confused I am. I don't know who I am or what I want in life but you are the one who knows me so well. I am not ashamed to tell you as you have seen me before with a different man every night. I can pay them to make me feel happy and as long as they make me feel great I don't care how much I have to pay. Since I came back to my own country I haven't had anyone and I can no longer do anything I want to do because of my family name. It is not like in London here; I am so sick of myself; you must know that I can't live without a man.

"How are feeling this morning?"

I said to him, "I am getting better, thank you." I could feel he was sat close to me but I kept my eyes closed.

"Are you missing London?

"Yes I am, very much. London means so much to me."

"I do understand," he said, "Why did you come back Lucy?"

"That is a good question, I often ask myself the same thing and I am still waiting for the right answer. I am sure that one day I will be able to give you the right one Mr. Ambassador."

"You are lucky to be Joe's sister."

"Why? If I wasn't Joe's sister what were you going to do with me Mr. Ambassador? Do you want to kill me?"

"No, I want to kiss you." I opened my eyes but it was too late, he was already kissing me; I don't know how long it was. Suddenly he said he had to go, as the others were waiting for him to go and play golf. He said he would see me later.

When they came back at lunchtime Mohamed took us for lunch in the town centre. I couldn't look into his eyes but I felt so fresh and I had hope. Natalie bought a lot of fashion accessories and said that in London everyone was crazy about seashell handy crafts. She had a great time shopping and Mohamed was kind enough to pay for everything and carry loads of bags for her. When we got back Robert said, "Don't forget to have a good rest ladies as we are going out dancing tonight. You can't get sick again," which made me laugh.

We had dinner at about 8.30 and then went to the ballroom. Natalie was wearing a pink, satin dress and looked really beautiful. I was in my white, cotton dress; it was very simple but so comfortable to move in. Robert and Natalie got drunk on champagne and red wine and Joe wasn't in a good state either and by 12.30 they couldn't dance any more. Mohamed took the opportunity to dance with me until 1.00 o'clock, he was so polite, but he intended something I didn't know about.

"Shall we go back to the hotel?" He asked, "I think we are all a bit drunk but I want to be with you all night," he said.

"I said to him, "You see? You are drunk and don't know what are you saying."

"I am not drunk," he replied, "I haven't had much to drink and I know what I want. I really want to talk to you."

I said to him, "Yes, we can talk tomorrow. Look at them, they are all sleeping." Mohamed carried Natalie to her room and Joe and Robert helped each other to their rooms. I went to my room by myself. I soaked in my bath for a long time thinking that he was in Natalie's room. Suddenly my room telephone rang.

"Hello, sorry, it's me; I couldn't sleep; could I talk with you?"

"What time is it now?"

"I am not sure," he said, "I promise I won't be long, don't open your door Lucy."

"Then how can you get in?"

"If you look next to the cupboard just unlock the connecting door."

"I am sorry, I didn't notice." Very soon Mohamed was in my room. That night I have to tell you; but it is so hard to explain; I can't find the right words to write and tell you. I thought it was all a dream, the most wonderful dream of my life. I went to paradise; for the rest of my life I will never forget it. Of course it was both rough and smooth; I was transported far away from this world; it was something I had only dreamed of and I wanted it to continue for ever until I died. It was what I had always wanted and now I can't live without it. We didn't stop for several minutes, I was working so hard to cross the divide and so was he; we were so strong until the sun shone and we could both see the way to cross the divide; we held hands and on all sides we could see the sun was drowned. We looked into each other's eyes and could see that we were at the same destination; we had arrived and I couldn't hear anything except the sea hitting the silver sand; it was so hard and so wet; it was so real and so powerful, we didn't want to stop our journey but we had to wake up and for a while, oh God! How wonderful to see the sun was drowned again.

The next morning, when I got down for breakfast it was very late. I saw Natalie was sitting alone; she waved to me with a big smile. "Good morning."

"Good morning," I said.

"I am so sorry Lucy."

"What about, Natalie?"

"I was speaking about last night," she said, "I think one of the gentleman put something in my drink; I have never felt so bad as I do this morning, I have such a headache. Last night I slept like a rock and I don't remember how I got to my room, it was terrible."

"I think we were all a bit drunk although I wasn't too bad. I think Mohamed took you to your room."

"Oh yes, he is so kind to me. He is my man and he has never changed since I have known him."

"Well you are lucky to know him."

"Well yes, but he is just my close friend, I mean very close, but in another way Mohamed's heart is deeper than the ocean; I can never read his mind. Shall we walk?"

"Yes of course."

"I don't want to go back to London," she said to me.

"Why don't you stay with Mohamed?"

"Do you know Lucy? Sometimes men are so difficult to understand, I thought I knew him well, then I got a big shock; I really know nothing about him; he is a very, very complicated person. Maybe he is a millionaire by birth or maybe through his job or perhaps he is just a playboy; I don't know; I just can't keep him."

"When did you meet him?"

"A few years ago; when I met him I was working for a French cosmetic company. He introduced me to his close friend Chris and since then I have been with Chris whilst Mohamed moved from place to place with his job. I stayed with Chris for a few years; he gave me everything I wanted but he is another mystery man."

"Why?" I asked Natalie.

"Chris is a millionaire through his family. He is the owner of the Unity Club in London, but to be honest with you Lucy I never know what he is doing. One day he is at home in Knightsbridge, the next day he is in New York. Most of the time he says he is working for his business and that is why he has to move around the world. You see Lucy; these are men I have known so well. Chris bought me an expensive flat in Chelsea and gave me a beautiful apartment in France. He was so sweet even though he had so many women in his life. He always came back to me but then, one night, he met a girl he called princess; I remember her so well. Her name was Nadia and he was very much in love with her."

"So where is Nadia?" I asked Natalie.

"Well Lucy, it is a long story. I hope I am not boring you with it Lucy?"

"Oh no, not at all Natalie; in fact I want to know because I sometimes don't understand men either. I haven't had much experience and I think men are very interesting, so I am sure it will be useful to me in the future. Please carry on and tell me more."

"Nadia was married to the U.S. Ambassador and had two sons. Just before her second son was born she had an affair with Mohamed."

"Did she divorce her husband?"

"Yes. The U.S. Ambassador got so angry when he found out that his dear wife was having an affair with the Ambassador of Saudi Arabia."

"Did she get custody of her sons?"

"No. I mean no way; the U.S. Ambassador won the case to keep his two sons with him. She could of course visit them or meet them at home but he doesn't allow them to stay with her."

"That is very cruel."

"I know but what could she do? She was the one who committed adultery with another man."

"So where does she live now?"

"Oh dear Lucy, I hope you won't tell anybody this story about Mohamed."

"Listen, I don't know anybody in this country, if you don't want me to tell that is okay with me Natalie."

"I mean, Mohamed told me because he was so hurt by Nadia."

"Really?"

"Yes, he was the most upset I had ever seen him and I realized he loved Nadia very much. He was so upset I thought he might have gone off marriage altogether."

"That is very serious Natalie."

"It was indeed Lucy. Mohamed adored Nadia. She is beautiful and clever and had her own apartment in New York. Mohamed visited her often."

"Is he still seeing her even now?"

"Well, I think he would if he could; for the rest of his life if it was possible but Nadia had more then Mohamed expected. I would like you to meet Nadia and make up your own mind. She is a remarkable woman; she can cook dinner for guests; I mean she can cook Cordon Bleu; she can make intelligent conversation with people and she always gave excellent advice to her husband or Mohamed; she was such a charming woman."

"I know what you mean. I can imagine Nadia."

"That is good Lucy, so you won't be too surprised when I tell you that Mohamed called me to see him at the Hilton Park Lane Hotel for dinner. He liked to stay there because his mother had a big flat in the Bayswater Road."

"So, you mean his mother lives in London?"

"Of course; since his father died his mother has returned to live in London. She is an English lady; that's why Mohamed is such a handsome man and why women can't keep their eyes off him. That day we had a nice time chatting and talking about old times. Mohamed asked me about Chris and I said, "To be honest Mohamed, I am not the only girl Chris goes out with.

In fact he has so many girlfriends that I am tired of chasing him and I am so fed up with him."

Mohamed looked into my eyes and said, "You are still very beautiful."

"Thank you," I said, "But I can't win his heart."

"Maybe he has got one particular woman in his heart."

"What do you mean Mohamed? Do you know who this luckiest woman in the whole world is?"

"Of course, and you know her."

"I have no idea Mohamed. As far as I know, for the past few years he has been messing around with blonds."

"No she is not a blond; he called her his princess."

"Nadia?"

"Yes it is."

"No, Mohamed that is impossible."

"I'm afraid it's true; he loves her so much." Mohamed told me everything. He said Chris went back to Nadia after she divorced. Mohamed didn't know himself; he said he went to visit Nadia without telling her first and when he opened the door Nadia and Chris were making love on the floor in the front room."

"Did he have a key?"

"Of course Lucy he bought that flat for Nadia to live in."

"Did he go back and see her again?"

"No I don't think so. He told me that a few months later he got a phone call from Chris saying that Nadia was in hospital and she wanted to see him."

"Did he go back?"

"Of course he did. I think he loved Nadia with all his heart. Mohamed flew back to New York immediately. He said Chris was by her bed when he got there. She was in a coma and they both held her hands until she took her last breath. Are you crying Lucy?"

"Yes I am; it is so sad."

"Yes it was sad, even for me."

"Why was her life so short?"

"She had cancer, but by the time the doctors found out it was too late; it had spread all over her body."

That evening, when the three men came back from playing golf, we had dinner. Robert reminded us that we are going dancing that evening and the next afternoon we were going back to Bangkok.

"I don't want to go back yet," Natalie said.

"You can stay here as long as you want Natalie, you don't need to go back to work," Robert said.

"That is not a nice thing to say to a lady," I said.

"It's okay Lucy, Robert is right."

"But you can't stay here on your own Natalie."

"I know Lucy but I have met a nice guy, he is French and very handsome."

"You have to come back with us tomorrow afternoon Natalie," said Mohamed.

I asked Joe if it was possible for me to do a tour round the place in morning, before we left. I wanted to know if there were any temples nearby in Hua Hin as I wanted to visit one.

"Yes sure," Joe said, "I will take you to see a temple in the morning." In our belief we pray to the soul of someone who has died and we ask a holy monk to send our best wishes to the spirit. I shall never forget that it was Nadia who helped me to recover from being a drug addict and trained me to be a businesswoman. I have made millions of pounds through her advice and I will never forget her.

We went to the dance; I was very quiet but Robert and Joe were happy and had a lot to drink. Natalie was crazy for the French guy and danced with him all night long. I danced with Mohamed until the last song: I Have to say Goodbye:

I want to tell you my darling when you are nearby, I feel so good even though I am so shy, I try to touch you I am so relieved that you don't mind. My darling I can tell you if you look into my eyes, I am so in love with you even though I am so shy. Please let me kiss you before I say goodbye. Darling I want to tell you I feel so good when you are nearby I want to be with you all night. Please let me kiss you even though I am so shy. Oh my darling I don't want to say goodbye,

I know that you are not mine, could I tell you that I love you? I wish you were nearby tonight I am sorry darling I have to say good bye, good bye my darling, good bye.

Mohamed said goodnight to me with a kiss on the lips and said he would not disturb me but would dream about me all night long. In the morning I met Joe and Mohamed in Reception. We had breakfast and I asked Joe where Robert and Natalie were. Joe said they were still in bed and just the three of us would go to the temple. We went in Mohamed's car, without his driver. He took us far away from the hotel and when I got out of the car I could tell it was a holy temple. It was such a beautiful and peaceful place. Joe went to the temple and said something to the monk. We all sat down and Joe gave me a small jar full of water. He told me that when the monk was praying I should pour the water into a small bowl and then wish for good things for a person. I did this and wished great power for Nadia. I wanted her to be happy and to find a peaceful place for her soul; I wished to be her friend again.

That afternoon Mohammed's driver took us from Hua Hin to Bangkok. We stopped on the way and had lunch. We all had our little thoughts but as for me, I knew I couldn't tell Natalie that I was a friend of Nadia and that I was so crazy for someone and that I wanted him so much, so much indeed.

I hope you are well and I am looking forward to seeing you very soon. I miss you and London so much

Love

Lucy

CHAPTER TWENTY-EIGHT

Dear Lucy

How delighted I was to open and read your lovely letter, it made me so happy. Since you left London I have been hoping that it won't be too long before I can go abroad to earn some money. I have been waiting eagerly for your news and get all excited when I see a postman coming.

"Do I have any letters?" I ask him.

"Yes you have love."

"Oh thank you." I was thinking about you and then I got your big news. I was very surprised; I was amazed that Natalie was with you in Bangkok. But now I think a black cloud has just passed the sun and I can see blue skies. I haven't seen Chris at all; he has sent me some postcards from various places; one was sent from South Africa, another from Canada. He says that as soon as he is back he will come to see me. I got a postcard one morning, before I went to the University and the same day I saw him at traffic lights in Baker Street; he was with a blond girl in his car but he didn't see me. You see Lucy this is a man I can never trust again. I have told myself that I am alone from now on and I don't need to worry about him any more. As soon as my final exam is completed I will come and see you.

David and Jim invited me for a special meal; they both look after me like I was their own family. They said that if I go abroad to live they will miss me so much; in fact they don't want me to go far away from England. For them, going to Spain is too far. David and Jim love me and they are both such nice people.

This year has gone so quickly; Christmas is coming soon and it seems to me that you only left London a few months ago.

London is still the same; it rains nearly every day, the fireman are not happy with their wages, the London underground is going on strike and the public have to put up with all this trouble. In the future, if a student wants to go to university, their parents will have to pay the fees; I think that is going to be a big problem. Even now I have to suffer so much to get my degree by using my own money. Soon we are going to have the status of a Third World Country. If parents don't have enough money, they won't be able to send their children to High School and get a degree from university. At the moment London is a place for rich people to live in; I am sorry to say that. I know you could come back to live in London anytime you like but I don't need to tell you that. I think you are a real Londoner but it is a very bad time for working class people like me to get to the top and earn a lot of money. At the moment we are lucky to get a one bedroom flat in a bad area like Kilburn or Camden Town and even then we would find it hard to pay back the mortgage. This is London life, you are lucky to be a millionaire and to have escaped.

I can't imagine what your man looks like; he must be handsome to win your heart but there you are, when you are in love you can sing a song day and night. I hope you and Mohamed will be happy together. I wish you a wonderful Christmas and I hope to see you soon. Thank you so much for your wonderful news and letter, it made me happy and I am waiting for the next one.

Have a Merry Christmas and a Happy New Year.

Thinking of you always

Louise

CHAPTER TWENTY-NINE

Chiang Rai   February

Dear Louise

Thank you for your lovely letter; it reminded me of the pub in Maida Vale; I really loved it. I do miss the old place that I used to live in there. This time I have so much to tell you I think you will still be reading it when you are travelling to Bangkok.

I arrived at Chiang Rai Airport before noon and want to spend Christmas with my uncle in the North of Thailand. I came by myself, without Joe or Robert. At first I wanted to take the train but Mohamed said that at the moment it was very dangerous as the weather was so cold and there was lots of fog on the mountain tops and he said it would take me two days and two nights. I wanted to see the view, which they said was beautiful, but I couldn't travel by train, so instead I came by plane. It took me about one hour and it was convenient for uncle to pick me at Chiang Rai Airport. Chiang Rai is the highest province in Thailand and is up in the North, near the Burmese border. When my uncle retired early from his job, he came to settle down in his second home here for a few years but he visits his International School in Bangkok every month.

"Hello uncle," I said.
"Hello my dear Lucy, this way. I don't think you have met Naree yet."
"No uncle I don't think I have."
"Naree, this is my niece Lucy. Naree is my Private Nurse."

"Nice to meet you Naree."

"I am pleased to meet you to; your uncle always talks about you."

"I hope it is in a nice way?"

"Yes, he says you are so intelligent and he is very proud of you."

"Oh thank you uncle."

This year in Chiang Rai it is so cold that it felt like it was January in London. My uncle had phoned me and told me to bring thick clothes but I think I made a mistake and I didn't believe him because it had been so hot in Bangkok. Uncle said that up North, from November until March, it was always cold, that was why he liked to live here; he said it reminded him of England.

"Are you hungry Lucy?" he asked.

"Not yet uncle," I replied.

"We will stop in a town on the way to the village where I live. My house is far away from the lowlands and it will take us nearly two hours to get there. We usually come into town every two weeks."

We went to a small breakfast café where everyone seemed to know uncle very well. We just had omelettes and tea. Uncle then took me to the Head Office of the Land Registry to pick up his letters. We went along a country road and there was a lot of fog and I couldn't see anything.

"Are you okay?" He asked.

"I am not sure uncle; I think I might be getting a cold."

"We won't be too long; you just put my jacket on." A short time later we were there.

"Here we are, let's get into the house."

"Oh uncle it is so beautiful. How wonderful, it is like houses in Canada; am I dreaming uncle?"

"No you are not. Let's get you warm first or you will get sick Lucy."

"I am okay uncle."

"I will make some green tea," Naree said.

"And I am going to make it warmer in here."

"Can I help you?"

"No thanks, it is quite complicated; it's not coal like in London. I have to use wood instead but you can watch how I make the fire." The house was in the middle of the Tribal area and the lowlands.

"Here is your tea."

"Thank you Naree."

"You are welcome."

"I am amazed at the life you lead here uncle; this is so different from Bangkok. This place is so far from the real world; it is in the middle of the jungle."

"I know but it is better than it was a few years ago; it was so dangerous before."

"Why do you live here uncle?"

"To protect Human Rights; I have to help the people because without me they haven't got a hope; no hospital, no school; I will tell you more later. Let's take your suitcase to your room."

"Thank you uncle, let me help."

When I looked round the house it had a huge sitting room with a lot of old pictures of various countries in Europe; England, France, Italy, Holland. He grows plants in the house, some quite big and other small ones with flowers. I walked to the back, past the guest room and found a large library with several hundred books in it. I turned right and there was my uncle's bedroom, next came the dining room and at the back was a big kitchen and a toilet. I walked to the left and saw four guest bedrooms. Behind the kitchen was a big room which was connected to the house. When I looked out of the back of the house I could see a high mountain with hundreds of trees and a beautiful lake. I went to my room thinking my uncle was the most special person in the world. In my room I had an en suite bathroom, a dressing table and a bed with a beautiful net over it. I thought I must be dreaming; how come I am in the jungle at the end of the world.

"Lunchtime Lucy," I heard him calling me from the sitting room.

"Yes uncle, I am coming."

"Lucy, this is Pa Ploy, she is my housekeeper and my cook and this is Lung Non, her husband and my driver. They used to work with me when I was Minister of Foreign Affairs.

"Hello Khun Lucy."

"Hello, nice to meet you both." They called me 'Khun' as in Thai it is a word used before mentioning someone's name, it is very polite to address people as 'Khun'.

"This is my niece, the one I sent to live in London. Perhaps you don't remember Lucy, Pa Ploy?"

"I do Minister," she cried out loud, "Oh yes, she is so beautiful now."

"Thank you Pa Ploy."

"What do you have for us?" Uncle asked.

"We have some salted fish, salted eggs and watercress soup."

"That is good." Then he turned to face me and asked, "Are you okay with this food Lucy?"

"Yes uncle, please don't worry."

"I should warn you that we live like everyone else here," he said, "Ten years ago we ate vegetables every day and were lucky if we had some dried meat and fish; it is a long story and I will tell you another time Lucy."

After lunch we went to sit in the living room; uncle pointed out of the window and said, "Can you see that building?"

"Yes uncle," I replied. It was not too far from the house.

"Can you ride a bicycle?"

"Yes uncle."

"Good, I will take you to see my project."

"Oh uncle, this is unbelievable is this your hospital?"

"Yes Lucy, we have forty beds and the building over there is a school; we have seventy students and two teachers."

"What uncle? You only have two teachers?"

"Yes, and I am very lucky to have them. It is very difficult to get people to live up here in the North."

"So how can they teach the students?"

"One teacher takes the students in a group and gives them work in their turn."

"So how many doctors do you have in the hospital?"

"I have got one doctor, one nurse and one midwife and that is all I have."

"How do you make a profit uncle?"

"My dear Lucy, sometimes you have to think about other human beings and if you have the chance you should help people who have no hope in life. I have given the hospital and school to a charity project that helps the tribes people; they don't have any money to pay for medical treatment when they are sick; they can't speak the Thai language when they visit the lowlands and I want them to be able to make contact outside their world. They don't need my help but I am willing to give them what they need; a proper doctor and the ability to read and write so they can understand the outside world."

"Do you have to pay for the doctor and teachers?"

"Of course; even though they help the poor they still have families to support; in fact I pay them more to live out here."

"Uncle, why are you so kind?"

"Sometimes we have to help each other; you can't let people suffer if you have the chance to help them. Today it is too late to take you to the tribal village. If you want to go I will take you there another time."

"Thank you uncle."

"This is the Reception area. Hello, is anybody in? Ah yes, here they are."

"Hello sir."

"Lucy this is Dr. Arun and these ladies are nurse Sunan and midwife Tara; this is my niece Lucy."

"Hello Khun Lucy."

"Nice to meet you all."

"How many patients do you have Dr. Arun?"

"We have two women who are expecting to deliver their babies; I have put them in a back ward as it is convenient for them to call us at night."

"That is good. Last month I heard that you were very busy."

"Yes sir, a lot of people came down from the village; many of them had bad chest infections."

"Do you need any medicines?"

"Yes sir, I have just ordered some from Chiang Mai Hospital. Dr. Smith and his group might come to visit us soon sir."

"Very good; if you need anything in case of emergency just let me know and I will go and collect it."

"Thank you sir."

"We are going to visit Mon and Nut at the school. I will see you all next week."

"Thank you for coming to see us sir and nice to meet you Khun Lucy."

"I am very lucky to meet all of you here in the Hospital."

"Hello Mon and Nut are you in?"

"Yes sir, we are in the living room sir."

"Ah there you are in front of the fire; this is my niece Lucy."

"Hello Khun Lucy."

"Hello Mon and Nut."

"Please sit down sir and I will make some green tea for you sir."

"Oh thank you Mon."

"We let the students go home early today as the weather was so bad; it is too cold. If you are going to Bangkok, I think we need some more thick clothes to give to them as they haven't got enough to keep them warm sir."

"Yes Nut, I spoke to my secretary in Bangkok this morning when I went to pick up Lucy at the airport. She will send the clothes to Head Office as soon as possible, so you will get them very soon."

"Thank you sir; this year the cold is really bad."

"I think that if the weather gets worse you might have to shut down the school for a few weeks, what do you think Mon?"

"Let's see about it sir. Here is Khun Lucy's tea and this is yours sir."

"Thank you Mon."

"The main problem is that the students have to walk from the village to the school, which takes one hour and then walk back; another hour."

"Why it is so far from the village?"

"Oh Khun Lucy they live at the top of the hill and sometimes we have to go and beg the parents to send their children back to school."

"Why?"

"The families need help; sometimes they want their children to work on their farms."

"Oh my goodness!"

"You see Khun Lucy it is not so easy, even when the classes are free."

"Do you have enough food Mon?"

"Just about sir; we have plenty of rice and dry food but we are short of fresh vegetables because the weather is cold and they have stopped growing. We also need some tinned food sir, but the food delivery from town will arrive soon, thank you sir."

"We had better leave you now; I think Lucy is very tired."

"I am not too bad uncle."

"Hello we are back, anybody in?"

"Yes dear we are in the kitchen. You look very tired Lucy, if you go and rest in your room I will send in a pot of tea for you. Dinner will be at about 6.30."

"Thank you uncle."

"Hello Lucy, you look very pale."

"Yes Naree, I have a bad sore throat."

"Oh then you need some ginger tea with honey; it is good for you and you will feel better."

"Thank you."

"Sit down please. Uncle asked me to introduce you to my family. Okay Pa Ploy; let them in." As she said this several dogs came running in. "Calm down calm down! This is Ruby; don't get so excited, I know you miss me but you have to behave as I have my niece here."

"Oh uncle you have such a big family."

"Yes I do; and here are Snow, Snob and Tiger. Someone gave Snow to me as a present; he came from Hongkok Tiger and is a Labrador cross, the same as Ruby. Snob is a real Siamese dog. I keep them out with Pa Ploy when I have guests but they are very good dogs really; except those two, Ruby and Tiger, they are both rather young."

"They are so lovely uncle but why is Snob so quite? I can tell you love her very much."

"I love them all equally but Snob is special to me, isn't she Naree?"

"Yes she is special to our family. She was the first dog in the family and loves your uncle very much."

"Is it really true Uncle?"

"Yes it is true; she saved my life."

"How uncle?"

"When I went to visit Professor Bee at Chang Mai University I saw Snob, at that time she was an ugly puppy; she had a skin diseases and no one was interested in her. I asked Professor Bee who the puppy belonged to.

"Oh no," he answered, "I don't think she has a master, she just runs around the University."

I said that was good and that I would take her with me.

"Oh no Minister, the puppy has a nasty skin disease."

"That's okay," I said, "I will look after her."

"Look!" said the professor, "she can understand what you are saying; she is licking your shoe."

"Okay Professor we will have another meeting before I make my decision."

"That is a good idea Minister. I hope to see you before next month."

"Yes Professor, take care."

"And you too."

When I left Chang Mai University that evening I took Snob with me. We had to drive across the mountains to get back to Chiang Rai, it was a long way and I was very tired. When I turned onto a narrow track I lost control and my car went away down into a ravine. I don't know how long I was unconscious but when I woke up I was in a hospital bed with a beautiful nurse beside me and Professor Bee.

"Where is my puppy?" I asked.

"Don't worry Minister; I will look after your ugly puppy although she is an intelligent dog Minister."

"How did I get here nurse?"

"I am not quite sure sir; I think Professor Bee called the ambulance and we went to pick you up sir."

"The last thing I remember is when my car went over the edge; then I don't remember anything."

Professor Bee explained what had happened. "I was in my house, reading a book after my dinner when I heard a dog barking, just a small noise like a puppy. It went on for a long time; then she stopped and tried to bark. It was annoying me so I opened the window and that is when I saw the ugly puppy run around trying to get inside. I thought something must have gone wrong because the Minister had taken the puppy with him. I went to open the door and asked her 'Where is your master?' She tried to bark outside in the street. I called the ambulance as I knew there must be something wrong with you."

"Is she okay?"

"Don't worry, her skin disease is clearing up and I am sure she will be fully recovered by the time her owner is better."

"Thank you Professor."

"No, no you should thank this beautiful nurse who is looking after you and your puppy."

"So uncle, you had a broken leg but you gained a private nurse for ever."

"Yes and I have Snob." We were all laughing at the same time.

Uncle said, "Tonight Pa Ploy will cook a special dinner for us; we are a long way from Bangkok so I hope you can eat our food."

"Of course uncle, I can eat anything you can; don't worry." I asked him, "Uncle, since you are in the countryside, why do you have a five-bedroom house?"

"Oh you will be surprised how many guests come to visit me in a mouth."

"Who are they?"

"I have groups like the professors from the University, student doctors from Chiang Mai University and sometimes I get groups of missionaries who come to visit the tribal village. I knew them before I set up the Charity School and Hospital. Now I have a new project helping people with HIV and I accommodate a group of visiting doctors. Sometimes I don't have enough room for them all. They have to come to visit the tribes, sometimes called Mountain People, and I send them to stay with Dr. Arun at the Charity Hospital. This mouth the Professor's group went to South Africa for a month. You will be surprise Lucy when you see them; they are a group of young doctors but they all work very hard.

After two days of my visit I couldn't get up from my bed as I had a bad cold. It was so foggy every day. I had Pa Ploy to look after me; she is such a wonderful lady.

"Where are uncle and Naree?"

"Oh they went to the northern village."

"Where is it?"

"You have to walk for about two days; it is across that mountain."

"Can we go by car?"

"No, you can't even use a bicycle up there; it is very high."

"Who lives up there?"

"There is a village for sick women."

"Sick women?"

"I am not quite sure; you had better ask Khun Naree."

On the Friday night I heard a lot of noise outside the house and a car coming from far away.

"Pa Ploy, Pa Ploy!" Someone was shouting outside the door, "Let me in please, it is very cold outside and we are hungry. Please open the door." I came out of my room and went to the front door; it was Robert's voice!

"Oops!" he said, "Surprise, surprise! She is not Pa Ploy. Here she is."

"Oh! Mohamed, Joe please come in."

"Thank you Lucy," Mohamed said.

"Come on Mohamed give her a big kiss and tell her how much you miss her."

"Shut it Robert," he said.

"Oh yes! Now you tell me to shut up. Why have Joe and I come here? Can I tell Lucy the truth?"

"Please bring the boxes in first Robert," Mohamed said, "We have several boxes in the car."

"Yes sir, Ambassador."

"We have brought so many boxes from the office to give to uncle," Joe said.

"There she is," Robert said, "Pa Ploy is coming and I did remember her bicycle bell. Hello Pa Ploy"

"Hello Ambassador, Khun Joe, Khun Robert, how nice to see you all here. I am sorry I have been at the hospital, is there anything I can help you with in the house?"

"No Pa Ploy, it is all done; shall we go inside?"

"Yes I'll make you some green tea."

"Thank you." Pa Ploy went into the kitchen for a while. When she returned she said dinner was ready.

"When are uncle and Naree coming back Pa Ploy?" Mohamed asked.

"They will be away for a few days."

"Oh no," Joe said, "and all of the family have gone with them?"

"Yes Khun Joe," Pa Ploy replied.

"I am hungry Pa Ploy," Robert said.

"Oh I have a special curry for you. I cooked salted pork with red curry and I put in some fresh grass leaves in it."

"That is jolly good Pa Ploy. It means Joe and I will laugh all night long."

"Then I have some grilled chicken with mint herbs."

"That is wonderful for tonight Pa Ploy," Mohamed said.

Robert turned to Pa Ploy and said, "You said you went to the hospital, was there any serious reason?"

"Oh yes, Dr. Arun his nurse and Ms. Tara had to work very hard. It took them nearly the whole day. A village woman came from the high mountains with her husband and a few other people but when they got to the hospital it was nearly too late. She was giving birth to a baby boy but instead of the head coming first his legs showed first."

"Oh no Pa Ploy."

"It was okay Khun Lucy; Dr. Arun, his nurse and the midwife Tara managed in the end. Her husband was so please; it was their first baby."

"Thank God," Joe said.

Mohamed said, "I have got a lot of presents for you Pa Ploy and for the people at the hospital. I will hand them out tomorrow. Are you okay Lucy?" he asked.

"Yes I feel better thank you."

"Of course you must be better," Robert said, "Look who is here! The Ambassador is better then any medicine." That raised another laugh.

This year has been so cold up in the North, so cold that our school had to shut down for a few weeks because the children had to walk from the hilltops and they didn't have enough to wear. I hoped we had some clothes in the boxes uncle had ordered, through his secretary in Bangkok, amongst the load of boxes sent to the Head Office that had been brought up by Joe, Robert and Mohamed the evening before.

"Thank you so much Pa Ploy, dinner was absolutely wonderful as usual."

"I have some desert for all of you; grilled ripe banana and an organic tea from the hilltop."

"Oh I love that tea Pa Ploy," Joe said, "By the way, where is Lung Non?" He asked.

"He went with the Minister to carry some of the dried meat."

"So you are here with Lucy?" Robert said.

"Yes Khun Robert."

That night I was so happy Louise; I stayed with Mohamed all night long as he cuddled me and kissed me. He said that since he had got back from Hua Hin he had been thinking of me. He asked me if I would go on holiday with him to Switzerland but I didn't give him an answer.

"Did you have a good sleep last night Mohamed?" Robert asked the next morning.

"Yes I did," Mohamed answered.

"You look deathly tired; perhaps you had better stay here with Lucy. We are going to visit the hospital and school, so you can look after each other," Joe said, "Pa Ploy is coming with us as we have a lot of canned food and clothes to deliver."

"When we come back in the evening we expect a very nice dinner," Robert said.

"Yes sir," Mohamed replied. We watched them go until they were far away from the house. I don't know how long I was enfolded in Mohamed's arms; I had missed him more then anything in the whole world.

"Do you need anything Lucy? We are going into town tomorrow morning."

"I need so many things my darling Robert; I need to make a list."

"I hope it is not too long because you are coming back to Bangkok with us next week."

"Who said that?"

"I don't know; ask Mohamed. Chiang Rai and Bangkok are not that close you know Lucy? Can you stay with uncle for a month without Mohamed?"

"Ha, ha, ha! Okay then, in that case I will change my mind; I don't need to make a list."

"Ooh, ooh! She accepts; good girl."

I asked, "Who is going into town?"

"Mon, Nut and me. Dr. Arun and Joe need a lot of canned food for the patients."

"I will get some fresh fruit for you."

"Oh thank you Robert."

"You are welcome."

Uncle, Naree and the family came back on the Friday evening. Uncle was so please to see Mohamed, Joe and Robert and when we were together I could tell how happy he was. He talked about so many things relating to his projects, which I didn't understand at all. Mohamed is very close to uncle and Naree; he looked like a part of the family.

"By the way," said Joe, "We went to the town with Dr. Arun. We had hundreds of salted eggs, rice and cans. We went to see the head of the office and he gave me a few letters from abroad."

"Oh, thank you Joe. How is Tiger Company business?"

"It is still very good uncle. Sales haven't dropped at all."

"That is lucky."

"Yes it is uncle. Where are you going on holiday this year uncle?" Joe asked.

"I don't know yet Joe; it could be any place that is safe for the time being. I think this year I might not go to Switzerland; I have been over there twice this year."

"Where will you go then uncle?"

"Maybe I will go to South Africa, if my project goes smoothly and I don't need to worry about the hill people and they can look after themselves. What about you and Robert?"

"Well, this year we plan to visit Canada. On the way back we might stop off and visit London; I haven't been to London before."

"That sounds great Joe."

"I think Mohamed wants to ask your permission about your niece uncle," he said laughing.

"My niece? Where are you going to take her Mohamed?"

"I think we might go to Switzerland."

"Very well, that is between you and Lucy but thank you for letting me know, Mohamed. I have known you for a long time. Before you make any commitments think about it; you are both grown up and are not teenagers anymore. Lucy is a Londoner and you are not Siamese; you grew up in London so I think you know what you are doing. I will be happy if both of you are happy. Oh and I nearly forgot, Lucy? About your friend in London, does she still want the job? The Headmistress, Mary, told me that one of her teachers is going back to Australia in July so we need to replace her."

"Yes uncle," I replied, "Louise has just confirmed that as soon as her final exam is completed she will be coming."

"Oh, that sounds interesting," Joe said.

"You will be surprised Robert; Louise has a very strong personality. You know, since her grandmother died when she was sixteen she has worked to support herself as a full-time student at university. When I met her she was working in a pub at night."

"Does she need any help Lucy? Uncle asked, "I can send her some money."

"No uncle, I once offered her money but she refused so thank you uncle but I think she will be alright."

"Do you know her well Lucy?" Joe asked.

"Yes Joe, Louise is a great girl."

"Make sure she does not have any problems and do what you can to help her to graduate," uncle said.

"I will uncle."

"If you are going to Switzerland please let me know; I want to send something to the Thai Ambassador, he is a good friend of mine."

"Yes I will uncle."

The next day we all packed our small suitcases into the Landrover, uncle sat with Mohamed and Naree sat with us in the back. Pa Ploy and Lung Non, her husband, Tiger, Ruby, Snow and Snob all stood at the front of the house to say goodbye Ruby and Snow tried to get into the car but Snob surprised me, she was an unusual dog, very claim, almost disinterested; her name certainly suits her.

"Bye, bye Tiger, Snow, Ruby and you too Lady Snob. See you again Pa Ploy," Robert said. When we got to Chiang Rai Airport it was so crowded with tourists.

"I will be coming to Bangkok at the end of this month," uncle said.

"I will see you uncle," Joe said.

"Thank you Naree, for everything," I said.

"You are welcome, we hope to see you all again soon."

"By the way, may I see you for a minute Mohamed," uncle asked.

We went to the plane but no one asked Mohamed what uncle had said to him but he looked so happy. When we arrived at Bangkok Airport Mohamed's driver was waiting for us.

"I will stay with Robert tonight," Joe said, "So we can go to Lucy's house for a cup of tea."

"Of course, you are all welcome."

They were gone for a long time. I can't sleep Louise, I am sick within myself; I want Mohamed to be with me. I want him so much but it is very difficult to read his mind. I really don't know what he thinks of me. In the morning when I woke up I was so depressed. There was a knock on my door.

"Khun Lucy, you have a guest in the living room."

"Okay Pa Chom I will be downstairs soon."

"Good morning Madam, how are you?"

"Oh Robert, I wondered who it could be coming to see me so early in the morning and it's you."

"Oh yes, you thought it might be Mohamed."

"That was my guess. Pa Cham, bring us a pot of tea please. Now tell me why you have come to see me Robert? You must have some news for me."

"Yes you are right Lucy. Someone has asked me if you would be prepared to help with a charity."

"What kind of charity?"

"I think it is an orphanage."

"Who is running it?"

"She is the wife of someone in the military; she is a close friend of mine."

"Actually I am very interested; I can donate some money to help her."

"No, that is not the point; she needs someone to give the project some ideas. Maybe I could bring her to see you and we can discuss the matter."

"That would be perfect."

"I will call you later this week."

"Is that the only reason you called so early?"

"No, I have something to do at the British Embassy this morning and besides this is not too early, it is mid-day already."

"Would you like to have lunch with me?"

"No thank you Lucy, I have to get back to my office. This week my paperwork is piled up after my holiday; it is a disaster."

"Will I see you at the weekend Robert?"

"Yes you will."

There you are Louise, that's my daily life in Bangkok. I will tell you more in my next letter or I will tell you myself when you get here. Take care of yourself and take it easy. Sometimes it is so hard and lonely, even though I am with my family. Just think, you are the only one to make things happen if you just put your mind to it. Happiness and sadness are close friends.

Miss you and London

Love

Lucy

CHAPTER THIRTY

London

Dear Lucy

I was very happy to get your letter; I read it often and keep it in my bag like a close friend. It made me so happy as you are the light of hope in my heart. Right now I am in love with Chiang Rai; I even imagine how beautiful it must be in spring. I wish I could be there now so I could help your uncle in Chiang Rai. I don't need to tell you about London life. The underground staff went on strike and then the fireman; they all want more pay. Also the teachers are threatening to go on strike. I think that very soon it is going to be us poor students at university who won't be able to afford to pay the fees. Thank God it is my final year; in the future students will have to work day and night to pay back the loans taken out to study for degrees at university. Students whose parents have to pay for accommodation, books and food now will soon have to pay the fees as well.

I got a postcard from Chris; he sent it from South Africa. I think he is coming back to London soon.

I will let you to know when my final exam is. At the moment I am fed up with London, the routine that we have to put up with, the rotten political situation, it all makes Londoners sick of the depressing, lunatic behaviour.

At the moment I am working very hard to prepare myself for my final exams. I have to work late at Uni and then read until late every night. I would give my life to pass these exams so I can get a good job in the future. I dream every night about going to work in Bangkok and would be so happy to see you again, I do hope it won't be long. I'm counting the days and it makes me happy when I think of it.

I have been to Jim and David's flat and they cooked me a very nice dinner. They have just come back from Spain after their holiday. They both love me and I am very happy to be with them both. They don't want me to go to work in Bangkok as they say they will miss me so much. I have told them I would write to let them know how I am and I want to go to work for a year. They are worried that I won't come back to London. I hope I will see you in Bangkok very soon and I hope you and Mohamed will be happy together. Just to remind you, it won't be too long before I see you in Bangkok.

Lots of love and see you soon

Louise

CHAPTER THIRTY-ONE

I was very nervous and excited. It was the first time in my life that I was going to travel abroad, far away from London. I would be on my own with no one else to talk to. I was going to a foreign place to work for a year. Even so I was also sad. I was fed up with London but London was the place I was born. Now I knew what Lucy meant in her letters when she said that she missed London so much. I checked in with British Airways a bit early. I didn't have a lot of things to pack, some books and a few gifts for Lucy and some things that I really liked. Jim and David didn't want to see me off at Heathrow Airport, they said they would cry.

"Hello, hello, this way," I heard someone shout. When I turned round I jumped.
"Hi Jason," I hugged him very tightly.
"I am so pleased to see you Jason."
"I'm pleased to see you," he said.
"I am very nervous Jason."
"Don't be silly, just pretend that you are going on holiday and don't forget, you are going to see your best friend Lucy. Soon you will forget London." For the past four years Jason and I had been very close, we understood each other so well and we shared the knowledge and talent to pass our exams. We were both extremely satisfied with our results It had been so hard and difficulty but we both walked through them.

"Promise you will come back for graduation next year?" Jason said.
"I promise you," I replied.
"If you need anything from London just let me know and I will send it to you."

"Thank you so much Jason, I hope we will remain friends."

"Of course Louise, I will be your friend for ever. We have been together for four years, how can I forget my best friend?"

"I don't trust men, they are all the same."

"Hey, be a good girl; there must be one man in the world that will be different? Listen, Louise if you don't have anyone I would like to be your boyfriend or am I too late; I have no one in my heart."

"You are so lucky Jason, you will go far in life; you have a good job, good pay."

"I can say the same about you Louise. Look back to the past when I had lots of problems, who helped me to sort myself out? It was you Louise, how can I ever forget you? I will write to you. Listen Louise, would you promise me one more thing?"

"Yes of course Jason."

"You must take care of yourself. Always remember, you are not in England, you are in a foreign country so think twice before you make any decisions and remember that Jim, David and I are here in London."

"Yes I will, I promise you."

"Where are your passport and ticket?"

"They are in my bag."

"Show me. Lucy's address is in my diary; do you have my mother's address that I gave you?"

"Yes I do, I put it in my diary."

"That is a good girl."

"Goodbye Jason and goodbye London."

"Give me a big hug. As soon as you get there send me a letter."

"Yes I will Jason."

"Are you ready?"

"Thank you for coming Jason."

"You are my best friend Louise. Good luck Louise; be strong and proud of yourself goodbye Louise."

CHAPTER THIRTY-TWO

As the plane flew through the sky I looked out of the window and wondered how I would be able to stay away for more then a year; I was missing London already. We had been flying for nearly twelve hours when I heard them announce that we were going to land in thirty minutes and that it was eight o'clock in the morning local time, I was so pleased. When I got through customs I noticed two gentlemen who appeared to be looking for someone. The younger one had a similar face to Lucy's, the other one had to be Robert.

"Excuse me, are you Miss Louise?"

"Yes I am."

"Oh that was a good guess," Joe said, "We have come to pick you up instead of Lucy. I am Joe and this is Robert."

"Nice to meet you both," I said.

"And we are pleased to meet you Miss Louise."

"Please just call me Louise."

"Okay we will," Joe said, "Shall we go and pick up your luggage?"

"I think it is down there," Robert pointed his finger at the carousel.

"You look much younger then we expected," said Joe.

"Thank you Joe."

"We thought you would be tall and pale; I mean white, like me," Robert said.

"I know, some people have said that I am not pure white because of my skin colour. I don't know why as my grandmother was Irish and my grandfather was English. I am not sure about my own father …," we were all laughing.

"Lucy asked me to apologise to you; she couldn't pick you up herself as she is in Switzerland at the moment. She will be back tomorrow. What on earth do you have in your suitcase?"

"Oh I am so sorry if it is heavy; I have a few books in there; they are all to help me when I am teaching in the school."

"Oh well, so you are prepared to be a teacher?"

"That is why I applied for the job."

"Okay Louise, our car is this way. Are you tired Louise?"

"A little bit; it is night time in London isn't it?"

"Yes I suppose it is. We are about seven hours different from London," Robert said, "You can have a rest Louise and we will come back to pick you up for dinner. In this house you have Pa Chom, she will look after you. Just make yourself comfortable as if you were in your own house."

"Thank you so much Joe."

When I was alone I walked around the house and fell in love with it. I realised that Lucy had told me a lot of things about it before I got here but from my first steps through the door I felt very comfortable. Pa Chom couldn't speak English but I could tell by her eyes and her smile that she liked me a lot.

"Wow! Two gentlemen and a beautiful lady, I am so proud," Robert said to Joe, "I am sure we will be in the gossip columns in tomorrow's newspapers, ha, ha."

"Where are we going Joe?"

"Where would you like to go Louise? The Oriental, the Hilton or the Sheraton?"

"The Oriental please. I heard it is very beautiful."

"That is right, shall we go?"

"I am so excited Joe, it is so beautiful and it is so real. I love the river; it reminds me of the Thames in London." Robert and Joe smiled widely.

I heard Joe say to Robert, "Don't look round but you have a senior British diplomat sitting behind you."

"Who is it?"

"The Ambassador, his wife, Professor Bee and Mary."

"No shit!"

"Just keep quite, they haven't seen us."

"There you are boys! What are you doing here?"

"Oh we are just having dinner. Louise, this is the British Ambassador's wife."

"How do you do madam?"

"How do you do Louise?"

"Louise just arrived this morning."

"I see, are you here on holiday?"

"Yes Madam."

"Excuse me Louise; I think I should go and say hello to the Ambassador," Robert said and he walked away with the Ambassador's wife. When he came back he was smiling at Joe.

He said, "They all think Louise is a very beautiful English lady." We looked at each other and smiled.

The next morning, when I woke up, Sumon was outside my bedroom with a tray of tea, toast and orange juice; I knew that she could speak a little English. I looked at my watch and saw that it was ten-thirty. When I went downstairs I walked past the sitting room and saw a big basket of fresh flowers. It had such a nice smell and the colours were so beautiful. I walked through to the back of the house to the kitchen and there was Joe.

"Good morning Joe."

"Good morning Louise."

"What are you doing?"

"I am just preparing lunch."

"Can you cook?"

"Yes of course."

"May I help you Joe?"

"No thanks Louise, just go and have a rest, it is nearly done. Robert will be here in a minute so you can chat with him. Here they are." When I went to the door I couldn't believe my eyes.

"Louise! Oh, Louise!" She shouted from the door; "I have missed you Louise; I have missed you so much. I am sorry I went away."

"I missed you too Lucy. How lovely to see you again Lucy, you look so well."

"Yes I have put on weight."

"You still look beautiful Lucy."

"Thank you Louise."

"Excuse me madam, there are three gentlemen standing here waiting to be introduced?" Mohamed said.

"I am so sorry Mohamed. This is Louise, my closest friend. This is Mohamed the Ambassador of Saudi Arabia."

"Nice to meet you sir." When I stopped talking Joe and Robert were rolling on the floor and couldn't stop laughing. Mohamed's face was red with embarrassment; I noticed that he looked very handsome when he was embarrassed and his face was so sweet. I smiled at him with my eyes and he knew my meaning. Lucy hit Joe and Robert and then they both looked at Mohamed's face.

They both said at the same time, "Sorry sir."

I gave my hand to Mohamed, "How do you do," he shook my hand so hard that it hurt. I took my hand back and he smiled.

"I am very pleased to meet you Miss Louise."

Mohamed told his driver to put Lucy's luggage in the house.

"Are you tired Lucy?" I asked.

"No not really. I have so many things to tell you Louise." Joe and Robert were in the kitchen and they called us for lunch. Mohamed just had a black coffee and I had a tuna salad. Lucy just had a pot of tea whilst Joe and Robert had roast beef. I noticed that Lucy was very much in love with Mohamed. She had changed from the old friend I remembered; she was not a very strong personality any more and was so quite in front of Mohamed. Joe and Robert were so close with him; he was so generous and I could see that Mohamed had a special personality.

After lunch Joe said to Robert, "We should let Lucy and Mohamed rest; they must be tired and we should go out and do some shopping for dinner." We went out together to the shopping centre and when we got back Joe went into the kitchen. Robert helped Joe to prepare the food and I stayed in the kitchen with them. When Mohamed came down he sat beside me.

"Can I give you a hand?" He asked me; his voice was so a powerful and very polite.

"I have nothing to do and they won't allow me to touch anything," I replied.

"So may I sit with you?"

"Please do." He looked me in the eyes and I looked at him. When I turned my eyes towards Joe I felt as though I had a fever; I was so cold.

"Are you okay Louise?" He asked.

"Yes I am thank you."

"How is London?"

"Oh it's just warm and is the same as ever, nothing much changes."

"Do you miss London?"

"I think I do." When I answered him I couldn't look him in the eyes, he seemed such an intelligent person. His eyes looked like an eagle's and seemed to be on fire; they could make me hot or cold but I liked to look at them. Once again I looked into his eyes and he looked straight at me and smiled.

"Oh here you are. I was looking for you," said Lucy from the kitchen, "So you are with Louise." "Yes, we are talking about London," Mohamed said to Lucy. He stood up and walked over to Joe and Robert. He said to them, "I didn't know both of you could cook; it must be a very special dinner. From now on both of you can be my private chefs."

"What are we having for dinner?" Lucy asked.

"Tonight we have roast potatoes, boiled green beans and real Aberdeen Steak with a fresh mixed salad.

"Wow! That sounds great Mohamed said.

CHAPTER THIRTY-THREE

They had all been gone for some time. Lucy and I were sitting in her bedroom and she said I could get up late the next day. I thought she looked happy but she was also sad.

"Do you have something to tell me Lucy?"

"Yes I do." She cuddled me and was crying. "Do you know Louise, when they say money can't buy everything it is true? I have got a lot of money but I can't buy happiness. I am not happy at all Louise."

"Why not? You should be happy; you have your family, you have a lot of money and you have Mohamed."

"Yes I appreciate my family and I am lucky with money but I need love and Mohamed doesn't love me."

"How do you know Lucy?"

"If he loved me he would have asked me to marry him when we were in Switzerland."

"But maybe it is not the right time to ask you."

"No, I know him and he hasn't given his heart to me. Mohamed loves his family more then anything and he can't marry me."

"If he doesn't love you why did he take you with him?"

"He just wanted to please me."

"Listen Lucy, if he can't marry you it doesn't matter, as long as he makes you happy. He has got a high position and I think he is an intelligent person; he carries great responsibilities with his job so give him a chance. He might not ask you to marry him today but in the future things can change. Marriage is just a piece of paper to show that in law you are husband and wife. To be together, understanding each other, helping each other and sharing that is real happiness. If he is not ready don't force him, one day he will ask you to marry him."

"Thank you Louise I am so happy to be with you again."

I went to my bedroom wondering if I had made the right decision in coming to this country to work. Was I really pleased to see Lucy? I tried to close my eyes but I could still see Mohamed's eyes looking at me. All night long he was in my mind. I wanted to escape from this man as soon as possible.

"Good morning Louise."
"Good morning Joe."
"Where is Lucy?"
"She is still in bed; she must be tired," I said.
"Oh Louise, I phoned the Head Teacher, Ms. Mary, at the International School but she has gone on holiday in the North; in fact she has gone to see my uncle in Chiang Rai. The school will be open for another week so I don't think there will be a problem if you want to move in as soon as she comes back. So don't worry about the job; if you want to see the place I can take you to see it; it's not too far from here, about twenty minutes by car."
"Thank you Joe, thank you so much."
"I had better phone Robert and tell him or he might come round here looking for us." He picked up the phone and dialled, "Hello Robert, it's Joe. I am going to take Louise to see the school, so I will see you this evening, is that okay? Yes I will and you will tell Mohamed? Yes, yes, thanks, see you. Bye."

Joe and I went in his car. He behaved like a businessman, so confident; he looked at me and laughed, "What are you thinking Louise?"

"I am just surprised. I have only known you for just a short time but it seems I have known you for ages."

"That is very strange. I feel the same, even Robert told me he felt close to you. Do you know Louise? Deep inside me I feel that you are one of the family."

"Thank you so much Joe."

"You are welcome; don't worry about anything; if you are in any doubt about anything you have me and Lucy to help you. Mary, the Head of the school, is a bit fussy and old fashioned but she is an honest person and very close to my uncle, so just make yourself comfortable.

"Thank you again Joe."

"I will park my car next to the guard house, which is close to the gate, and we can walk from there."

"This is a very big building Joe."

"Yes, the first building used to be an old house. Half of the house is for the teachers who live-in. The second building is for seven to eleven year olds; they all live outside the school. I think at the moment there are about five hundred students."

"That is a lot."

"Yes it is. The right-hand side here is for girls who are going to do O Levels; there are about two hundred at the moment and at the back of the building is a hostel. Most of the students live at home but we have some who live-in; I think there are about thirty of them, I am not sure. Ms. Mary will tell you, but I think they will be the students whose parents live in the countryside. This school is smaller than the new branch and was the first school in Bangkok for seven to sixteen year olds whose parents wanted them to study, write and read in English only. Uncle has made a great success with his first project. He had to open a new school for the juniors because we didn't have enough places for them. People have to book for places two years in advance because the parents have been so impressed with their children's' progress in speaking English so well that they have told all their friends. Originally everyone was against uncle's idea, even the newspapers tried to ban his school. They said it was too expensive and seven years old was too young to learn to read and write in English. Uncle was the Minister of Foreign Affairs so he went to the High Court and eventually he won his case. At that time the government only allowed International Schools for foreigners. Since uncle won his case they now allow all citizens to learn to read and write in English."

"I like the location so much Joe. It is as if I was standing in a jungle; there are so many big trees and hundreds of flowers."

"These big trees are many, many years old. Uncle loves the forest and he has banned the cutting of any tree unless it is replaced. I think he loves England and is trying to keep the natural habitat as best he can. He has said that in the future he wants his students to speak perfect English and go to university in London."

"Joe, look at that tree, it just has pink flowers and that one over there just has yellow flowers, but there are no leaves; they are so beautiful. What is that tree called?"

"Oh that is a guava tree, you can eat the fruit. It has got a lot of seeds inside and when it's ripe it is quite sweet and has a funny smell. The other one is a mango tree."
"I know about mangos, Lucy likes to eat them. Who lives in those two bungalows over there?"

"One is for the gardener and the other one is for the guard. Are you hungry Louise?"

"No, not yet. I would just like to walk around."

"We are a long way from the gate and you will get tired Louise."

"Okay, if we haven't got much time we can go back Joe."

"I promise you if you want to walk around some more I will bring you back Louise."

"Thank you Joe, you are so kind."

When we got back from the school the house was empty, but then I saw Robert driving up behind us. When we got out of the car we went into the sitting room.

"Pa Chom, Pa Chom," Joe called.

"Yes I am coming Khun Joe."

"Where is everybody?" He asked.

"I think Khun Mohamed is upstairs"

"I didn't see his car."

"I saw his driver drop him off and drive away."

"Oh I see. Can we have some lunch Pa Chom?"

"Yes of course Khun Joe, I have roast chicken with salad and we have coconut ice cream in the fridge."

"Oh that is lovely Pa Chom."

"Robert, I am afraid you will have to look after Louise for a week."

"Why? What is going on?" Robert asked quickly.

"I have to go to Singapore on a business trip. Actually I haven't been there before as my brother is dealing with it but last week he wasn't well."

"I promise I will take care of Louise."

"Oh is that Mohamed coming down from upstairs? Would you like anything for lunch?" Joe asked.

"Oh no thanks Joe, I would prefer a black coffee, thank you PaChom."

"How is she?" Joe asked again.

"She is just tired."

"So Joe and I will go to the club without you this evening?"

"No, no I will come with you as usual. Do you want to come with us Louise?" Mohamed asked.

"No thank you, I think I will stay with Lucy."

I was not sure what was going on in this situation; Lucy called me to her bedroom and said, "I think it would be better if you stayed with me in this house Louise, you can drive my car to work."

I answered her very politely, "Thank you Lucy but I think I had better live in the school with the Head Teacher for a while, at least until I get used to it. This is my first job and I am a bit worried. I promise I will come and see you. After all I am not in London anymore. I am just round the corner from your house."

"But I am so alone in this house."

"No you are not alone Lucy, you have Mohamed, he will be with you."

"But Mohamed only comes in the evenings. He never stays here but goes back to his place."

"I know, you told me Lucy, but this is not London and Mohamed is the Ambassador; he has to be at home in his place in case they need him to go on duty."

"Okay Louise I can't win. If you want to stay at the school you can."

"Thank you Lucy."

"But you must come to see me often."

"Of course Lucy, I will do that."

CHAPTER THIRTY-FOUR

I was so excited. Mohamed and Robert carried my suitcase and Lucy walked with me. She had lost weight since she came back from Switzerland and looked so sick.

"I hope you get better soon Lucy," I said, "I will call on you as soon as I have settled in. Tell Joe I am very grateful to him, he has been so kind to me."

"I will Louise, I will tell Joe." I kissed her goodbye and got into the back seat of Mohamed's car. When we arrived at the school Ms. Mary was outside to greet us."

"Good morning Ambassador and Mister Robert."

"Good morning Headmistress," Mohamed and Robert replied.

"This must be Miss Louise." She came close to me and looked at me for a long time. Robert coughed, "Oh I am so sorry," she said, "Please come inside all of you, this way please." Mohamed looked at me with his private smile. Ms. Mary looked more then fifty years old, she was quite plump but elegant. She looked quite good for her age and I could tell she was a very strict person but with a good heart.

"Please sit down," she said, "Charlie, Charlie," she called, "Please bring some drinks for everybody. Thank you Charlie." When the owner of the name came out we nearly burst out laughing; she was such a sweet person but appeared with a dark expression on her face; she looked very sour. Her hair was very curly and she appeared to be about nine years old. She looked at me with her big, beautiful eyes and I think she wanted to speak to me but Ms. Mary said. "Thank Charlie, you can go now." She turned to us and said, "I have just come back from the North and the Minister told me about Louise; he is very pleased and sent his best regards to the Ambassador and Robert. He said he might be coming to Bangkok very soon."

"Did you enjoy your holiday Headmistress?" Mohamed asked.

"Oh yes, very much. When you get old the best way to relax is to see your old friends and chat about old times."

"But you look so young," Robert said.

"Oh you have made my day sir. I also went to see Dr. Tony and we met up with Professor Bee in Chiang Mai. Then we went to see the Minister and the American Missionaries John and Ann, it was very pleasant."

"I think we must leave you and Louise to talk; we will be back again soon," Mohamed said.

"Oh yes Ambassador, please do."

"This is for you Headmistress, I went to Switzerland and I thought of you."

"Oh you shouldn't have Ambassador, what is it?"

"You can open it later. I hope you will like it."

"Thank you so much," she said with a big smile. Robert gave me a kiss to say goodbye and Mohamed just looked at me but I couldn't work out his meaning at all.

When we got back to the room she came very close to me and looked into my face again, then she put her glasses on and took them off, then she sighed, "I think I know you Louise; you look so familiar." Someone knocked at the door, "Yes, come in," she answered to the person who was knocking, "Oh Julia and Maria come in; this is Miss Louise from London. She will be staying with us. Louise, this is Maria from Australia and Julia from New Zealand."

"Hello Miss Louise."

"Hello Julia, Maria."

"It is good that you are here, both of you can show Miss Louise to her room so she can have time to prepare herself. We have two more days of school left before the end of term. I will talk to you later Miss Louise."

"Thank you Headmistress." We left the front room and walked along to the end of the building.

"This is your room Miss Louise," Maria said.

"Please call me Louise."

"Okay, I think it will be easy for us," Julia said, "This room is smaller than ours but you have your own private toilet and bath. It's very nice for one person. We live together in the same room next to you. If you need anything just knock."

"Thank you Maria, Julia."

"You are welcome Louise."

CHAPTER THIRTY-FIVE

The next day the Headmistress called me to her office. "Please sit down Miss Louise."

"Thank you Headmistress."

"The Minister has agreed your wages already and here is your pay-in-book. In this school we have a very strict rule; you must never tell anyone else what your salary is; this is because salaries depend on the qualifications of the teacher and most of them live outside the school. Another rule is; if you are going to stay away for the weekend you must let me know where you are going. Oh, and one more rule is that no visitors are allowed inside your room. If you have a visitor you must meet them in the front room only."

"We have two holidays, summer and Christmas, plus bank holidays. At the end of the year the Minister will give everyone a share-out depending on how much profit we make. We have thirty students who live in the school; they are senior students only and they are in that building out front in the left hand wing. We have nearly eight hundred students altogether but the rest live outside the school. If you want to have a free dinner in the evening you can do so, but you have to join the students in the dining room at five o'clock. If you want to buy your own dinner there is a big restaurant just outside the school, but don't stay out much after six o'clock as we shut the main gate at six-thirty. If you have any trouble my room is behind the office."

"As for your duties, you are responsible for five classes; you will teach a junior class at nine-thirty, then we have lunch for one hour. After that you will teach a senior class English and history. Tomorrow morning I would like you to come to see me in this room, and one more thing Miss Louise, I recommend that you do something with your hair; you look much younger than I expected, in fact you look more like a senior student than a teacher."

"Yes Headmistress."

The first day of my new career I was very nervous. I told myself I could do it; I was an Englishwoman who had been to a London University and I was educated enough to be a teacher. I am who I am. Thank God I had no problems with the junior classes, they were so lovely. In the afternoon, I had to teach the senior students and the Headmistress went with me. She introduced me to the class; "This is your new teacher, Miss Louise, she comes from London and is going to be your permanent teacher from now on." Then she went away. I could tell all of them are quite young girls but some were taller then me. I called their names out one by one. Because their names were so long and my pronunciation so poor I made them laugh so many times.

"Why do you have such long names?" I asked them. They told me they derived from the Indian and Balinese languages; it would take me a while to remember them all.

Someone knocked on my door. "Come in," I said, "Oh Julia and Maria, please sit down."

"Thank you Miss Louise."

"Just call me Louise," I said.

"Oh yes I forgot. How was your first day?"

"Not too bad at all. I especially liked the juniors, they were so good but I am quite tired; I gave them some homework so let's see what happens tomorrow morning. How long have you been teaching here Maria?"

"Almost two years, I came at the same time as Julia."

"I see and do you like it here?"

"Yes, but the Headmistress is so strict."

"I thought she was okay."

"Yes, maybe with you Louise because you are a friend of the Minister's niece. Don't you think so Julia?" Maria asked.

"Oh yes I agree with you," Julia replied, "Did you know Louise, she never allows men to visit us?"

"But I think it is okay as the rule is not after six-thirty. I do understand that the rules must be strict; we are teachers and the students need us to be leaders; if we break the rules who will obey us?"

"Anyway Louise you seem to be on her side."

"Oh well, I am just telling you the truth Maria."

"Are you hungry Louise?"

"I can't eat much at the moment Julia. I haven't got used to the food yet. I think by next week I should be okay."

"Never mind Louise, I will make you a pot of tea."

"Thank you so much Maria. I haven't got any tea or coffee in my room."

"I know Louise, don't worry about it; maybe this Friday evening we can go out together and do some shopping? I need a lot of things as well, what do you think?"

"Yes."

"Maybe the Headmistress will be in a good mood on Friday and we might even go out and see a film."

"That would be great Maria, Julia. Could we go on Saturday morning instead of Friday evening?"

"Why Louise?"

"I would like to buy a special dinner for both of you and then we can have a drink in our rooms later."

"That is a good idea Louise."

I was really looking forward to this special occasion. Julia and Maria took me to the Shopping Centre in Silom; they had everything there, it was such a huge supermarket. I bought a lot of tea and coffee and some chocolate for the Headmistress. I liked dried fruit as it was good for my stomach. I thought of Lucy and wondered if she might like some fresh fruit. *'What kind of fruit could I buy for her?'* I asked myself. When we went outside in the street I stopped Julia and Maria.

"Please, please, stop for a minute!"

"Yes Louise, what is it?"

"I want to buy some fresh mangos."

"Okay, how much are they?" Maria asked.

"Eighty baht for one kilo."

"No, no that is too expensive, sixty baht per kilo and if you buy two kilos it should be fifty baht per kilo."

"Okay I will buy two kilos."

"Oh Louise it is quite heavy, may I help you with that bag?"

"Thank you Julia, but you have five bags to carry already."

"It's okay Louise, pass it to me and we will call a taxi to go back." I heard two blasts on a car horn, "Look Louise, someone is pointing his finger at you."

"Where are they?"

"In that car, two men in that grey Mercedes." It was Joe and Robert.

"Hello Louise, this way please Louise."

"Hi Joe, Robert. May I introduce Maria and Julia, we are working together. This is Robert and Joe."

"Nice to meet you both."

"Pleased to meet you too. We went to see you at the school but the Headmistress said you had all gone out shopping so Joe and I had to guess where you would be."

"You made a good guess," Julia said.

"Are you hungry?"

"No, we just had our lunch in the Shopping Centre thank you Joe."

"Please get in the car and we will take you back. How is your new job?" Robert asked.

"Oh a bit tiring but I will get used to it. How is Lucy? I think I will call her tonight."

"She is miserable, she is not very well and wants to see you," Joe said.

"Well I want to be with her and comfort her. I really do want to see her but I can't make it until I know I will be okay with my new position. I am not confident with my duties yet but I think after two or three weeks I should know what I am doing."

"We understand Louise."

"Thank you both. Please go into the guest room and I will make a pot of tea."

"No, you stay with them Louise, we will make the tea for you."

"Thank you Maria and Julia."

"You are welcome and thank you for taking us home."

"I hope to see again Julia, Maria," Robert said.

"You will," Julia answered.

"Here is your pot of tea."

"Thank you," I said. "Please tell Lucy that I can't use the phone for a private call; I have to use a phone box but I will go round to see her in the next couple of weeks."

"We will," Joe said.

"Please could you give this bag to her?"

"What is it?" Joe asked."

"It is very heavy and contains mangos I bought for Lucy. She liked mangos when she was in London but they were very expensive."

"She will be pleased," said Joe as he took the bag. "Since she came back from Switzerland she has not been well," Joe continued.

"I see. Has she seen a doctor?"

"No, but I think Mohamed is taking one to see her tomorrow."

CHAPTER THIRTY-SIX

The Headmistress had adopted Charlie from the Orphan House and she lived next door to Ms. Mary's room. Charlie was a very cleaver girl; she looked half Thai with dark coloured skin, curly hair and big eyes. Sometimes her behaviour towards Maria and Julia was very strange; she would treat them as her enemies one minute and good friends the next. She was very scared of Ms. Mary but she liked me and wanted to look after me

"Would you like some tea Miss Louise?" she asked me.

"No thanks," I said to her, "Have you finished your homework Charlie?"

"Yes I have," she replied.

"Maybe the Headmistress would like some tea."

"Oh no, after six-thirty she doesn't want me to disturb her."

"Oh I see. So you can read the book that I gave you."

"I always read it Miss Louise. It has good cartoons and I love it but I wanted to speak with you, your English voice is so beautiful, much better than Maria's."

"First I thank you for the compliment but it is not nice to criticise someone behind her back."

"I am sorry Miss Louise."

"I forgive you this time but don't do it again."

"No Miss Louise, I won't."

"That is a good girl. Where are you going Charlie? I asked as she went towards the stairs at the back of the building. Instead of speaking she put her finger to her lips and pulled me by the hand. It was about eight o'clock at night and we walked for a long time until we arrived behind the gardener's and guard's houses. There were so many big trees and flowers. At first it was so dark I couldn't see anything until I heard a voice.

"Oh God, please, please don't stop. Oh yes you are superb. Oh please, yes that is so nice. Oh God it is so wonderful" Charlie pulled at my hand and we moved to the next bush; I couldn't see anything as it was too dark but this time there was no noise; instead the ground was shaking and we could hear only heavy breathing. Then she said, "I am dying, it is something I have never had in my life, you are so great." I was with Charlie for a long time but they continued doing it for what seemed to be the whole night long. When we got back to my room I told Charlie that it was not good to see somebody doing that kind of business, it was very naughty.

She said "No, no."

"You won't tell the Headmistress? Promise me Charlie?"

"Yes I promise."

"That is a good girl. One day, when you are grown up you will understand. I have something for you Charlie, this is from London."

"I love dogs."

"It is yours; you can cuddle him when you are in bed."

"Thank you Miss Louise."

I had been a teacher for only a few weeks but I soon learned that my students in the senior class were separating into two groups. I tried very hard to keep them from fighting. One Friday, at the start of a long bank holiday weekend, I said to the Head Girl, "You know, I already feel sad that you will be leaving me to go to your family for a few days. I will have no one to have dinner with."

"But Miss Louise, we will come back after the bank holiday," she said.

"I know, but I keep thinking that very soon you will be doing your A Levels and you will leave me for ever; how sad that will be. Time is so short; we only have one more year."

"Yes you are so right Miss Louise."

"So why is class divided? You should all be pulling together, trying to get top grades so you can be the top school in Bangkok."

"That is a good idea Miss Louise. I promise that when we come back we will all try to stick together and help each other to get good grades and be friends together."

"Thank you; that would make me very happy. I hope that all of you in my class will get high grades and go on to study at university or get good jobs in a big company and use your knowledge of English. I hope I will be very proud of my students."

"I promise that when we come back we will all do our best."

"Thank you again. I hope you all have a very nice long weekend with your families."

"Goodbye Miss Louise."

"Goodbye and see you very soon."

"Maria, Julia, are you free after dinner?"

"Yes Louise."

"May I see you both in my room? Don't bring anything, I will make a pot of tea and I have a lot of dried fruit for you to enjoy."

"Thank you Louise."

"Okay, I will see you both later."

"This is a very nice cup of tea and the dried fruit is so tasty."

"That is good; I am so glad you like it. I have these silk scarves from London, I gave one to the Headmistress and I have two left; you can have them."

"Thank you Louise, they are so beautiful. May I have the pink one Julia?"

"Yes, you have the pink one and I will have the peach one."

"You know Julia, Maria? We have a very difficult job as teachers. I mean, to be a good teacher is not easy. Sometimes, if we do something wrong and the students know about it, they won't respect us or we might lose our jobs. It can cause great embarrassment. All I am saying is be careful; do you both understand?"

"Yes Miss Louise. Can we call you Miss from now on? We would prefer to call you Miss."

"Yes that will be okay, if you are happier with that. This weekend I'm not in, so please take care. Good night to you both."

"Good night Miss Louise."

Charlie came to help me with my small bag and when I got to the guest room I saw Mohamed and the Headmistress. They were laughing and Mohamed stood up and bent his head and whispered something, which annoyed me.

"Oh Miss Louise, come in and sit down please."

"Thank you Headmistress," I said.

"The Ambassador has come to pick you up and he has brought a big box of chocolates from Switzerland for me."

"How nice."

"Are you coming back on Monday Miss Louise?" She asked.

"No Headmistress, I will be back on Sunday evening."

"I see. If you change your mind you can just call me."

"Yes I will do, thank you Headmistress."

"Are you ready now Miss Louise?" Mohamed asked.

"Yes I am Ambassador," I said.

"I will see you again Ambassador?"

"Yes Ms. Mary, you will. It's been nice to see you."

"Yes, please come and visit us at any time Ambassador."

"Thank you again."

When we left Mohamed carried my bag which I didn't want him to do.

"I can carry it by myself, it's not too heavy," I said.

"Do you want me to carry your handbag and you?" He asked. I had to give my bag to him immediately and he smiled at me.

"That is a good girl."

"I am not a girl, I am a teacher and I teach girls," I said.

"Oh yes, you are a big girl to me and naughty." My face felt hot as we got to the car. He opened the door for me and I was alone with him. My heart was beating so loud; his eyes, his face; the man was the most handsome in the world, so intelligent and so suited to his job. I was standing beside the door and he said, "Are you okay Louise?" When he asked me this he just whispered it into my ear and I could feel his warm breath on my neck. I couldn't answer him; I just wanted to stay like that for ever. I didn't know who I was. "You must be tired," he said again in a soft voice, "Let me help you," he said. He shut the door and then went to his seat. That day it was very hot and I was just wearing a white tee shirt, which was see-through, and a pair of jeans from Camden Market. I told myself I shouldn't do this. He was in the car but still looking at me.

"I am cold," I said, "I think I am not well."

"Take my jacket."

"Thank you." He drove the car past Sukhumvit Road.

"How is Lucy?"

"She is okay; she can't wait to see you. She has missed you and I have missed you too." When he said that I looked at him but he kept looking straight ahead at the road. "Are you enjoying your new career?"

"Very much," I said.

"That is good. How long will you stay there?"

"I don't know for sure. I will make my own decision after my graduation next year."

"Do you miss London?"

"Not exactly; I have a long way to go. I am only twenty two."

"You are so young Louise, like a child learning how to swim." I wanted to hit him but he looked at me and said, "You are so sweet Louise."

We arrived at the house and as the car was being parked I could see Lucy standing in front of the house.

"I have missed you Louise, I really missed you," she said.

"I missed you too Lucy. You seem to have lost so much weight. Let's see who is in the house. Oh! Joe and Robert. Oh look, you have so many fresh fruits, mangos, pineapples."

"We knew you liked fruit so we picked them for you."

"Thank you all."

"And thank you for the fresh mangos Louise. I have eaten them all."

"When are you going back Louise?" Joe asked.

"I will go back on Sunday evening."

"But you have a long weekend," Robert said.

"I know but I have a lot of paperwork to do."

"Oh I forgot, she is a teacher now," Robert said, at which everyone started laughing. I looked at Mohamed and I could tell at a glance that he was very cheeky. His eyes were sharp as a laser.

"I will take you back on Sunday," Joe said.

"Thank you Joe." I could tell that Lucy loved Mohamed very much. More than that she adored him, but what about him? It was hard to tell. He did not seem to have changed since I had known him; he was deep and calm, I didn't really know what kind of person he was. When he was with Ms. Mary he was the handsome Ambassador, when he was with me he was so crafty.

In the evening we went out to a restaurant and went on to a dance club. I danced with Joe and Robert and Lucy was with Mohamed all evening until the last minute; just as the club was closing. It was very crowded at three o'clock in the morning and it was difficult to make out individual people but suddenly I felt someone was beside me; I was in his arms, the music was slow and it was very dark. I only knew him by the smell of his perfume; I did not struggle to protect myself; it was all so real. He kissed me on the forehead, then my ear, then my neck. He kissed me on my lips for a long time and then he said he wanted to be with me until he died; just the two of us. I don't know why I let him; I felt I wanted him so much. Our bodies were so close together I could feel his heart beating next to mine. Once more he kissed me on the lips and all over my face; how could I ever forget his kisses? They will be with me for the rest of my life.

"Louise, I need you forever."

"I need you too." Those were the last words I spoke to him.

CHAPTER THIRTY-SEVEN

Since I came back from visiting Lucy I phoned her at the weekends. She was very sick and told me she had decided to stay in Switzerland but she didn't know when she would be back. Joe and Robert were still my best friends and sometimes they would come and take me out for dinner or Maria and Julia and I would go with them to see a film. There was one person that I always thought about but I never asked Joe or Robert about him. Maybe he would go and visit Lucy in Switzerland. I sent a long letter to David and Jim and told them all about my job and what I had seen in this country. I also sent a letter to my best friend Jason.

After a few months I was very happy with my teaching; all my students were great. That year we had a big school party, I made a very special effort for all of them and the Headmistress was really pleased with my organization. We had at least two months off and some of the students said they wanted to come and visit me before school reopened but I had to tell them that I was going away up North on the Friday evening. Before we went off, I was sitting underneath a big tree with a load of student paperwork; I wanted to finish it off so that I didn't need to worry whilst I was away. I was going to visit the Minister in Chiang Rai together with the Headmistress, Maria and Julia. Joe and Robert were going to join us later. I heard someone walking up behind me and stop.

"Is that you Charlie? You are just in time, I have nearly finished my paperwork and you can help me carry it inside; it is quite heavy and I need you to help me." There was no answer. "Good, just stay there and help me when I am ready." Still no answer. I turned to face the person behind me; Oh god! It was the Ambassador.

"Please sit down." I pushed all my paperwork away.

"How long have you been here?"

"More then twenty minutes."

"How is Lucy?"

"I think she is okay. I have missed you Louise. I missed you so much I had to come and see you."

"Ambassador!"

"I known you have tried to keep yourself far away from me."

"Please don't, don't say anything at all."

"Louise, we are of the same mind, the same soul. We understand each other. Why you are killing me without saying a word? We both have the same feelings."

"I understand Ambassador but we both have to do our duty, we are responsible people. I don't want anything more then I have got."

"Can I come and visit you?"

"Yes you can."

"Thank you Louise I am so happy just to see your face I can't live without you."

"Ambassador!"

"It will be dark soon; you had better go into the building. I will help you to carry your paperwork."

"Thank you Ambassador."

"I won't see you for a few weeks. Please take care when you are in Chiang Rai."

"I will." When he picked up all the paper he came close to me and I put my face to his chest.

"You must wait Louise, one day I will protect you for life." He kissed the tears from my face and kissed my lips, and then he went away.

In the morning I received a letter from Lucy:

Dear Louise

I have to tell you that I have made my decision. I am going to stay in Switzerland for good. I love living over here and I will forget Mohamed. I love him more than my own life but I am not quite sure about him. I didn't love his money; I love him because he is a real gentleman. I don't know when I will see you again Louise but I hope you will be okay.

Miss you

Lucy

When I finished reading her letter I felt guilty and so sick, why did it have to be me and Mohamed? Lucy was my best friend. I had a bad headache and was crying in my bed when I heard a knock at my door.
"Please come in Headmistress. Please sit down."
"I have come to make sure that you are alright because we have to leave early tomorrow morning and you don't look well."
"I just have a bad headache."
"I know, if a man loves you it is not your fault but if you love him it doesn't matter if he has got someone else, at first it is not real love. I think you have to understand love; it means both of you in your hearts must feel that you are together day and night, even if you are far away from each other. Love is inside you both. Why don't you go to bed, have a good sleep and don't cry any more?"
"Thank you Headmistress."
"Good night Louise."
"Good night Headmistress.

CHAPTER THIRTY-EIGHT

When we got off the plane at Chiang Rai Airport it was very foggy but not too cold. We saw two Landrovers waiting and Maria, Julia and Charlie got into one and Ms. Mary, Joe, Robert and I got into the other.

"Elisabeth Louise," someone called out. I turned round immediately. Who could have called my name? No one else knew my full name. "Are you Elisabeth Louise?"

"That was my mother's first name."

"Do you know Louise uncle?"

"No I don't know her Joe and I don't know why I called her by that name."

"This is the Minister Louise."

"I am so sorry sir; I got a bit confused as no one calls me by my full name. First of all I must thank you so much, sir, for giving me the job. I appreciate your kindness."

"You are welcome Louise."

"What is going on Minister?"

"Let's get home first." Ms. Mary said.

When we arrived at the front of the house I was introduced to Naree and four big dogs.

"Naree this is Louise," the Headmistress said, "Louise this is the Minister's private nurse and these are Snob, Snow, Ruby and Tiger." Snob come up to me with her friendly face, which surprised everyone, her tail was wagging as if she had known me before; she licked my face and was very friendly.

"What a surprise," Joe said, "Snob obviously likes English ladies; she is a very strange dog. She never did this with Lucy or anyone else." We were all laughing. Joe said, "I am serious." The Headmistress then introduced me to Professor Bee.

"He is an old friend of mine," she said.

"How do you do sir?" He looked at me and nodded his head and called me Elisabeth Louise.

Joe and Robert shared one of the guest rooms whilst Maria, Julia, Charlie and I shared the big room. I was surprised that Ms. Mary was in the room next to Professor Bee. I liked the house; it was so big and comfortable. We put our clothes into the cupboard and then Charlie and I walked to the library. I looked at the pictures, one by one, until I came to the last one, it was a very old black and white photo and at first I was not quite sure what I was looking at. Somebody called out that tea was ready so I went and sat down. I could tell the Minister was looking at me and so were the Professor, Ms. Mary, Joe and Robert, they were all looking at me.

I said, "I saw a picture in the library, is it of you Headmistress?"

"Yes Miss Louise, it was me at the Minister's wedding in London."

"But, but that was my mother's wedding. I have got the same picture in my album in Bangkok."

"What did you say?"

"That picture, it is of my granddad, grandma and my mother."

"Oh God, Jesus Christ, Mary and Joseph, I was right!"

"Yes Ms. Mary."

"I was right, Minister, Elizabeth Louise is your daughter!"

"Naree, help Ms. Mary to sit down before she falls on the floor."

"Yes Minister."

"Why did you leave my mother?"

"Sit down Louise. If that photo is of your real family I must explain very clearly. I have a long story to tell you. More then twenty-five years ago I was a student at Oxford University. I met your mother and fell in love with her, she was so beautiful. About the time I finished university she became pregnant and promised that she would come with me. Before I left her I gave her all of my money to look after the family. After the baby girl was born she sent me lots of photos and I sent her more money. I think it was after about six months that she stopped answering my letters. I wrote again and again but all my letters came back to me. A few years later I saw Ms. Mary in Singapore and asked about your mother it was the same answer that it was the truth. What happen to Elizabeth?"

"I was told that when granddad died they had to move away and not too long after my birth Mum was diagnosed with cancer and died very soon after granddad."

"Why did granddad die so early?"

"He had a heart attack, grandma said. When the doctor found out that mother had cancer it was too late, they couldn't cure her."

"And what about grandma?"

"One night when I was sixteen, grandma went to sleep and didn't wake up again."

"Who sent you to university?" The Headmistress asked.

"I had to work in a pub at night to pay for my tuition."

"I recognised her face when I first met her but I wasn't quite sure. She looked like the Minister and Elizabeth."

"That is why you called me Elizabeth Louise at the airport."

"So you are my cousin," Joe said.

Robert was laughing, "A broken heart again, poor Joe."

"I have got my locket, do you want to see? Here it is; mother and I when I was a baby."

"Oh she was a beautiful lady."

"She is always in my heart. I have got an album full of photos of when you were married to Mum with all of your friends. It is in my room in Bangkok."

"You should have told me a long time ago," the Headmistress said.

"I have a lot of things to tell you my daughter."

"Ms. Mary please don't cry; I will cry with you," Naree said.

"I am so happy; look the dog is happy as well, look at Snob."

"Shall we have our dinner?"

"I don't think I could eat anything."

"But you better have dinner Ms. Mary or you will faint on the floor," Professor Bee said.

Pa Ploy said, "I am so happy Minister, I can look after her from now on."

"I wish I could have a beautiful daughter like you Minister," Professor Bee said, "It was Ms. Mary's fault, I asked her to marry me nearly twenty years ago but she never said yes. She always told me next year." That made everybody laugh.

After dinner we planned a trip to a hill village. The sitting room was so comfy and at the same time it was so crowded. Charlie lay on the floor playing with Ruby and Tiger. Ms. Mary sat next to Professor Bee and Naree and the Minister sat side by side. Snow was on the Minister's lap. They were looking at old photo albums dating from when my father was in England. Maria, Julia, Joe and Robert were playing cards and I was with Snob. She was sitting on my lap until Pa Ploy and her husband, Long Non came in.

"Would you like any tea or coffee?" Everybody put their hands up and we all said at the same time; "Yes please."

"And I want some ice-cream," Charlie said. We all looked at her, "I mean ice water please."

"I have some sweets for you Charlie," Pa Ploy said.

"Oh that is great in the jungle like this. I will have some sweets." Everyone laughed. She was so funny sometimes and such a clever little girl. During tea time the Minister said to Professor Bee,

"Tomorrow morning we will take two jeeps to the village. We will leave the jeeps with the Head Man and then we will walk to the high hills."

CHAPTER THIRTY-NINE

In the morning we were all dressed like a climbing group, except for Charlie. "Are you going skiing?" Joe asked. She looked at Joe with her green eyes.

"I bet it is cold on the top of the world." All of us had to laugh, she was so lovely.

"Good morning everyone," Ms. Mary said.

"Good morning Ma'am."

"Are we ready? Shall we go?" When we got to the first village it was before noon. When we stopped I saw the Head of the village; he gave respect to the Minister and shook hands with all of us. My father spoke to him in a different language. I met a couple of white people who came to see us; they knew some of us in the group.

My father said, "Louise, this is Sam and Heidi, this is Louise my daughter, she has just come from London."

"Hello, she looks like you Minister."

"Of course, she is my blood." Then he laughed, "Heidi and Sam are American and work for The Red Cross. They have worked here for more than thirty years. Next to Louise are my school teachers, Maria and Julia the rest you already know."

"No, no, no sir, I am Charlie."

"Oh sorry, I forgot about you." We all clapped our hands for her.

"Sam and Heidi are coming with us. Don't carry any heavy stuff; just carry your own bags. As for drinks, cans and rice, the village men will bring them for us." I looked at the village, it was so beautiful. There were about fifty small houses. My father said, "Don't worry Louise, when we come back we will stay here so you can look around."

"Thank you sir."

"We all went off, my father, the Professor, Sam, Heidi, Naree Ms. Mary, followed by Joe, Robert and I. We all climbed up very carefully; sometimes it was quite a dangerous hill. I could hear the birds singing and see the flowers and plants with so many hundreds of colours. It was such a wonderful jungle. Several times Joe and Robert stopped to take photos of deer, monkeys and big birds. After an hour we reached a big pool and when we looked up to the hilltop we all sat down with our eyes wide open. A waterfall came down from the high mountain and it looked like paradise. My father turned to look behind him and said, "Okay girls you can rest here for half an hour then we must go on." Charlie took out her sweets from her bag and walked around offering them to everyone.

"Oh how nice to have you with us," Joe said.

"By the way, where did you get them from?" Ms Mary asked.

"Pa Ploy gave them to me."

"They are bad for your teeth," Julia said, "Give them back if you don't like them," Charlie said.

"Sorry it is too late, I have put them in my month already," she said, "May I have one more please?"

"You said they were bad."

"I meant for children, not for adults."

"Here, it's the last one for you Miss Julia."

"Thank you Charlie."

"Shall we go?"

"Yes we are ready sir."

When we passed the waterfall we walked easily across green land and then we passed through a landscape with hundreds of huge trees. After that we could see a village which had a number of small huts, in the middle was one big one. When we arrived we went into the big hut; inside it was made of hardwood and had a wooden floor. It could fit twenty people and at the back there were a few small rooms. We all lay down in the hall.

"It is so big and comfy," I said.

Ms. Mary said, "Girls I will take you to your room. If you want the loo it is inside at the back; come along with me."

At dinner time we saw a lady who was reporting some news to the Minister, Sam and Heidi.

She said, "We had some good news last week, one of the patients was so sick we thought she would die; she had a fever and couldn't sleep or eat. She lost her memory and we didn't know what to do. I looked for some medicine but I couldn't find any. Eventually I found a few dried herbs and put them in a pot of water and boiled them up for a long time. When I thought it was ready I made her drink some, we had to force open her mouth and pour it in because it was so bitter. After about an hour she managed to go the toilet, her fever went down and now she can walk and eat but we are still making her drink the bitter water."

"What herbs did you use? Can you remember?" The Minister asked.

"There was bitter cucumber, dried mint, lemon grass and dried yellow roots sir."

"That is very good; we will have to write it down in our Medicine Book." The Minister took us on a tour of the hill village. He said, "This village is where we grow experimental herbs and organic vegetables, all free from chemicals. The villagers grow lots of herbs for themselves."

"What kind of herbs, sir?" Julia asked.

"We have lemon grass, holy basil, ginger, galanga, turmeric, mentha, chillies and garlic but they are not growing enough yet, they need to grow much more if they are to cure themselves. As I said, we are doing experiments. These people should already be dead; they had no one to help them. Five years ago they came to see me saying that they had no place to live and no place to die, they had no hope."

"Where did they come from sir?"

"From Bangkok."

"What do you mean sir?"

"They are all HIV carriers. Don't be afraid Julia. In the past five years only two have died and that was only because they came to me too late."

"When we saw them in the hall we were very surprised as the people looked so healthy."

"Yes, I think maybe it is because up here the air is pure and there is no pollution and they mostly eat vegetables and herbs. We are still not quite sure about our experiments into HIV, that is why we don't want the outside world to know. There are only a few of us involved and we are not quite sure exactly what is going to happen in the long term. As a result of modern technology and new developments by scientist they might discover a good medicine that is even better than herbs.

At dinner time we all sat in the middle of the hall near the fire place. The Minister noticed that Julia and Maria didn't eat much. He said, "Don't worry about the food, it is very clean, Naree cooked it. This is salted meat, grilled with lemon grass, lime, fresh onion and fresh mint, it is good for your stomach, and that is sadin soup with lemon grass, lime juice and coriander with some small, chopped chillies to make you warm. Be careful with the chilli it is hot. That dish over there is an omelette with tomatoes, mixed herbs and fish sauce. I promise you it is pure and clean." It made everybody laugh. "And we have a good drink made of fresh ginger with honey which is good if you have a cold. For Charlie we have a lot of dried bananas with honey."

"Thank you sir," she said.

That night we went to bed very late. When I got up I looked at Julia, Maria and Charlie but they were all sleeping like logs. I walked to the hilltop. Where were they all? When I looked down at the landscape I could see everything on such a beautiful morning. I could see the first village, so far away with the sun shining in between a screen of fog. The villagers were doing their exercises; I think I am right in saying they were doing a Chinese style of exercise called Tai Chi. When I got back Ms. Mary said, "If there was a tiger living near here he could have eaten Miss Julia, Maria and Charlie. Look, we went around the world they have just got up."

"Oh no, the tiger wouldn't eat me," Charlie said.

"Why not?" Joe asked her.

"Because after eating Julia and Maria the tiger would be full up." This time Joe and Robert laughed so much they were on the floor. After breakfast we were going to the hilltop.

"Breakfast is ready," Naree said, "We have some fried eggs, sausage and baked beans."

"Yum, yum," Charlie said. She made everyone happy.

We walked away from the top village where all the sick women lived but not too far away we could see hundreds of plants. The Minister pointed out the various plants to us. "This one is a lychee tree and those are longang trees. The next one is a mongo tree and over there are citrus trees, coffee, and tea plants."

"How long have you known this place Minister?" Maria asked.

"More than fifteen years. Then it was worthless land at the end of Thailand. It was jungle and if you walked for a day you could get into Burma. There used to be poppy fields but when the King of Thailand started to help the tribes people he tried to get rid of the heroin. He introduced them to growing citrus trees and other fruit and vegetables. At that time I was a Minister and thought it was a good idea to plant fruit trees. Professor Bee helped me a lot."

Ms. Mary picked beans, Joe and Robert helped the village women to pick tea and Julia, Maria and Charlie picked mangos. When Naree come to us with the leader of the women she said, "Suda, this is Miss Louise, she is the Minister's daughter, I forgot to introduce you earlier." She greeted me with the traditional wai and I just said hello. I walked away with Suda, she was a very attractive person and her face was still very beautiful. She spoke to me in English.

"You are so beautiful, from head to toe."

"Oh thank you so much Suda. You can speak English?"

"Yes Miss Louise but I have forgotten so much since I came to live here."

"You speak very well."

"Thank you."

"Excuse me for asking but did you used to work in Bangkok?"

"No, I used to work in a five star hotel in Pattaya, as a manageress in Reception."

"That was a good job."

"Yes it was. I was able to send my brother to university."

"That was a great responsibility for you."

"He never appreciated it, even my family didn't want to know me. They said I had HIV; it was so embarrassing for them." She looked straight into my face and said, "Do you know Miss Louise? You and your father have come to us from haven. You and he are so kind and are very rare in this country. No one wants to know us or help us. People hate the thought of HIV; they think HIV is very easy to catch so they don't understand. In this country, if you have a lot of money, people adore you, if you don't they don't want to know you or say hello." She carried on picking tea and said, "Once I used to drive a BMW, I had a fiancé who was very powerful, he was a policeman and I loved him very much. One night he came to see me, it was my day off. He told me to close my eyes and count to three. When I opened my eyes I saw a big diamond ring. He told me to put it on; it looked so perfect. I asked him if it was for me and he said it was. He took me out for dinner and he stayed at my place. He was with me several times a week until he moved to Bangkok but he promised he would come to see me twice a month. For the first two months he managed to keep his promise but then he disappeared. I went to visit him without telling him and I saw him with another woman. I felt so sick for a few weeks until I had a blood test. I remember so well when the doctor told me; I wanted to commit suicide, I had no hope, I wanted to kill him. I left my job and went to the police station intending to give them all free sex as a revenge on all policemen. Above all

I felt regret. I went back to see my family in Chiang Mai but they hated me and sent me away."

"How did you end up in this place?"

"I went to see my teacher at my old school. She introduced me to Sam and Heidi and they took me to see the Minister. He built this place for women with HIV. At first I was all alone but then a friend from Pattaya arrived and now, as you can see, there are about fifty women here."

"Did you go and have a blood test again?"

"No Miss Louise. We don't want to mix with the world outside anymore, we have our own little world here and we are very happy. When we die we will die in peace." She looked at me and smiled.

I continued to pick tea and said to her, "Who knows, you might not carry HIV in your blood after five years?"

"Oh if that is true it would be a miracle from God." We both smiled.

In the afternoon, after we had rested, we were all together and we shared our lunch. Naree and the women opened a big plastic container; there were fresh vegetables and they made a grill of dried meat and potatoes. It took over an hour to grill the potatoes, they were really nice. Charlie went around offering her mangos but no one wanted them as they were so sour.

"You can have them all Charlie," Joe said to her.

"No, no it's not fair. I want some meat please. I can't eat my mangos, they are so sour."

"Who told you to pick them?"

"I saw Miss Louise, she likes them so she can have them," she said.

"Okay I will have some but you will have to carry them for me," I told her.

"Okay, I will do that. Just give me more grilled meat please." We all loved her as she was so sweet sometimes.

On the last day of our visit we had had a special dinner and Naree was the one who prepared it.

Suda said to me, "Will you come back to visit us again?"

"Of course I will be back Suda."

The next morning we walked back down the valley to the village. The Head of the village was waiting for us and Sam and Heidi said to the Minister, "This year the Headman will give you a special thank you sir. It is in recognition of your kindness and your help to the village over nearly twenty years."

When we arrived at the village we all stayed in the Headman's big house. The entertainment started in the evening and the Headman give some spirits to my father and then they served roasted meat. The village people joined us for the buffet and the village girls danced with the village man. We all sat together and the world was at peace in the jungle. We got back to my father's house the next morning. Joe and Robert were so drunk with dry grass and Maria and Julia didn't get up until midday. Charlie was counting her stones, which she said were diamonds and I went to the back of the house with the four dogs. When I went back in Joe and Robert were in the sitting room drinking a pot of tea.

"We must go back tomorrow."

"I haven't seen the hospital or school yet," I said to them.

"They are on holiday now Louise," Joe said.

"I just want to have a look at them, can we go?"

"Okay, jump on a bicycle and we can go."

"There is Ananta Hospital, we don't want to go in yet so I will try and take you to see the school. No, I am afraid it is locked up; let's go this way. Hello? Is anybody home?"

"Come in, we are in the sitting room."

"Oh, how lucky we are to see you both. Mon and Nut, this is Miss Louise, she is the daughter of my uncle."

"Hello Miss Louise, nice to meet you. Please take a seat I am going make some green tea for Miss Louise and for Khun Joe."

"Thank you Mon, how has it been this year?" Joe asked.

"This year has not been too cold but at the moment we have nearly eighty students."

"Have you told the Minister?"

"Yes we have but he said no one has applied for the job."

"I am not surprised. No TV, no electricity; thank God you have battery operated radios. I suppose it is very romantic to use oil lamps but you must have amazing spirit to live here Mon and Nut."

"Yes we do, we love the innocence of the children, they need to learn to read and write. If we were not here they would have no one else."

"Do you want to join them Louise?"

"Yes, very much. This is how I dreamed I would live."

"When Mon and Nut finished at Chiang Mai University they taught in a few schools before they came to stay with uncle."

"What about you Miss Louise?"

"I have just finished at London University and I came to Thailand to work in the Minister's International School."

"Oh that is very clever of you Miss Louise."

"Thank you."

"We would be so happy to have you here."

"I promise that as soon as I have repaid my debts I will come and be with you."

"We can wait until you are ready Miss Louise."

"Do you need anything Mon?" Joe asked.

"We need a lot of books for the students."

"Okay I will tell uncle."

"Thank you Khun Joe."

In the morning everyone was so busy. Miss Maria, Julia and Charlie carried a lot of bags and Ms. Mary said to Charlie, "What is in your bag Charlie?"

"Nothing, nothing at all, just a few stones from the hilltop."

"Stones?" Ms. Mary said.

"Yes."

"Give them to me. It is stupid to carry them on the plane, they are worthless."

"No, I like them."

"Shall we go?" The Minister said.

"Yes, we are ready sir."

When we got to the airport the Minister said to Ms. Mary, "I will see you next week. You too my dear daughter." Everybody said goodbye and thanked the Minister and Naree. When we got to Bangkok Airport we saw Mohamed's driver waiting for us.

"Where is Mohamed?" Joe asked.

"I am not sure sir; the Ambassador just left me a message to pick you up sir."

"Okay thank you. Let's get the ladies home first."

CHAPTER FORTY

A week later, after I had finished work, Julia called to me, "Miss Louise you have a visitor." When I went to the door I saw Joe and Robert were waiting for me.

"Hi there," I said, "How are you both?"

"We missed you. Uncle sent us to pick you up, you don't need to tell Ms. Mary, uncle will speak to her on the phone, she will be okay."

"Give me five minutes and I will be with you."

On the Saturday night, after dinner, Naree and the Minister were sitting together in the sitting room looking through all the photo albums. When they reached the last one he asked me, "Do you want to do a Masters Degree Louise?"

"No Minister, I don't think so."

"Please call me father; after all I am your dad."

"Yes, thank you. You see, I have got a big debt to pay back for the loan I got from the government for my tuition. When I was in my final year I didn't work."

"Do you have any other debts to pay?"

"No sir."

"I think you are going back to England in July aren't you?"

"Yes, I am going to my graduation."

"Very good. Do you want to live in this house? No one lives in this place."

"I would like that, thank you, but if you don't mind I would like to go and teach at the Chiang Rai Charity School." At that moment everyone was quite.

"Are you sure Louise?"

"I am positive sir."

"Okay, if you really want to go there, give me two months to build a small cottage for you."

"Thank you so much father."

"Oh we will miss you," Robert said. Joe just looked sad but kept quiet.

When I got back to the International School I didn't hear from anyone at all. I didn't know where everyone was and felt very much alone. I wanted to know where Mohamed was. Was he in Switzerland with Lucy I wondered? Why did I miss him? There was a knock on my door.

"Yes," I said.

"Miss Louise, it's me, Charlie. Can I come in?"

"Yes, come in please and take a seat."

"Thank you. The Headmistress has gone out with Doctor Tony and I am all alone."

"So you need a friend?"

"No, no I wanted to see you."

"Oh I see."

"I wanted to tell you Miss Louise that I will miss you so much when you go to Chiang Rai."

"Thank you Charlie."

"Do you know Miss Louise? The Headmistress adopted me. I don't know who my father and mother were. I want to be like you and have a very rich father."

"If you want to be like me you must study very hard and learn many things so that you can become well educated and then we will all be very proud of you."

"But I want to live in the jungle."

"Oh Charlie you are too young to know about life. Go and do your homework, be a good girl for me."

"Okay then, goodbye." There was another knock on my door.

"Is that you again Charlie?"

"No Miss Louise, it is Maria."

"Come in Maria."

"Miss Louise, you have a visitor, he is waiting in the front room."

"Okay, thank you Maria." I was expecting Joe and Robert when I got there but my heart was beating so loudly; the Ambassador! We shook hands for a long time."

"I'll make you a cup of tea."

"No, no Miss Louise."

"Please sit down. Where are Joe and Robert and how is Lucy?"

"Which question do you want me to answer first? It is a very long story. Joe misunderstands me, Robert is fine and Lucy is very upset."

"So what is going on?"

"Joe thought I broke Lucy's heart, I can't even explain it to him as he won't listen to me. One day he will understand that Lucy wanted to marry me."

"So why don't you?"

"I can't. There is someone else in my heart."

"I see. So Lucy's heart is broken?"

"Miss Louise, I can't marry a woman I don't love."

"So why were you with her?"

"I explained the situation to her and she accepted it."

"But the way you treated her, we all thought you were going to marry her. Do you know how hurtful it can be when a man refuses to marry a woman Mr. Ambassador?"

"I know Miss Louise."

"You know Ambassador, now is not like the old days, when you and your friends went out with blond ladies and could sleep with them and then change them like a pair of shoes. You have had so many women but never chose even one. I think your time has passed."

"Miss Louise!"

"Let me tell you one more thing, real love is to die for a beautiful woman, who is the only person you want to marry, you would never give your heart to anyone else." I smiled at him as I knew he was hurting inside.

"Louise you will never understand me. One day I hope I can explain it to you," he said. I went to the door to say goodbye; we both shook hands but I felt I wanted to be sick. I went to my bedroom and cried so much. I didn't know why and I was hurting inside my own heart.

CHAPTER FORTY-ONE

I continued with my job and Maria and Julia were my close friends; they both looked after me. The Headmistress was kind to me and one Friday evening I heard a noise coming from the front room. The Headmistress, Maria and Julia came and invited me to go in and when I walked into the room I jumped with surprise. "Oh, Joe and Robert, it has been a long time since I have seen you, where have you been?"

"We have been to Switzerland, we went to visit Lucy."

"How is she?"

"She is getting better, she is much happier. Look, we have so many things for all of you."

"Thank you both, but you must tell me the story; no one is telling me the truth."

"Oh yes," Robert said, "Joe punched the Ambassador in the face, a few times I think."

"Oh God! You punched his face?"

"Yes and Mohamed told the police it was a private matter but Joe was arrested."

"Oh poor thing. How is he?"

"Do you mean Mohamed?"

"Yes, was he hurt?"

"Of course he got hurt Louise."

"I mean was he really hurt?"

"Oh no."

"What had he done wrong?"

"Everything went wrong until we met Lucy in Switzerland. Lucy explained everything to us so we now know the true story. When we got back we both had to apologise to Mohamed and we are friends again. You will see him with us next time I promise," Joe said, "Uncle telephoned me and asked me to tell you to pack your suitcase as your cottage is nearly finished."

"Oh thank you Joe."

When they had all gone I was alone in my room. I missed him so much, I wanted to know how he was and I regretted that I had been so rude to him the last time I saw him. At the end of the month I went to Chiang Rai, up in the North. I had my own place, which was not far from Mon and Nut's cottage. It had two bedrooms and I had my own library. When I walked into the sitting room I saw it had a fireplace and at the back was the kitchen.

I remembered my last day at the International School, the Headmistress was crying, Maria and Julia were very tearful and Charlie wanted to come with me. I gave a gold pen to the Headmistress, a cosmetic box to Maria and Julia and to Charlie I gave a Big Ben clock. So many things were happening to me at the same time, Mon and Nut were so happy to have me with them.

"Hello Miss Louise, are you in?"

"Yes, please come in Mon, Nut."

"What are you doing Miss Louise?"

"Please sit down; you are just in time as I need your ideas. I am planning a schedule for our school and I want to ask the Minister to build an extension. We need one more room for the library so that we can lock up the classroom when the students go home. One more thing, I don't like it when the students have to eat their food in the classroom, it is not hygienic. We need a small canteen to make it easy for them so they can sit at long tables."

"But it might be too much for us to ask the Minister."

"Don't worry Mon. I will write a very nice letter of application for planning permission and I will show it to him."

"Oh God you are an angle Miss Louise."

"Thank you Nut. This is our plan for the class. You can carry on doing what you did before but I think I will have a problem with communication so I will teach drawing in the English language. I have a lot of picture books so the students might be able to understand what I am talking about."

"Oh you are so wonderful Miss Louise; we love you and are so happy to have you here."

"Thank you Mon."

One Friday evening my father came with Naree to see me whilst I was having tea with Mon and Nut in my sitting room.

"Oh good evening sir."

"Good evening to you all. Please stay, Mon and you Nut, I want to have a meeting with you all."

"Yes sir." The Minister opened an envelop that was in his hand, it was my letter asking for planning permission and he was laughing so much.

"What are you laughing at father?"

"You are my dearest daughter and a good organiser and straight forward. You remind me of the Councils in London, you have to ask for planning permission before you can do anything. I am very impressed with my daughter. I will send the workmen to see you tomorrow and you can give them this plan."

"Thank you so much father."

"You can do anything you like, this is your project. One day, when I am dead, I want someone else to look after the poor instead of me. Do you like your cottage?"

"Yes father, thanks again."

"Naree and I are going to South Africa for a holiday and we might go and visit Lucy in Switzerland, do you need anything?"

"I do father, but it is in England."

"In that case you will have to wait as I want you to go back to London for your graduation. Oh by the way, I forgot to mention, Louise, I went to the Head Office in the lowlands I saw you have a few letters from England. When I get home I will ask Lung Non to bring them to you."

"Thank you father."

CHAPTER FORTY-TWO

One day I received two letters. I had been waiting for them for months:

London

Dear Princess Louise

I am sorry it has taken me so long to send an answer to your postcard and letter but I am not in London. After you left England I got a job in Saudi Arabia. At first I didn't want it but the pay was so good that I had to take it and since then I haven't been back home. I am really having a great time, I love it there. I have to work between these two countries. I have a few stories to tell you but not at the moment as they are extremely secret. If you want me to send you anything from England please ask. I have got my own place now; don't ask about girls, I just muck around. What about???? Hope to see you in a few months. Don't forget graduation in July.

Thinking of you always

Jason xx

Dearest Louise

We both miss you so much and are sorry that we haven't written to you before. Let us explain - not too long after you left David had health problems and he was not well at all. I decide to rent out the shop, although we kept our flat on the top floor, and we bought a house in Spain; we have just come back to visit London.

We wanted to send you a letter but we didn't have your address. David misses you very much and so do I. We are so pleased to hear about your new job and we want to see you so much. I will give you our address in Spain as well so you can keep in contact in the future. We love living in Spain and are so happy together, we don't want for anything and as long as we have good health that will make David and I very happy. We both want to see you back here in the long term.

We will leave all we have to you as we have no one except you so please keep in touch. We hope you will come to visit us when you come back to London so please let us know when you are coming. We hope and pray for you to meet a very good, kind man who will look after you for life because you are our princess. We still go to the church every Sunday and ask God to look after you. We thank God and hope you will let us know that you are okay and hope to see you very soon.

God bless you

David and Jim

I was so happy to read the letters, how nice to have such good friends when I lived so far away from them. I wanted to tell them my story; that what was happening to me was like a dream; my father, a very rich, kind and considerate man. How could I tell them even now? I sometimes thought none of it was true; it must be God helping me to see my own father. I promised myself I would tell David, Jim and Jason when I saw them in London.

In the morning, outside the classroom I told the students that we were going to grow our own vegetables and flowers and that they had to look after them so they would learn how to grow plants. I was very pleased with my drawings, they were such clever children and they understood. They were so quiet and they loved me with their innocent eyes. I said to them, "This is my arm," and they repeated it. "These are my eyes and this is my mouth, for talking to you." I was sure they would remember soon. When we finished teaching, Mon and Nut would sometimes come to my cottage to have a chat or I cooked them dinner."

"Hello Mon, Nut I have some salted eggs for you, I can't eat much today."

"Why Miss Louise, are you sick?"

"I look at the children and they have nothing to eat but sticky rice and salt. It makes me ill and get upset."

"Oh Miss Louise, this is the way things are, we can't help them any more than we do already."

"I have to do something better, Mon and Nut. Are you free this weekend?"

"Yes we are."

"I think we should go to the town as we need a lot of food."

"But we haven't got enough money Miss Louise."

"My father has gone on holiday and he gave me a card to use. Please Mon, could you ask Doctor Arun and the nurse if they want some food and they can make a list?"

"Yes Miss Louise."

We went to the lowland town where there was a big market. We walked around the market and then went into a shop and bought a lot of dried meat, dried fish and tinned vegetables. When Mon and Nut went to check the cash machine a piece of paper come out, I could see their eyes wide open and Mon's face was so happy."

"What happened Mon?"

"The Minister has put up our wages."

"Congratulations, you both deserve it, you give your life to the poor, who have no other opportunity to learn how to read and write in the jungles of Thailand. No one wants to come here except you two."

"I promise you Miss Louise, we will stay here until we retire."

"It is good that you help these people."

"What about you Miss Louise?"

"Oh well, I don't get any wages. My father just gave me the cash card." We laughed.

When we got home we had so much tinned food and dried meat. Mon bought some fresh meat and said he would cook a special dinner for me. I was in the kitchen but they didn't allow me to help. It was about five o'clock in the evening when we heard a lot of noise.

"Hello there, are you in?"

"Look Miss Louise, Khun Joe and Mr. Robert and behind them must be the Ambassador. Hello, this way sirs. The Minister is on holiday," Mon said.

"We had to hire a truck."

"Please come in. I will make you some green tea," Mon said.

"And I am going back to the kitchen," Nut said, "I am cooking a special dinner."

Joe opened a bottle of red wine and Mon cut some dried grass. Robert went to pick up a pipe.

He said, "Well I haven't smoked for a long, long time so am I going to smoke real cannabis tonight?" Nut told me the beef curry for me was separate and I was not to touch the one for the others because he had put fresh grass leaves into their curry so they would go to the toilet all night long.

"Do you want to join us Ambassador?" Mon asked.

"Oh no thank you. I will just drink some red wine." I looked at them each smoking sitting in a circle. It was not even nine o'clock and they were laughing and telling stories.

"Would you like to go for a walk?" The Ambassador asked me.

"Yes, I wanted to show you the school."

"It is too dark, we can go tomorrow. I just wanted to walk with you."

"Have you heard from Lucy?"

"Yes I have. She is happy and has met her old friend from London, Abdul."

"Abdul, how come? She was trying to escape from him in London because he never told her about himself."

"Yes, Abdul is my cousin, did you know him?"

"Yes I did."

"They are all drunk, shall we walk far?"

"Yes, we can walk up the hill."

"Did you get hurt?"

"Yes I did. Joe didn't listen to me until he went to see Lucy, but I am fine now. I have to say congratulations to you."

"What for?"

"For being the beautiful daughter of the ex-Minister of Foreign Affairs."

"That was a coincidence Ambassador."

"I see. Please could you call me by my name?"

"I want to but I think I have got used to calling you Ambassador."

"How long will you stay here?"

"I don't know I love it here."

"Can I come to visit you?"

"Yes you can but you will give up. Bangkok is a long way from Chiang Rai."

"If I can go to New York every month for several years, I can certainly come to visit you here; it just takes me forty five minutes by plane."

"Do you still miss her?"

"No, not any more. Once I thought no one could replace her but now that time has passed I realise that love is coming back to me again but it is a different person."

"So you have forgotten her?"

"No, there is a different reason. When you love someone your love is in your heart, when she or he dies you suffer and it has taken me a long time but I am alive and I need someone to understand me and love me so I can share real love and be a real family."

"So have you seen her?"

"I think I did, it was the first time since Nadia died."

CHAPTER FORTY-THREE

At Bangkok Airport, Joe and Robert had special permission to take me to the plane.

"Where is he?" Joe moaned.

"He said he was coming," Robert said, "Maybe he is stuck in a traffic jam. You will forgive him Louise," Joe was worried.

"Yes of course I'll forgive him Joe."

"So how long will you stay in London?" Robert asked.

"I will be back as soon as possible after my graduation as I have nothing else to do."

"You promise?" Joe said.

"I promise."

"We will miss you," Joe said, "There is the last call for your flight, you had better go." Suddenly, there he was, running like a tiger.

"I am so sorry everyone."

"You better be; where were you?" Joe asked.

"I couldn't leave my meeting, it was rather important."

"Okay, you can give her one kiss to say goodbye," Joe said.

"Not more than one," Robert insisted.

"We all want one, that is enough," Joe said.

"Oh let him have two, they won't see each other for at least two months," Robert said.

"Oh no I can't wait that long, I will go to England and bring you back," Mohamed said, "Please Louise could you arrange to deliver this box to this address for me?"

"Yes Ambassador I will."

"Thanks darling." He kissed my ear, "I will miss you a lot," he whispered.

"Here you go Louise," Robert said, "If you are not careful the captain will come, Ambassador, because you are delaying the plane."

"Goodbye Joe and Robert."

"See you soon Louise," Joe said.

I was travelling in Business Class, it was very comfortable and when I think back I was dreaming of when I left London a year earlier. Jason had seen me off then and I was going back to England feeling that I now had a wonderful life.

I hadn't seen my father since I was born; I never even knew he was alive. I suffered so much when my grandma died and I had wished I could die with her. I was alone, sad and quiet. I always had God but I was lonely in my heart. I had no one to talk to and tell my problems to, I had to cry by myself nearly every night. The first person who helped me was Dr. Padachee. Yes, he was the first person who was kind to me and he left me in real life. I suffered for four years, working in a pub at night and working in Camden Town Market at the weekends, even in winter when it was so cold. I had no social life in my teenage years, no spare money to buy cigarettes, so I didn't smoke, I had no money to go and see a film. I didn't even know how to go to discotheques. I had to count every penny to pay for my dinner and I had to make a list of how much I could spend on potatoes. When I thought of that I remembered one evening when I had to drink half a can of soup so I could keep the other half for the next day. I prayed to God, if he was there, and really thanked Him so much for looking after me.

I don't know how long I slept but I woke up again when the captain announced that we were in London and the local time was 7.45. I looked out of the window. London was always beautiful to me, I was very glad to be going back to my motherland, I missed London so much. When I stepped off the plane I was the happiest person in the world.

I had arranged with the agency, who rented out my flat for me, to keep it free for two months. When I opened the door to the flat I found it so clean. I lit a candle and drank a bottle of red wine. I got up late the next morning and when I opened the French windows I looked over to the next door flat and wondered who owned it now. My life was strange I thought to myself. I didn't see anybody on the balcony but I was still thinking of him, one of the richest men in London, Chris. I walked from my flat to the church and paid my respects to God. After I finished my prayers I went to David and Jim's shop and discovered that they were both still in Spain. The new tenant was very nice and I had a tuna sandwich and a cappuccino. Then I jumped onto the underground and went to the university.

I wanted to make sure that my wages were being paid into my account every month so I went into my bank. "Excuse me? May I see the bank manager without an appointment?"

"Of course you can. Just wait one moment please."

"Please sit down Miss Elizabeth Louise, how may I help you?"

"I think you have made a big mistake with my account. You see I shouldn't have that much money. You must have put someone else's money in my account. Such a large amount of money must belong to someone else. I haven't got four million pounds."

"Let me check for you Miss Louise. No Miss Louise, there is no mistake."

"It's not a mistake?" I repeated.

"I guarantee that it is your money."

"Where did the money come from?"

"It was transferred into your account from a Swiss Bank two weeks ago. I can guarantee that it is your money."

"Thank you so much."

"My pleasure Miss Louise."

I took a taxi back to my flat. It was impossible, why had my father given me so much money? I was happy to have it but

I still couldn't believe that it was true. I picked up the phone and dialled the number, it rang for a while.

"Hello, Jason speaking, hey Louise where are you?"

"I am in London."

"When did you get back?"

"Yesterday evening."

"Can I see you tomorrow after I finish work?"

"Okay then. Where do you live Jason?"

"Between St. John's Wood and Baker Street, not too far from your place."

"Okay Jason, I'll let you go, we can talk tomorrow."

"Okay Louise, I can't wait to see you."

"Me too Jason, bye for now."

"Bye."

CHAPTER FORTY-FOUR

On the Friday evening Jason was coming to pick me up. At about six o'clock my door bell rang.

"I am coming Jason." When I opened the door there he was.

"Hello princess."

"Hi Jason. Wow! You have a sports car."

"Do you like it?"

"Yes it is beautiful."

"Like you," he said.

"Jason I am your friend."

"I know, my dearest friend Louise. Can't I tell you that you are beautiful?"

"Of course you can. And you are so smart and charming."

"Oh thank you Louise, you make me feel so good. Shall we go?"

"Yes."

"I will take you to have dinner first and then we can pop in to see my place, is that okay?"

"It's okay Jason."

"How is life in Siam?"

"Too much to tell Jason."

"Here we are," he said as we drew up outside a Chinese restaurant. "Let me park my car next to the door."

"Hello Mr. Jason, this way please."

"Thanks."

"I will let you order Jason. You must be a regular customer. Don't order too much as I feel a little sick."

"Maybe you have jet lag."

"I think it is the different time zone so my body is a bit confused."

"So tell me about your life in a different world."

"I don't know where to begin Jason."

"Never mind, let's have dinner first; we have the whole night to be together."

"Jason!"

"I'm joking Louise. This is sweet and sour chicken, roast duck with honey and steamed fish with lemon. What would you like to drink? I always have Chinese tea."

"I will have the same as you Jason."

"Maybe Chinese tea will help make you feel better."

"It is very nice food Jason."

"But you have only eaten a little bit Louise."

"I am sorry Jason."

"It's okay; I know you are not feeling well. Would you like some fresh fruit Louise?"

"No Jason, thank you so much, I can't eat anymore. I think I need to go and relax."

"Waiter, the bill please."

"Here is my place. I'm on the first floor"

"Oh it is such a beautiful place, it is very cosy."

"Do you like it?"

"Yes I do."

"Please sit down Louise, I'll go and make you a hot cup of tea."

"Have you heard any news from Alison?"

"Yes I have. A friend told me that after she left Uni she was very upset. She had a baby girl but left the baby with her parents and then ran away. When I first got my job I was working day and night in order to afford this place and I stayed away from London. As my job is with an oil company I had to move to another country, that is why I answered your letters so late. When I came back from the Middle East I went out with some friends to a night club in Park Lane and I met her in the club. She was a lap dancer; she looked really beautiful and was great at her job."

"Did you talk to her?"

"No I didn't have a chance that night. The next night I went there again and this time she saw me but she pretended she didn't know me. I asked my friend about her, he is a member of the club, and he told me that if I fancied Alison I would have to be a millionaire as she was one of the owner's girls. I asked who he was and he said he was a very rich man called Chris, who was the owner of The Unity Club as well. I went there a few times and I met Chris, he was in his late forties, dark hair, good looking guy but he was a playboy Louise. I tell you Louise, he would never marry Alison, he likes sleeping around, a different blond girl every night. Are you all right Louise?"

"Yes I am."

"And what about you? How are you getting on with your job?"

"I suppose it is going okay, but how can I explain it to you? It was just a coincidence."

"What do you mean Louise?"

I told Jason my story from beginning to end. He was so impressed and said it must be a gift from God. He was very happy that my life had turned out well and took me home. We promised to see each other at the university.

CHAPTER FORTY-FIVE

I was walking along the Bayswater Road, looking for the address that Mohamed had given me to hand deliver the letter to Mrs. Anna. I pressed the door bell.

"Hello."

"Hello, Mrs, Anna? I have a letter for you."

"Okay, can you give it to the porter?"

"But it has come from the Ambassador."

"Pardon?"

"The letter has come from the Ambassador."

"Okay, wait for me down there and I will come down to you. Are you the young lady with the letter?"

"Yes madam."

"Please come in to my place, it's just on the corner. Please sit down."

"Thank you madam."

"Would you like anything to drink?"

"No thank you madam. Here is your letter from the Ambassador."

"Can you wait for a few minutes?"

"Yes madam."

"How do you know the Ambassador?"

"I work overseas."

"When are you going back?"

"After my graduation."

"Would you mind if I contacted you before you go back?"

"Not at all madam."

I left Mrs. Anna and went for a long walk. I thought the lady was very beautiful, even though she was quite old. She looked a bit like Mohamed. I walk across Hyde Park to Marble

Arch and thought of so many things. The week before I had been in the jungle with no gas and no light but now I was in the centre of London. I went to a bookshop and spent the whole day picking out hundreds of books to send back to Chiang Rai for the school library. Then I ran to the department store where I used to work.

"Excuse me; do you know Many? Does he still work in this department?"

"Yes he does. He just went down to the stock room but will be back in a few minutes."

"Hello Many."

"Oh Louise, how are you?"

"I am okay, nice to see you. You haven't contacted me for a long time, what happened to you?"

"Oh Louise, I will be finished in ten minutes, maybe I can ask the Section Manager if I can leave early. Can you wait for me?"

"Yes."

"Just wait for me at the front door and I will go and get my coat."

"Where shall we go?"

"Out the back, it's more quite. Oh Louise, thank God, you have come just in time. I thought we would never see each other again. I am very sorry that I haven't been in touch."

"Me too, I am really sorry."

"I am under so much strain, I'm so depressed. My mother died."

"I am sorry to hear that Many."

"I am under so much pressure Louise, at work and in my private life. I can't cope with things at work; there are not enough staff as they want to save money. Sales have not been successful and they opened a new branch. Then our bonus was less than before and I couldn't pay for my holiday. I am so depressed; I wish I had Andy to help me."

"I am so sorry Many."

"I have had a bad time Louise. God has sent you to me Louise. At the end of the month I am going to live in Australia with Andy, he has a farm over there. I sold my mother's house and put half the money in the bank. I will take the other half with me."

"That is good Many."

"You promise to keep in touch Louise."

"I promise you Many."

I told him what had been happening in my life and he said that it must be God helping me, nothing else. He was very excited and kept saying how lucky I was.

On the Friday evening I had two messages on my answer phone, one from Jason and the other from Mrs. Anna. I listened to Jason's first. 'Hello stranger, you promised that after graduation you would take me to the Theatre. I've been waiting to hear from you, bye, Jason.'

Mrs. Anna's message was: 'Hello Miss Louise, just to remind you, before you go back, please come and have afternoon tea with me, thank you, goodbye, Mrs. Anna.' I phoned Jason and said we could go to the Queen's Theatre in Soho on Saturday evening. That afternoon I went to visit Mrs. Anna.

"Please sit down Miss Louise; I am so pleased you came to see me. This is Peter, my partner. This is Miss Louise."

"Nice to meet you Miss Louise."

"And I'm pleased to meet you Peter."

"Nina, you can bring tea and biscuit now please."

I could tell that when she was younger she must have been a very beautiful lady. Her flat was huge and she must like antiques as she had a number of fine items. Mrs. Anna herself was a very fashionable person, she was so elegant. She said, "I want to thank you Miss Louise, for bringing my son's letter to me. It was so wonderful and I read it again and again. I was so happy that even if I die now I will die smiling. I have waited to hear from him for nearly four years."

"Why has it taken such a long time?"

"Yes it does seem a long time. After his father died he didn't expect me to find a new man, he loved his father very much."

"So you are the Ambassador's mother?"

"Yes I am. His father had a business in the Middle East and travelled between England and Saudi Arabia before he died. Mohamed was born here and his father sent him to boarding school until he finished his degree at Oxford University. He went to stay in the Middle East for a while, until he got his job. He used to come and visit me before but he stopped when I met Peter. He had never even sent me a letter until you came and delivered this one and the happiness came with you and I can now die with my eyes closed. Peter and I want to thank you so much."

"Do you want me to take anything back for him?"

"Yes please. I have prepared it already. Here is a letter and a small box. Please look after this box."

"I will. I promise I will give it to him when I get back."

CHAPTER FORTY-SIX

"Hey! This way Louise."

"You are just in time; I thought you were never late."

"No, I never am big head."

"Who's got a big head?"

"You have Miss Louise."

"Will you keep your promise and not touch your wallet? Tonight it is my turn Jason and if you pay for me you won't see me again."

"Okay Madam Louise. I want to see you again please." His phone rang, "Excuse me Louise. Hello babe, I told you I am out with my best friend. No she is not my girlfriend, I wish she was but she is my very close friend. Listen, I will see you tomorrow I promise. No, I can't make it tonight. Yes I do love you but I love my close friend to. We spent four years together at Uni. Listen, Anita; I have to be with her tonight as we are going to the theatre after dinner. I can be with you every night but she is going abroad in a few days. I will call you tonight. Okay, bye Anita."

"Are you okay Jason?"

"Oh women!"

"Are you mucking around Jason?"

"No Louise. I think I will give her up but she is such a strong personality. She has so much confidence."

"Who is she?"

"She is the owner of a fashion shop in Marylebone High Street."

"How did you meet her?"

"Through a friend."

"I heard you call her Anita."

"Yes, do you want to find out all about her Louise?"

"Yes I do. What does she look like?"

"Oh women ask so many questions. You have already asked one, two, three, four... How many? I think her family came from India but she was born here. Do you want to interview her on your own?"

"Yes. Can I meet her after the theatre?"

"Do you mean tonight? No Louise, that's not possible, she is in a bad mood. She always gets her own way."

"Where does she live?"

"In Belsize Park." He pressed the button for the front door intercom.

"Hello it's Jason. Could you let me in?"

"Okay, just push the door."

"Hello Anita."

"Hi Jason."

"I have someone with me, my close friend. She wants to meet you."

"Come on in."

"Anita, this is Louise, Louise this is Anita."

"Oh my God! Louise!"

"Anita!"

"What is going on here?"

"We will tell you Jason."

"Let me make you a pot of tea."

"I have told you all about myself Anita; it is your turn to tell me about yourself."

"Yes Louise. Do you remember Louise, after my birthday party my family wanted me to marry the Indian man, he was very rich and wanted to set up a business in this country. After I finished my A Levels, my parents didn't want me to go to university. I thought I could look after myself so I ran away to work in a fashion shop for a while. Do you remember my brother, Dr. Pada?"

"Yes I do."

"I went to him and borrowed money from him to buy my own shop and that's where I am now Louise."

"Oh you are still the same old Anita."

"Yes, I never change Louise."

"And how is Dr. Pada?"

"He has two boys and my parents have stopped following me. I often go to see him at the Royal Free Hospital, he is happy with his family. What about your close friend Jason Louise? You better tell him not to muck around with me."

"I have warned him already Anita."

"Do you know you were so terrible to me Louise? You never contacted me; you just disappeared from my life."

"I am sorry Anita. As I told you, I was working seven days and three nights a week. I was so sick for several weeks and it was only because I had a good friend like Jason and a few others in our group, who helped me, that I managed to get my degree."

"I must congratulate you Louise."

"And my congratulations to you on the success of your business at the shop."

CHAPTER FORTY-SEVEN

This time at Heathrow Airport I had my dear friends Anita and Jason. "Please Louise; promise you will write to us."

"I promise you both. As for you Jason, we were very close for four years and you know me very well. You two must take care of each other, remember, if you have only one wing you can't fly, you need two wings."

"Thanks Louise."

"Thank you both for being here." I hugged them both before I went through the main gate. I turned to face them and blew a kiss.

The plane was taking of from Heathrow Airport and I was so happy. I dreamed about the Charity School in Chiang Rai, it was going to have the perfect library as I had sent nearly two hundred books to Northern Thailand. I had some beautiful gifts for everybody, including my father's dogs Snob, Snow, Ruby and Tiger; they could chew on their bones until their teeth were white. I had also bought a lot of vegetable seeds for the students to grow and I had lots of postcards of London so that they could see what it looked like. I had a beautiful gift for the HIV women on the hilltop. I bought a medicine book for the Charity Hospital and hoped Doctor Arun would like it. It had been fun choosing the right present for everyone except for one person, he was so difficult, I didn't know if he would appreciate it or not. I didn't think his heart would melt but never mind, he was my.... what? I didn't know – maybe just my good friend or maybe I was thinking too much. He was a very deep person, deeper than the ocean; I could never read his mind or his heart. I had to admit to myself that in fact I missed him so much, I really did.

When the plane landed at Bangkok Airport I felt so strange. There was nobody to greet me inside the airport. I had sent them a message but maybe they didn't get it. I heard a voice calling me, "Miss Louise, this way please,"

"Ali," I called to him. When I saw his face it looked like he had been crying for some time, his eyes were so red.

"Do you have any more luggage Miss Louise?"

"No Ali, that is all."

"Come this way Miss." I knew something was wrong but I just kept quiet. Ali drove away from the airport and cut through to the west, which was not the way to my house. When the car arrived at some gates my heart nearly stopped when I saw the sign, it said: Missionary Hospital. It was nearly 7.45 local time. I went to the private reception room and I could see my father, Robert, Joe, the British Ambassador and his wife and Ms. Mary.

"Where is Mohamed?" Doctor Tony came out, he was shaking his head from side to side and his eyes were red.

"He has lost a lot of blood. I phoned round to see if I could find any blood from another hospital but they didn't have blood group A. if we can't find some soon it may be too late."

My father went up to Doctor Tony, "I am blood group A."

In the dark of the night it was so cold and still. I looked up at the sky and saw hundreds and thousands of stars covering the Universe. Some were flashing and so far away, others seemed to stay still, what is up there above the atmosphere? Scientists believe there is no life there but my grandma used to tell me, 'Oh don't do anything bad, God is up there and he is looking down at you. If you are a good girl he will look after you and when you are in trouble he will come to help even if you haven't asked him to.'

Oh God! I prayed to Him and said that if He was looking at me at that moment I would always be a good girl, even at that moment I would give my life to Him but could He please help him, please allow him to live longer. I would never ask Him again if He helped him in that moment. He was dying, with a bullet in his chest. Please God, just give him one more chance and let him live. I had nothing else to believe in, I only had Him and I begged God. I promised that if He helped him I would serve Him more than I had done in the past. Amen.

My father came out of the Operating Theatre and stood behind me. He said, "Louise, he will be alright, you go home and rest. Ali will pick you up tomorrow."
"What about you father?"
"Dr. Tony said I have to stay here because I'm not strong enough to go yet," he said, "They needed more of my blood than they expected." For the first time in my life I hugged my father and cried on his shoulder.

CHAPTER FORTY-EIGHT

When Mohamed got out of the hospital he sent Ali to pick me up for breakfast and I stayed until dinner. He had lost so much weight since he came out of hospital. Doctor Tony said it would take him a few months to recover because he had lost a lot of blood. He always lay down in his bedroom with a beautiful, white net. He liked me to read a book to him until he fell asleep. Sometimes he asked Ali to set a table for two by the French windows and we would have a pot of tea. He liked to look at the Chao Phraya River, which was always busy with water traffic. He said he liked water as it was so calm and beautiful. He liked to look at me but he didn't talk much, he just held my hand and closed his eyes.

"Please Joe, tell me what happened."

"Oh, it was terrifying that night; I shall never forget it in my life Louise. That night we went to a high society party, it was mostly for diplomats and rich businessmen in Bangkok. We left the party at about 3.00 am in the morning. I think the gunman shot the wrong person; he was only a short distance away. The British Ambassador was right next to Mohamed and he called the guard straight away. Robert got him to lie down the police caught the gunman; I think he was involved in some political protest. When we got to the hospital Mohamed was unconscious for several hours, the bullet passed close to his heart and he lost a lot of blood. At that time we had no hope, the British Ambassador's wife was crying and went to the church at the back of the Hospital, she was very close to Mohamed. Once you came back his breathing improved and we believe he is still alive because he was waiting for you.

I went back to Chiang Rai with my father. The Charity School library was ready for the books that I had sent from London and the canteen for the students to eat their lunch in was so nice with long tables and long bench seats. Mon and Nut were very happy and my father thought that when the new term started maybe the tribes people would send more of their children to learn. We all hoped he was right. The hospital was busier with several new born babies. My father and Naree stayed with the HIV women in their hilltop village because they had found out how to cure the virus. I sometimes had to stay with the family dogs, they were all so clever and they made me laugh. They are my best friends, especially Snob, who is a very good dog. After I came back to the jungle Joe and Robert didn't come to visit me for a month. Maybe they were too busy in Bangkok. I enjoyed myself with the project where we grew a lot of vegetables and flowers. One day I ask the students to invite their parents for a party at our school. We cooked the vegetables that we had grown and we had games and a music competition. We had a number of good singers in the school and they made up their own song. I encouraged them to enjoy using their own abilities. Mon and Nut were the referees and we gave a lot of presents out to them. They loved it so much that those who could speak English very well said to me, "Please Miss Louise, can we have more parties? We all enjoyed this one so much."

"Let's see, if you all behave yourselves we might have another party sometime."

"We promise we will be good."

"It would be wonderful if you could all go to the Secondary School in Chiang Mai."

CHAPTER FORTY-NINE

I remember so well when I was sitting in my front room with Mon and Nut after our dinner. Mon and Nut wanted me to tell them about the history of England and Scotland. I showed them a few books and then we heard Naree with all of the dogs; they were jumping up and barking outside the house. I went to open the door. "Please come in Naree."

"Thank you Miss Louise, I came to pick you up as the Minister wants to see you immediately."

"My father?"

"Yes."

"Is he okay?"

"Yes Miss Louise, nothing serious. He just misses you."

"Okay Naree. Let me tell Mon and Nut first."

When I got inside the house I saw my father smoking the pipe I had bought him from London. He was relaxing on the sofa looking through the photo albums. He looked at some of the photos for a long time. He told me he liked looking back to the old times. It was the same album I had given to him and a lot of the photos were of my mother and his wedding day.

"Please sit down Louise."

"Thanks father."

"I hear that you have more students from the hilltop than before."

"Yes father it's true."

"Can you manage?"

"Yes, it's no problem father."

"Do you like your library?"

"Oh very much and I thank you very much for your kindness."

"I must go and visit your school next week."

"Please, you must father. It would be so lovely if you could come."

"I am very pleased with your success and I am very proud of you."

"Thank you father. Can I ask you something father?"

"Yes of course."

"Why did you transfer so much money into my bank account? I don't need so much and I will never be able to spend it all as long as I live."

"It is a present to you. I haven't looked after you since you were born. You had a hard time in your early life and you got your degree by your own ability. It is not too much for me to give to my own flesh and blood. I have given millions to charity, so why can't I give some to my daughter? I called you over here as I have some news to tell you. This morning I was talking to the British Ambassador in Bangkok, he contacted me instead of the Ambassador of Saudi Arabia. Mohamed has asked permission to marry you. I told the British Ambassador that I would have to ask you first."

"But I love living here father; I want to be here with you."

"Think about it and ask yourself if you love Mohamed or not. I will always be your father and this land is yours, you can come and live here anytime you want to. I know you love Chiang Rai, Louise but you are still young, you have far to go and who knows, one day you might come back to live here? Mohamed is a great man; he is a gentleman in every respect. Don't cry, I am only asking you to think about it. I am going back to Bangkok this weekend but you have two more days. I love you and I have only one daughter but I want you to be happy in your life."

I was so confused about marriage. I still loved my independence, I loved being single but Mohamed was a man who could look after me and I thought it would be very difficult to find another man like him. I thought that what my father said was true. He was a man with power and a lot of people respected him. Even my own father, who used to be the Minister of Foreign Affairs before he took early retirement, still has power and people still pay respect to him, maybe I am still too young.

The day my father went to Bangkok, Joe and Robert came up to the North. They both said they missed me. Joe told me that Mohamed was still not strong enough to come with them. Also it was not so easy for him to travel as before because he had to have close security until the political situation improved."

"So we are both his companions," Robert said.

"We don't want to interfere with your decision and we want you to make up your mind on your own," Joe said.

"Could you both promise me something?"

"Of course, if we can," Robert said.

"Please be my friends for ever."

They both replied at the same time, "Yes we will."

"I was very sad when I lost my best friend and my cousin Lucy. Do you know how she is, Joe?"

Joe and Robert looked at each other, "Yes she is fine," Joe answered.

CHAPTER FIFTY

I had to return to Bangkok with Joe and Robert on the Sunday. At noon, in my father's house next to the British Embassy, my father, the British Ambassador and his wife were all there and witnessed Mohamed put his diamond ring on my finger. I returned to teach at the Charity School and as usual Mohamed, Joe and Robert came to visit me and my father every three weeks. One day before Christmas, when I was sitting with Mon and Nut discussing how to improve the school in the future, my father and Naree came to join us.

"Please sit down sir," Mon said.

"Thank you Mon," he said, "Are you discussing next years project to recruit a new teacher and get more students for the new class?"

"Yes father."

When we had finished he said, "My dear daughter I have some good news for you. You must come to Bangkok with me next week."

I can remember every day that I was with Mohamed, since the first day we were married. Our wedding day was a very private affair. The British Ambassador and his wife were there as witnesses and my father's close friend the Minister of Defence and his wife. Also Professor Bee, Doctor Tony, the Headmistress, Joe and Robert. Mohamed didn't have anyone from his family. My father gave a dinner party at the Oriental Hotel. The next morning Mohamed and I went on our honeymoon to London and because his four years of duty in Bangkok had come to an end he was going to move to another country. He was preparing for the future and bought a five-bedroom house near South Kensington and said that one day I would come back to live there.

I remember so well our first night on honeymoon. We were on the plane and kissed each other, that was all we did and he whispered in my ear that I would have to wait until we got to London. When we arrived we checked into the traditional Hotel, the Hilton in the Bayswater Road, he said it was near to his mother's place. When I close my eyes and think of him, he is in my blood, he is in my body and he is the breath of my life. That first night I was with him I shall remember until I die. I didn't know how to please him but he started to kiss me from my head to my toes, every inch of my body. He was so experienced and expert with his lips. I was so thrilled that he was a passionate person and at that moment I knew I was in heaven. We travelled to heaven and then we reached paradise until 2.30 in the morning, then we started again in the early sunrise. We didn't go outside the hotel for four days and four nights.

He went out to see his mother and his friend, the Saudi Arabian Ambassador in London. He had a few close friends and they helped us a lot in finding the house. Mohamed was so fussy about buying a property where we could live saying that it was going to be the place where he would die. When he bought the house, it seems such a long time ago now, it cost him a fortune. I said to him, "Please, Mohamed let me help? You can use half the money my father gave me, I will never spend it."

He looked at me and kissed me on the cheek, "Listen my beautiful wife, if I can't look after you and my family I should never have got married. My father-in-law will laugh at me. I bought this house for my wife and children. We had better invest in property right now as in the future it is going to be worth a hundred times more. So many years have gone by and one thing I realize is that he was a hundred times correct. He went to visit his mother again before we left London, she was so happy and he loved his mother very much. I was sick on the way home.

CHAPTER FIFTY-ONE

Not too long after we came back from London we had to move to Malaysia. Mohamed had his own people on duty with him, Ali the driver, the chef and the cleaning staff, all five moved with us. When I got back from London I was so sick. Joe and Robert came to visit us to help me move in and to comfort me because I missed Chiang Rai. One Saturday morning Joe said to Robert, "Are we going to be uncles?" He had noticed that I was vomiting.

Robert laughed, "It is too early Joe, but if it's true I bet Mohamed will have to work day and night." Because of what Joe and Robert said Mohamed sent for a doctor to come and see me. After the doctor had given me some medicine to stop the sickness Mohamed was so happy. He said to Joe and Robert, "Soon you will be Godfathers to my two sons."

"How do you know you are going to have twin sons?" I asked.

"Darling, I made them myself, I should know."

I was sick for the first three months. Mohamed was so passionate in his sexual activity that we had never missed a night from our honeymoon until the seventh month of my pregnancy. He said he needed me and wanted to be inside me. I will never tell anyone about his high sexual activity. Maybe I might have been wrong about him being so many years older than me. I let him do what he liked, even though I was sometimes so tired. He arranged for me to go into a private hospital in London as the babies had to be delivered by caesarean section and not by natural birth. I returned to England with him and whilst he dealt with the doctor he arranged for a lady called Renia to look after me in the South Kensington home and then went back to Malaysia.

I sent letters to all of my friends. To Many in Australia and to David and Jim. I had lots of visitors like Jason and Anita. Jason was so special to me because we had known each other for so many years. Sometimes he came to see me by himself and treated me like his wife, which Renia didn't like. Renia was a very quiet person and very honest but she was a very strict woman. One morning I heard a lot of noise outside and when I looked out of the window I wanted to run downstairs but I couldn't because my stomach was so big. "Oh thank God you have come father." Naree, Joe and Robert were with him and I couldn't stop crying as I was so happy.

Two weeks later Mohamed came to join us. I was so excited to see him. He whispered in my ear that he loved me and he was dying to be inside me again. Mohamed gave his elder son the name Bentham and the younger son Bernstein. They were both beautiful babies. Joe was a Godfather to Ben and Robert was a Godfather to Bern.

When I used to see someone else's baby I didn't feel anything but once I became a mother, I can't explain how a real mother feels. I can only say I loved them so much that I would die for them. I didn't want to go back to live in Malaysia but Mohamed said I must and that after four years we would move again and he said he would try to obtain a better position. My life in Malaysia was very quite and we almost stayed together except when I had to be a diplomatic party wife. Joe and Robert came to see us often. My father loved his grandsons and was always popping in. Mohamed was still crazy in love with me and I didn't need to do anything. I had a nanny for Ben and Bern and all I had to do was to keep myself ready to be his lover and keep him happy at night. He never looked at any other women and I am certain that if I hadn't used birth control I would have got pregnant every year.

Sometimes I couldn't cope, he was so emotional and a very possessive person. If a young man came and talked to me he would get upset and accuse me of wanting a toy boy. Even when we were arguing in bed he had such deep feelings and made love longer then usual. I was so happy with his high sexual ability, he had so much energy and he never stopped until he was completely exhausted.

After two years everyone said to me that I should get off the pill and he said he wanted a daughter. Ben and Bern were just two years old and he said we could pay for a nanny as he wanted a beautiful girl. Sometimes he was so sweet and told me he wanted to make love to me until he died. When I stopped taking the pill he worked so hard to make a little one. He was a very strict person; after dinner he liked to be with his sons until their bedtime, then no one was allowed into our private area. Everyone had their own private life and he would lock the door so there would just be the two of us. Sometimes he worked so late in his writing room that I had to go and kiss him otherwise he would say he would not be too long. He would light candles and he liked to make love to me with my clothes on. I had to wear a different nightdress. We sometimes made love on the floor with him behind me. He also liked to suck and bite at my chest. We had to double-glaze the windows in our bedroom as he sometime liked to make a lot of noise as we travelled to heaven. We both loved to scream. As he got older his sexual prowess got stronger than before and I worried about the scaring caused by the bullet fired into his chest by the gunman.

CHAPTER FIFTY-TWO

When I gave birth to our only daughter, Sophia, I was in London for two months with the children and the nanny. Mohamed came to take us back to Malaysia but I really wanted to live in London. Joe and Robert kept me going and my father visited me every month until we had to move to the next country, which turned out to be Cuba. I couldn't settle down in my life as I had to move with him because I loved him so much. When Ben and Bern were six years old and Sophia was four I couldn't tell Mohamed to be fair to Ben and Bern, he loved Sophia so much more than his own life, even more than me, which upset me.

"Oh darling she is the youngest leave her be," he said.
"But you spoil her." I was crying and he kissed my tears away.
"Oh don't let Sophia see you cry, she might ask why."
"You see, you love her so much more than Ben and Bern."
"No darling I love them all equally."
"That is not true, you have bought her so many dresses and the twins don't get anything."
"Okay, okay I won't do it again."

But after a few weeks he would do it again. Ever since she was born he called her a little princess. He arranged our family life and he hired a special teacher to teach the children French and Arabic. It seemed that Ben and Bern were only good at English.

"They are so young darling," I said.
"No they are not too young. They are both nearly seven and it is the right time for them to learn another language. Look at Sophia, she is five and half and can speak Arabic to the nanny."

I couldn't say anything as it was true. No one had taught her but she had picked it up from our staff.

I liked Cuba, the country was beautiful and the people were so nice. I was very happy and soon I could understand the environment and the people. We were happy with the social whirl and the children enjoyed their school. Mohamed was very strict with his two sons and forced the staff to speak Arabic to them. He got very upset and was disappointed with the two boys as they were not good enough at their second language. His only joy in life was his daughter; she was the one in the family who made him happy. At six years old she was fluent in English, Arabic and Spanish.

I prayed to God every night before bed and begged Him to help make England the next country we moved to. I knew Mohamed would send the twins to boarding school when they were eight; in fact he had wanted to send them when they were six but I cried and kissed his feet every night and told him they are too young to go and live with some one they didn't know. I loved them so much and if he had sent them away I would have died.

CHAPTER FIFTY-THREE

After four years we moved to Germany, I was so delighted. One day after dinner we were together in the leaving room and Mohamed asked Bentham, "What do you want to be when you grow up son?"

"I want to be a doctor father."

"What about you Bernstein?"

"I think I want to be a medical doctor too father."

"Very good, and what about you princess?"

"I want to be like you father. I would like to travel around from place to place and see the world, it is in my blood."

"Well boys, next month you will be going to England to study for whatever you want to be. I have arranged for you both to go to boarding school."

"But Mohamed!"

"No buts my darling, they are old enough, after all they are eight years old now."

"I will miss them so much."

"We will all miss them but you can go and visit them darling. England is just next door to Germany."

"And what about me Daddy? I want to go with them as well."

"No my sweetheart you are too young. You will stay with us until you are older; anyway, you told me you wanted to learn German."

"Oh yes daddy, I had better stay here." I was so upset with Mohamed but I couldn't fight with him as he was the head of the family.

Father and Naree and Joe and Robert came to visit us three times a year. They all agreed with Mohamed.

"Don't cry my darling, listen to me, the boys must go away to learn for themselves, it is for their future. You can't stay with them for ever and one day they will have their own lives to lead. They are not boys anymore, they are growing up and I want them to become good, intelligent human beings. Don't be stubborn; I think I spoil you too much darling. Look at your husband and tell me what would happen if I died tomorrow? Would you cry for me?"

"Oh no, please don't say that. I don't want to hear such things."

"I love you Louise, so don't worry. I have planned everything for everybody. You and my children will be happy without me; I don't want my wife and my children to be short of money."

"But I want you my dearest husband, I don't want anything and I don't want to live without you. I need you to hug me and bite me for ever." We were so madly in love when we argued that night that we didn't go to bed until we finished the second game.

When we arrived in London in the July, Mohamed had organised everything for the two boys. I had no idea as I had never been to a boarding school before. Mohamed arranged for a lady to stay in the house in South Kensington and I could see he was a very powerful man and I was so proud of him. I was so sad, the children had made the house such a happy place and I loved them so much even when they sometimes made too much noise. Sophia, who was always so happy, said to her two brothers, "Don't worry Ben and Bern, I will send you a box of choccies every month and I will comfort mum."

CHAPTER FIFTY-FOUR

After I returned to Germany my life was less happy. I was so sick and, to tell the truth, I loved the twins more then my life. For the first year I went back to London every two weeks to visit them. I realised that sometimes God allows people to be born with everything they need in life. I saw that since her birth Sophia had got whatever she wanted. If Mohamed could have given her the moon or the stars, he would have got them for her. Maybe when I was young I didn't have my father to look after me but Sophia was so self-confident, so intelligent and so beautiful. I saw that Mohamed gave his life to her. By the time she was ten she could read and write in five languages and tried to be the boss, like her father. "You spoil her too much Mohamed," I said.

"Oh darling she deserves it. Her studies are all Grade A and she is a good girl."

"But you didn't buy everything for the twins."

"That's true, I didn't buy them everything, but you did. It is the same darling. Look, here she comes don't mention anything or she will get upset. I don't want my daughter to be unhappy. Hello princess, how was your day?" He asked her.

"Oh Dad, it's the boys, I get fed up with them. I have told them to leave me alone but they keep trying to invite me to their parties," she said to him, "But Daddy it is not the right time. My boyfriend must be like you Daddy. He must be good looking, a real gentleman and look just like you as well Daddy."

At the end of Mohamed's duty in Germany we were all lucky to move to England. I gave a lot of things to God to thank him for sending us to live together and I promised Him I would never forget Him until my last breath. I remember it was the first time I had been really happy in the last four years. I knew Mohamed didn't want to send Sophia to boarding school and it was his turn to be worried even though she was fourteen. "You promised me Dad," she said.

"But you will forget how to speak Arabic."

"I promise I won't. I have the tape you bought me Dad."

"What about German?"

"It is still in my memory and I won't forget it. As for French, I will have to learn that at school. I won't let you down Dad." When all the children were away at school I looked forward to Friday evenings when they all come back. Mohamed and I were so happy to see them and they talked about their life at boarding school, our house in South Kensington was so alive then. Ali, the driver, found it tiring as he had to pick everyone up from school but he loved his young masters so much.

After we moved from Germany to live in England, Mohamed had to travel to Saudi Arabia every month. He said it was for business trips so he went there without me. It was a year after Sophia started school that he said he couldn't live without his daughter. "I will take her out of boarding school," he said, "I will arrange to give her private tuition as I am not sure how much longer I will see her growing up."

"Don't say that darling. You can do anything you like if it makes you happy."

"Thank you Louise for understanding how much I love my daughter."

When Sophia left boarding school she would come back from her private tuition each evening. Father and daughter spoke French, Arabic, German and Spanish together and were both so close. He never let her out of his sight and Ali acted as Sophia's bodyguard.

Mohamed had all his old staff with him and they loved him as their master. Sometimes I felt that they were all keeping a secret from me because they spoke in another language in front of me but when the twins came back from school all the staff had to speak in English only and the young masters would fight back.

"It is not fair Daddy, you and Sophia are so good at foreign languages but we are not. Besides, we are going to be doctors so we don't need to know lots of different languages. Maybe Sophia needs to but when I am in this house, English only please."

"Yes sir boss," said Mohamed.

As I have mentioned before, I shall never forget the last four years in London. The five of us were so happy in our house in South Kensington. One Friday night we were waiting for Mohamed to come back for dinner, he was very late. Sophia made a joke, "Maybe Daddy has gone out with a blond Mum?"

"No Sophia Daddy loves Mum only," Ben said. At about 9.00 o'clock Mohamed came back, he look very tired.

"I am so sorry everyone. I was busy at work and I didn't have time to give you a call."

"I thought you were out with a blond Dad," Sophia said to him. We didn't know what he said to Sophia in Arabic but she kept quite. That Friday night he didn't stay with the children but went to the bedroom and had a long bath.

"I am going to look after Daddy," I said to the children and went upstairs. When I got there he was still in bath.

Every Friday night since we were married I would light a candle in our bedroom and put white lilies beside our bed. The white net had to decorate the bed as Mohamed loved the ritual with his bed and my night dress. When he opened the white nets I was asleep.

He woke me and held my hand and said, "I am so sorry but tonight I have no energy to make love to you."

"That is okay darling you rest as you are tired." At about 2.30 in the morning he was kissing my lower regions when he moved up and said, "I love you my dear wife but I can't breathe, could you call Sophia for me please?" I ran to her bedroom and when I got to her door she was waiting for me.

"Is it time for me to be with Dad?" She asked.

"He wants to see you."

"Mum, you go down and call Ali and everyone and call for an ambulance. I will go to him now." She went away and when we returned to my bedroom, Sophia was kissing his feet.

She said, "Daddy, I want to be your daughter in every life and I will be with your soul wherever you are. You need never be afraid of where are you going and you will have a very beautiful place of your own." She kissed his face and the ambulance came.

It was too late, he had left us. The whole family was there when he died and he held my hand and Sophia's but he never came back. The doctor said it was heart failure. The Saudi Arabian government gave him the honour and dignity befitting his long service. When he left us he was over fifty and so many from the diplomatic community came to pay their respects. When my father, Joe and Robert came they all said he was too young to leave us. His mother, Anna, came and cried as her heart was broken. She had her two grandsons to comfort her. The only person who never came to see him was Lucy.

CHAPTER FIFTY-FIVE

I didn't know all the facts until the solicitor read the will. He said, "The oil company in Saudi Arabia, along with five hundred million pounds, is bequeathed to his first son, Mr. Mohamed Alkhaleej, who is a graduate at Harvard University in the USA. The balance of his account in Switzerland is to go to his second son, Alexander, who is Lucy's son. All five of the staff who have served him, including Ali, are to receive one million pounds each. As for his dearest wife and children…" I didn't hear what he said as I was unconscious before he completed his sentence.

I only have my twin sons and my dearest daughter to comfort me. I was so hurt, I had been with him for sixteen years and I didn't know anything at all. Now I knew why, for the last four years he had kept returning to Saudi Arabia and that is why Lucy hated me. I wanted to know more, I wanted someone to tell me the truth about Mohamed.

Ali and his staff wanted to stay with me. They said they wanted to be with their young masters. The only people who knew Mohamed's secret were Ali and my daughter.

"Ali, please sit down. Please don't disappoint me, you have known me for more than sixteen years and I know you adored your master more than your life and you would die for him. Please tell me about his life before he married me."

"The Ambassador met his first wife when he went on holiday but she wanted to stay in Saudi Arabia and did not want to move from country to country with him. When his first son was four years old his wife died of cancer and his son grew up with his cousin. When he moved to the USA, the next lady we all knew he was very much in love with was an American diplomat's wife. When he met her she had two sons by her husband but soon the Ambassador had an affair with her. She divorced her husband and they lived in New York for a few years. Sadly she died of cancer as well."

"What about Lucy?"

"Ms Lucy loved the Ambassador so much she wanted to marry him but the Ambassador didn't love her. They went to Switzerland together and later on when Abdul, the Ambassador's cousin, found out Lucy was his girlfriend in London he told the Ambassador everything but it was too late, Ms Lucy was already pregnant by the Ambassador. When the Ambassador explained to Ms. Lucy she accepted it and asked the Ambassador to keep it secret so she could live in Switzerland with her son. However she did not want to marry Abdul."

"So she just made up the story that she was happy with Abdul?"

"Yes."

"Poor Lucy."

I wanted to tell the whole world how I felt. I don't think anyone can understand such deep feelings until they have experienced such things themselves. I went to visit his grave every Friday. He had been with me for so long in the house. I would prepare a new nightdress for him every night as if he was next to me and for many years I could almost feel he was really with me, my heart will never change. The twins went to university and we were all together. It was Sophia's idea. When her Dad had gone she encouraged me to go to evening classes.

"Mum you should go and do something. You are still young and Daddy's soul won't mind if you find a friend."

"No I don't want to meet anyone," I said.

"But you should go and do some studies Mum. You will find it very interesting." I was so sick in my mind. I missed Mohamed so much I wanted to die so I could go to see him. He had treated me badly in love. I stayed in my bedroom for so long and I remembered him from our first night of marriage until I couldn't cope with my sickness. I suppose that if I hadn't had any children I might have done something stupid like committing suicide because of the loneliness.

CHAPTER FIFTY-SIX

Later I took Sophia's advice and went back to university. I went to evening classes and studied Human Geography and through this work my life improved. I wrote a letter to Alkhaleej, Mohamed's first son, and invited him to come and join us for Christmas in London. I told him his half brothers and sister would be happy to see him. I also wrote a long letter to Lucy and said that I was very sorry about the past and that I never meant to keep Mohamed for myself but I had not known what was happening. I asked her to forgive me and if she would like to come to pay her respects to Mohamed at his grave she could come any time she liked. I also invited her and her son Alexander to join us in London. I received a letter from Alkhaleej saying that he would be very pleased to come but that he was very busy with the oil company in Saudi and he would let me know when he could make it.

The twins did so well in their medical studies. Ben got a place in the Royal Free Hospital and Bern was accepted at St. Mary's Hospital. I never worried about Sophia, she was so determined to go to Oxford University like her father and she planned her own future as to what she was going to be. When she sat alone I liked to look at her, she was very beautiful and as her father liked to call her, a princess. She was the one who had all the brains in the family and I wanted so much to know what her life would be like, I was sure she wanted to be a British diplomat.

Just before Christmas we had a letter from Alkhaleej telling us that he would be coming to London. Sophia suggested that she and Ali should pick him up at Heathrow Airport as she couldn't wait to see what her half-brother looked like. I remember we all got very excited. The whole family, including the old staff, wanted to greet him and we all stood near the door as if a prince was coming. When the car passed through the gate and stopped in front of the house Ali got out first. He then opened the door for Sophia and Alkhaleej was the last person to get out. When he stood up we were all in shock. No one could speak a word. He looked so much like Mohamed he could have been a twin, but younger. I couldn't move at all. I looked at him from head to toe until Sophia said, "This is my mother Louise, the older twin is my brother Bentham and the younger one is Bernstein, they are both training to be doctors. I would also like to introduce you to our staff.

After dinner he returned to his Five Star Hotel but he came to visit us every day. The twins loved him very much and he behaved just like Mohamed. He talked with them till late every night and told us about his life in the USA, about the time he spent with his cousin, Abdul, and when he was at university and he told us how his oil company made millions all over the world. He said that it was his first time in England and he loved London very much and that he wished Mohamed had sent him to study in London.

"If you love London you should live with us," the twins suggested.

"Thank you both, I wish I could but there is no one else to look after the oil company," he said, "I think that even when I am not in London I will leave my heart behind this time. When I go back it will just be my body as I think someone will keep my heart with her," he joked. We all laughed but we never thought he was really joking.

Before Christmas Day Sophia took him out to do his Christmas shopping and the twins went out with their friends. When I heard a car arrive at the front of the house it was very late. I just open the curtains and peeped through, my heart fell through the floor. My goodness I thought as I saw Alkhaleej get out and open the door for Sophia and when she got out she stood so close to him and then hugged him and kissed him on the cheek for a long time. Maybe it is just her innocence; she was only just eighteen and had never let any boy touch her since she was a little girl. But then he moved close and started kissing her all over.

"Sorry we are late Mum, it was my fault. I took Alkhaleej around London and we had dinner. Where are my two brothers?"

"They have not come in yet." I looked at Alkhaleej's face, he was very quite and deep and it is very difficult to read his mind, he had a very powerful mind, like his father.

On Christmas Day we were all together for dinner. Ali was the first one to pay his respects to his young master and I could tell he loved Alkhaleej. Alkhaleej had bought beautiful and expensive presents for everyone.

"Mum, you open one first. Oh please, I want to know what he has given you."

"Oh! Thank you Alkhaleej. Oh these diamond earrings are so beautiful they are too much for me."

"They are for you as I don't know when I will be able to be with you again, so please accept them."

"Thank you again."

"You are welcome Mrs. Louise. Your turn Ben and Bern."

"Oh thank you brother, I will keep it until I finish my medical training. I will put it on my tie every day."

"So will I," Bern said, "But I might take the diamond out and sell it." Everybody laughed at his joke.

"What about you princess?" Ben called her like his father did. "Come on, it is not fair for you to see our presents, you have to open yours as well."

"Okay, okay be patient."

"Oh look Mum, look!" Ben said, "A big, heart-shaped diamond ring." Sophia spoke in Arabic to Alkhaleej without looking at me and then she translated into English.

"Don't worry everyone; this ring belonged to Alkhaleej's mother. He will take it back from me when he gets married. For now he just wants me to look after it for him. Don't worry, I will return it to him although it's a perfect fit on my finger.

CHAPTER FIFTY-SEVEN

Christmas came and went and Sophia was working very hard at her studies, even more than before. She kept herself away from everybody and locked herself in her room with hundreds of books. One thing that did make her happy was when she got a letter from Alkhaleej. I couldn't read it as it was in Arabic. One day I asked Ali to read it to me. Ali translated for me and in it Alkhaleej told Sophia that he was missing her very much and he wanted to see her again. I asked Ali if that was all it said as it was such a long letter. Ali read on and said that Alkhaleej wanted Sophia to be like their father. I spoke to Ali again and told him I wanted to know every word in the letter. Unfortunately Sophia came back and was so angry. She spoke in Arabic to Ali and she was crying so much and Ali was crying as well. She accused me of being very rude, as it was her private letter. How dare I try to find out what was in it. She said I had no right to ask someone to read it for me and in the end I had to apologise to her. Since then I never saw her letter again as she locked it up in her safe.

When she left us to study at Oxford University she was very polite and calm. She said, "I will miss you mother. I do love you and even though I may never show you my love is inside me. I will have to work very hard at Oxford so you might not see me during the holidays. I ask your permission to go and see Alkhaleej during the holiday at the end of my first term."

I couldn't say a word. She looked thin and seemed to have lost weight. I think she was suffering inside. I just wished that she would get better when she moved to her new place in Oxford. Her first holiday from university she went away and

I had a postcard from her saying that she very much enjoyed her holiday with him. I could never understand her; she was so clever, so beautiful and had everything she could want in life. I wanted to know what she was doing with her half-brother.

A few years later I began to divide my time between England and Chiang Rai. I went back to my old school to help my father do charity work in the HIV village. Joe and Robert, my best friends, were with me and Mon and Nut were still working with me at the Charity for the tribes people. I returned to London four or five times a year and still wrote to Jim and David in Spain. I got a few letters from Many in Australia but the two people I didn't hear from were Jason and Anita. Perhaps they had both gone away and I didn't want to disturb them. Joe told me about Lucy and her son, he said Lucy had married a businessman and had given birth to another son. She hated Bangkok and had never been back since. She told Joe that she had forgiven me but she didn't want to see me again.

Doctors Bentham and Bernstein often came to see their granddad and I. They were both amazed by granddad's project that helped the poor and the HIV village. After Sophia graduated with a First Class Honours Degree from Oxford in Politics and International Affairs and joined the Civil Service to train as a diplomat. The first country she was assigned to was Israel and one day I got a letter from her. She wanted me to go back to London as she wanted to give me a birthday party at our home in South Kensington. She told me that there were only the twin doctors staying as neither of them was married yet. She also told me that all of Mohamed's staff had gone to work for her in Israel although she had got a new chef as Mohamed's chef was too old. She said she still looked after him. They had all wanted to be with the Master's Daughter and Ali was still her driver.

I returned to the London home in May and was so happy to be in my old bedroom. I talked to Mohamed and told him that

I would die next to him and I wanted to be with him always. I shall never forget the way he loved me and when I closed my eyes I could feel him kissing me from head to toe.

Sophia organised everything for the party. She invited granddad and Naree, all of Mohamed's staff, Jim and David, Jason and Anita, Uncle Joe and uncle Robert. At about nine o'clock she announced that we had a special guest. I was very shocked and couldn't believe my eyes when Sophia introduced me to Uncle Michael, the husband of Auntie Lucy. "And this is my half-brother Alexander and here is a close friend of yours Mum, Uncle Chris." I cried so much with happiness, I didn't know what to say. Chris hadn't changed much and we chatted happily.

The next day Chris came back to visit me and said he was sorry to hear about Mohamed. He said he was an unlucky person from the past and I would never have been happy with him but could we be friends again. I told him I didn't live in London and that I was in between two countries but yes, he could still be my friend. Before Lucy went back to Switzerland she and her son went to pay their respects to Mohamed.

"Thank you so much Sophia for giving me this happiness If your father was still alive he would be very happy with me and I am sure he would be very proud of you because you never let him down."

"Thank you Mum. I still have you to be my real Mum. Life is too short, once God gave me a good chance I have everything I want, I am so lucky but one life to live and survive for me is too long. I want to tell God what I want and who I want to be with until I die. God is punishing me, I can't have him, nobody is perfect. Sometimes life is too complicated and strange. All we can do is do our duty, be honest and play the right character. I am very lucky to be the daughter of the Ambassador, Mohamed and Miss Louise, but somehow I am unfortunate in another way."

I looked at her left hand and saw that she was still wearing the big, heart-shaped diamond ring. It was big enough that even in the dark you could see that it was of the best quality. I wanted to ask her so many questions about the owner of that ring. Not just me, I bet the twin doctors wanted to know about their half-brother as well. We nearly did but nobody dared to ask, we all had to be respectful of her as she was the British Ambassador to Israel. She was so young, bright, intelligent, elegant and so beautiful. As long as I live I will write and tell you about all of my family. I still have my doubts about who is going to be my son-in-law in the future, I am not quite sure and I can't even write his name but yes, I suspect it must be him, the millionaire owner of a Saudi Arabian oil company.

Anthony Lewis trained as a Practical Nurse at M.D. Hospital in Bangkok and is now working for the John Lewis Partnership in London

ISBN 142510253-0